RETRIBUTION

By the same author

Death and Deception
A Game of Murder
A Fear of Vengeance

RETRIBUTION

Ray Alan

ROBERT HALE · LONDON

ISBN 978-0-7090-9318-3

Robert Hale Limited
Clerkenwell House
Clerkenwell Green
London EC1R 0HT

www.halebooks.com

2 4 6 8 10 9 7 5 3 1

Typeset in 10/13.5pt New Century Schoolbook
Printed and bound in Great Britain by
Biddles Limited, King's Lynn

N icky Bains sat alone in the cell at Winchester Crown Court, knowing that he would soon be taken up to face the jury and hear their verdict. He was innocent of the charge against him, but as the judge was known to be severe with previous offenders, Nicky felt that he had little hope of any justice.

He nervously ran his fingers through his long fair hair. He feared what the future had in store for him. If he was found guilty and the judge was as hard as everyone said, then he might be sent away for a long time.

Despite these thoughts going round in his mind, Nicky knew that his parents believed he was innocent. Seeing them each day in the public gallery had helped him through the ordeal of the trial.

His previous criminal activity had been considered petty. But now, at twenty-three years of age, he was in real danger of establishing a police record that would brand him a hardened criminal. Since he was eleven he had been in trouble with the law and had now graduated from the remand homes to the better-known penal establishments including Pentonville, where he had recently spent six months on a charge of burglary.

Now he expected to be found guilty of a crime he had not committed. A crime carried out by someone who, in an attempt to steal alcohol from a warehouse, had struck a nightwatchman on the head, a blow from which the man had died. Nicky could not get the memory of that night out of his mind.

He had dressed himself up in his best clothes to meet a girlfriend for a drink at her local pub, and because he would be drinking, he had decided not to take his car. When he got off the bus he took a short cut through an alley that ran along the side of a warehouse. Halfway along the alley he heard someone running and saw a figure dashing across the yard. The shadowy outline of a man climbed a wire fence, then dropped to the ground on the other side and ran out of sight.

Nicky noticed that a side door of the building was open and his curiosity got the better of him. Satisfied nobody was about, he climbed over the wire fence with all the dexterity of an acrobat. He reached the open door in seconds and moved cautiously inside. Believing that he was alone, he quietly walked to the main area where hundreds of boxes were stacked. Each one contained twelve bottles of whisky.

He was just about to open one of the boxes when he heard a groan. Turning quickly, he saw a man's leg protruding from behind a packing case. His first instinct was to get away as fast as he could. But he was too inquisitive and, despite his nervousness, he had to see who was there.

What he saw behind the packing case made Nicky feel sick. The watchman was lying with his head in a pool of blood but apparently alive. Although anxious to get away, he knew that he couldn't leave without doing something. He decided to call for an ambulance and then get out as quickly as he could. He hurried to a telephone on the wall and, using his handkerchief so as not to leave fingerprints, he removed the handset and punched in the numbers 999 with his biro. After calling for help, he hurried away.

He leapt over the fence and back into the alley, hoping he had called the ambulance in time. Nicky had committed various burglaries in his life but was against using violence and had never hurt anyone. The sight of the watchman lying in blood was all he could think of as he ran from the building and into a side road. He was just yards from the pub where he had arranged to meet the girl for a drink. Still in a nervous state, he looked forward to getting a large, stiff drink inside him to calm his nerves.

Inside the pub there was no sign of his girlfriend Katie. He sat down with a double brandy and waited.

He had just got up to order another large brandy when he felt a tap on his shoulder. He looked round expecting to see Katie. When he saw the uniform he realized that someone had seen him running and that he was in serious trouble.

*

Nicky sat in his cell thinking back on how he had come to be in this mess. He realized his mistake was in going into the warehouse. He knew all that. But he hadn't stolen anything. If only the night-watchman had lived – perhaps he would have been able to identify the person that hit him. And if only he hadn't admitted to the police that he was actually there and had telephoned for the ambulance. And why had the prosecution made it sound as if *he* was a killer? Nicky's mind went back to that moment in the witness box when Richard Eaves, counsel for the prosecution, had got him so confused.

'You admit that you were in the warehouse on the evening that the watchman was attacked and that your reason for being there, according to your statement to the police, was because you heard a cry for help. Is that correct?'

Nicky knew it was an exaggeration of the truth but needed a logical reason for his climbing the fence and entering the ware-house.

'Yes, it is,' Nicky answered, trying to appear calm.

'And being a good citizen, when you found the watchman had been injured, you immediately telephoned for an ambulance by using the telephone that was on the wall.'

'Yes.' Nicky's throat was getting dry.

'Can you explain to the court why no fingerprints appeared on any part of the telephone?'

'I told the police.'

'But I want you to tell the court.'

'I used my handkerchief when I picked it up.'

'Now why would you do that?' Richard Eaves asked. 'Why would an innocent man who had answered a cry for help take the trouble to avoid his fingerprints being discovered on a telephone?'

Nicky was frightened and fell into the trap.

'Because I knew that with my record they'd stitch me up as the bloke's killer!'

There was a gasp from the public gallery where his mother and father were sitting.

Richard Eaves looked satisfied. Then Judge Thornton, a tall, slim man in his mid sixties, addressed the jury.

'Ladies and gentlemen. You will disregard the fact that, on his own admission, the defendant has a police record. It is the law of this land that any previous police record that the accused may have shall not be made known or considered relevant to this particular case, no matter how serious any previous convictions may be.'

Nicky's defence counsel Andrew Wilson jumped to his feet.

'My Lord, I must object.'

'To what?' Judge Thornton enquired with a glare.

'To the fact that the jury is now *unable* to disregard the fact that the defendant has a police record. In English law—'

'Mr Wilson!' the judge snarled. 'I am perfectly aware of the law! It was your client who decided to inform this court that he actually *has* a police record. I am merely doing my duty in instructing the jury to disregard that unfortunate fact. Whether or not they do so is outside my control.'

There was a threatening stare from his steely blue eyes, one that counsel for the defence had witnessed before.

Andrew Wilson gave a reluctant nod of acceptance and sat, knowing that to argue with Judge Thornton would be fighting a lost cause. He had experienced the judge's wrath on a previous case and had concluded that his lordship was only interested in conviction, not justice.

Nicky looked nervously up at his parents and gave them a helpless shrug. His father gave a warm smile and a confident wink, trying to reassure him. But despite having put on a brave face, his parents were far from confident that the outcome would be in their son's favour.

Judge Thornton looked at Richard Eaves and nodded.

'Please continue.'

Richard Eaves gave a calculated look of despair and said, 'I have no more questions, my lord.'

He sat down, leaving his colleague for the defence the impossible task of convincing the jury that his client was innocent.

Nicky was mentally kicking himself for mentioning the fact that he had a police record when the cell door opened and he was escorted back into the court.

He stood nervously watching the jury take their seats. Then everyone rose and Judge Thornton took his place on the bench. Once everyone was sitting, the judge gave a nod for the clerk to proceed.

The clerk of the court turned to the jury and asked their foreman, 'Have you the jury reached your verdict?'

The foreman stood. 'We have.'

'How do you find the defendant? Guilty or not guilty?'

Nicky began trembling and his parents squeezed each others hands as they waited for the foreman to answer.

'Guilty.'

'And that is the verdict of you all?'

'It is.'

Nicky cried out, 'No! I never did it! I never touched him!' He looked at the judge and pleaded, 'Please. Please, you must believe me. I never did it.' He broke down and wept.

His mother cried and his father bit his lip as he watched his son looking helplessly at his defence counsel.

The judge was quite unmoved at the young man's plea, which he considered typical of a criminal who had committed such an offence. Judge Thornton was going to punish this young man according to the law. No cries for leniency were going to make him deliver a lesser sentence. He despised cowardice, especially in a young hooligan like Nicky Bains. He banged his gavel and called for order. Nicky stood trembling as he waited to hear his fate.

'Nicholas Jonathan Bains. You have been found guilty of manslaughter, which is a heinous crime, second only to that of premeditated murder. And it is the duty of this court to pronounce sentence.'

The tension in the courtroom increased as he continued.

'It seems that young men such as yourself believe that it is their right to break into private property and steal. And should an innocent guardian of that property get in your way you have no hesitation in violently disposing of them. It is my duty to show you that you are wrong and to punish you for the wrong that you have done to others. It is the sentence of this court that you go to prison for twelve years. Take him down.'

As Nicky was escorted from the court, he looked towards his parents in total shock. His mother blew him a kiss and began crying. His father stared at his son in disbelief.

CHAPTER TWO

It had been the perfect morning for a game of golf, with a clear sky and only a slight breeze. One of those days when he could get some exercise and much-needed fresh air, away from a stuffy court-room.

Judge Thornton had enjoyed his eighteen holes with Chief Constable James MacCormack. Apart from being in the company of a good friend, he had beaten his opponent by seven points and the judge was a man who liked to win. Being slimly built with silver-grey hair gave him the appearance of a kind man, but beneath that genial presence was the judge that had given long sentences in the belief that severe punishment acted as a deterrent to committing crime.

The two men lived near each other in Guildford, Surrey, and had similar views on the way criminals should be treated – which in their opinion was more harshly than the current laws allowed. Although privately a fair man, William Thornton had a reputation for seldom showing leniency to anyone who was found guilty of a serious offence, particularly if the crime had resulted in a person being seriously injured or killed.

He had always promised himself that, finances permitting, he would retire when he reached his mid sixties. And now, here he was, three weeks away from his sixty-sixth birthday, preparing to cele-brate both the birthday and retirement at a party that his daughter Alison was organizing for him.

As they walked towards the clubhouse, James MacCormack commented on the forthcoming event.

'Thank you for the invitation to your retirement bash.'

'I wouldn't dream of having it without you. I trust that you will be able to make it?'

'Unless someone shoots the mayor or tries to blow up the town hall, wild horses won't keep me away,' James said. 'But I don't know why you want to retire. I mean, it isn't as if you *have* to. You could go on for a few more years yet.'

Judge Thornton smiled. 'I could. But I don't want to. I shall look forward to pottering about and spending more time with my grand-daughter while she's still growing up.'

'Ah yes, Jody is certainly a lovely little girl. She likes being with you as much as you like being with her. But you'll miss being on the bench after all these years, surely?'

'Perhaps. But I don't want to end up an old fuddy-duddy who looks and sounds like a character from one of Gilbert and Sullivan's operettas.'

James MacCormack laughed. 'I know what you mean. I've come in contact with a few of those in my time. I suppose one or two villains will be glad to see the back of you though.'

The judge answered proudly, 'Oh yes. I'm sure most of them will be delighted to see the back of me. After all, I refused them the freedom to benefit from their crimes.'

James nodded in agreement. 'Absolutely.'

They arrived at the men's locker room and, after taking a hot shower, changed into their street clothes. When they met up at the bar it was James MacCormack who ordered the round of whiskies with plain water, and two ham sandwiches. Being creatures of habit, they sat at their usual corner table and raised their glasses to each other.

'Cheers,' James said.

The judge touched James's glass. 'Your good health.'

After they had sampled their drinks, the chief constable asked his friend, 'This next case of yours will be the last before you pack it all in, I assume?'

The judge gave a pleasurable sigh as he answered, 'It most certainly will.'

'Be over before the party, will it?' James asked with an impish grin.

The judge shrugged as he replied, 'I've got Phillip Burns acting for the defence, and when he gets on his feet there's no telling *how* long the case will take. However, with a bit of luck it should be all settled within two weeks. That will allow me time to rest up before the shindig.'

'What sort of case is it? Interesting or boring?'

'The only thing I find boring in a case is when counsel try to earn their fee by time wasting. That I find boring and extremely irritating,' the judge replied. Then, finishing his drink, he smiled and said, 'I think one more will still keep us within the limit.'

He ordered two more whiskies and they began eating their sandwiches.

'Your Alison has really gone to town on this party, hasn't she? Not many daughters would go to all the trouble that she has for their father.'

The judge smiled. 'I am a very lucky man. Alison has been a wonderful daughter.' Then with regret he added, 'Her mother would have been so proud of her. Alison was only four when Angela died. But she's turned out a gem.'

'Being the only child, I'm sure you spoilt her to bits.'

'I tried not to but it was inevitable I suppose. Mind you, when I employed Emma as my housekeeper, Alison became rather resentful. She thought I was trying to replace her mother.'

'Perfectly natural,' James said. 'Not easy for a child to come to terms with that situation. Probably thought the woman would take your attention away from her. Never mind, the way things worked out it couldn't be better. The two of them get on so well that I always think of Emma as a member of the family.'

The judge nodded in agreement. 'Finding Emma Roberts was certainly a lucky day for me. I don't know what I would have done without her looking after things for us. She won Alison over in no time.' Then thoughtfully he added, 'I suppose in a way she really *did* replace Angela, as far as taking care of Alison was concerned. Been a damned good woman, has Emma. Kept her looks too. I like a woman to take care of her appearance. It shows character.'

James smiled and jokingly asked, 'Do I detect a secret desire for the lovely Emma?'

'Don't be ridiculous.' The judge finished his drink. 'Time I was off. I promised Jody I would take her to see the baby elephant at the children's zoo. Don't want her to think that I have forgotten.' He stood up and shook his friend's hand. 'See you next weekend, if not before.'

'I'll get my revenge next week,' said James MacCormack.

'Not unless you practise hitting a straight ball,' Judge Thornton laughed. 'Drive carefully.' He waved and left by the side door that led into the car park.

Four Oaks was an impressive family house that stood at the end of a long drive in the village of Bell Green just outside Guildford. Built in 1924, it gave the impression of a small stately home of an earlier period. Its large double oak doors were the main feature at the front and any first-time visitor could be forgiven for expecting the house to include several servants, such was the effect it gave.

William Thornton had bought it after his marriage and had never considered living anywhere else. Standing as it did in four acres of delightful grounds, it was the one place he was able to get away from everyday problems. Apart from an unused area shielded by a spinney, the garden was mainly lawn with a series of rose beds carefully planted to produce eye-catching features. The large borders of shrubs and rhododendrons gave the effect of a perfect frame to the garden he considered his private park.

As he turned into the driveway he saw Jody dressed, ready and waiting by the front porch. She was a pretty eight-year-old with shiny dark hair and her mother's brown eyes, full of expression. He waved and when she saw him approaching she smiled and waved back. As he got out of the car, Jody ran and greeted him with a kiss.

'Always nice to be welcomed with a kiss from my favourite girl,' he said, returning her kiss with one of his own on her forehead. 'I hope you haven't been waiting very long.'

'No, Grandpa. I just came out as you arrived.' She held his hand as he walked into the house. 'Are we going soon?'

'As soon as I've had a cup of tea and a rock cake. Is Emma about?'

'She's in the kitchen. Shall I call her?'

'No. See if she can make me a cup of tea before we go out and ask her for *two* of her rock cakes. One for me and one for you.' Then, teasing her, he added, 'If you've got room for one after your lunch, that is?'

As Jody ran to the kitchen with enthusiasm, her grandfather smiled at the way children always got excited when cake was forthcoming. He was looking forward more than anything to spending more time with Jody. She made him happy when he was with her; he could forget everything else. Just one more case and he could hang up his robes, he reflected. But first, he had a date with a young lady to see a baby elephant, and the thought of that gave him great pleasure.

Alison and her husband Gary lived in the apartment over the old stables, next to her father's house. William Thornton had thought of converting the building into living accommodation for several years and when his daughter intended to marry he had the work carried out – partly in order to give his daughter a home but mainly so that she would not be miles away from him. Alison was happy being near her father, especially when she saw him with her daughter Jody. Judge Thornton was a different person when he was with his granddaughter and Alison was very proud of her father and always grateful for the love that he and Jody shared.

The one regret William Thornton had was that his daughter had chosen Gary Hanley for a husband. He thought of him as 'a failed entertainer' and never considered him suitable as the son-in-law of a Crown Court judge. He would have preferred his daughter to have married a man in a secure and respectable profession, not someone who earned his living impersonating famous people and appearing at working men's clubs where only dirty jokes and innuendo appeared to amuse the clientele that frequented them. And the thing that aggravated Judge Thornton more than anything about Gary Hanley was the way he referred to him as 'Pops'. But Alison had made her choice and despite her father's reservations, her husband had fathered a lovely child in Jody. Judge Thornton would always be grateful to him for that.

Their visit to the zoo had been a great success, with the baby elephant being the main attraction. Jody's amazement at the actual size of an elephant's offspring had amused her grandfather and, as always, the little girl's company had made him a happy man.

When they arrived back at the house, Jody couldn't wait to run and tell her mother about the wonderful outing she'd had, while Judge Thornton went to his study to examine the delivery of mail that had arrived after he'd left for his game of golf.

He was about to open a letter from the Prime Minister's office when there was a knock at the door. Without looking up he called, 'Come in.'

The door opened and his daughter Alison came into the room with an anxious look on her attractive face.

'Sorry to bother you, Father, but I thought you should know that Uncle Bernie just called on his mobile phone to say that he's on his way and will be here in a few minutes.'

'Oh God, so he's back,' sighed her father. 'What on earth brings him here?'

'When he arrives, shall I tell him you're out?'

'No. I'll have to see him. Let's just hope that he's on his way somewhere and won't be staying long.'

'Will you see him in here or in the sitting room?' Alison asked.

'In here, I think. I don't want him in the sitting room. If he gets too comfortable in an armchair he'll be here for the day.'

Alison smiled. 'I know what you mean.' Walking to the door, she turned and said, 'Jody had a lovely time, thank you.'

'We *both* had a lovely time,' he said with a half smile. 'Up to now this has been a very nice day. Trust Bernard to arrive like a bad penny and spoil it. As no doubt he will.'

'Perhaps he won't,' she said hopefully.

'Pigs might fly,' he replied with a grunt.

Alison left the study, leaving her father deep in thought.

His brother was the last person he wanted to see now. Bernard Thornton was the black sheep of the family and had a habit of turning up when least expected. The youngest of the brothers, he had been an embarrassment to his parents from his early days at university where, instead of studying, he preferred drinking and womanizing. Having failed to make the necessary grades to become an equal partner in their father's law firm, Bernard gave up any idea of a legal career and made it his sole ambition in life to become rich. He had a dream that his latter years would be spent living in luxury surrounded by beautiful women but, like every dream Bernard had, it only existed in the befuddled brain of an alcoholic. Now, after a two-year absence overseas, during which time no one had any idea where he was, he had returned. Judge Thornton's regret was that Bernard had ever come back to England at all, and he wished, as he had many times, that his brother was someone of whom he could be proud instead of the embarrassment that he had become.

The door burst open and Bernard Thornton breezed into the room as if it was his own.

He was tall but more portly than his brother and although three years younger he looked a lot older due to the intake of alcohol his body had endured over the years. His eyes were blue but the white area had now become the yellowish red of a drinker. He walked across to his brother and gave him a hearty slap on the back. 'How are you, old man?'

The judge politely held out his hand and, trying to appear friendly, said, 'I'm very well.'

Ignoring his brother's hand, Bernard noticed a decanter of whisky on the bureau and went straight to it.

'Don't mind, do you?' he asked as he poured a large amount into a glass. 'Care to join me?'

'Good heavens, no. For goodness' sake, Bernard, it's not even teatime yet!'

Bernard drank a large mouthful and smacked his lips.

'Perfect time for a heart-starter.' He grinned. 'You ought to try it sometime.'

'I'm surprised that your heart hasn't stopped before now,' said the judge with sarcasm.

'Touché.' Bernard suddenly seemed uncomfortable.

'To what do I owe this surprise visit?' asked his brother.

'Arrived back in the UK last week and thought how nice it would be to see my big brother. So I got my neighbour to jump-lead the old car and here I am.'

He finished his whisky and poured himself another.

William tried not to show his annoyance as he asked, 'And where have you come from this time?'

Bernard took his replenished glass and sat on the opposite side of the desk, facing his brother.

'Nigeria. The country's riddled with corruption but they wouldn't let me in on it so I came home!' His raucous laughter made the judge wince. 'What about you?' he asked. 'I suppose you're still sending the law breakers to purgatory?' He drank half the whisky from his glass.

William ignored the question, preferring one of his own.

'How long do you intend staying in England?'

Bernard shrugged. 'That all depends.'

'On what?'

'You, big brother.'

'What do you mean?'

Bernard finished his drink and got up, taking his empty glass back to the decanter for a refill.

'It's like this,' he said awkwardly. 'I've got myself in a bit of bother, old man. Nothing serious, you understand, but rather a nuisance nevertheless. Thought you might help me out of a hole.' He returned to his chair and smiled nervously at his brother. 'Don't like to worry you, old man, but, er, well, naturally I came to the one person I knew I could rely on.' His hand shook as he lifted the glass to his lips.

William looked at him with trepidation as he spoke. 'What exactly is this bother you refer to?'

Clearing his throat, Bernard said, 'Silly really. My fault of course. Had too much to drink, I'm afraid. You know how it is.'

'No, Bernard, I *don't* know. But I do wish you would get to the point and tell me. I am rather busy.'

'Absolutely. Point taken. It's like this.' He finished his drink and put the empty glass down on the desk. 'Met this chap at the hotel bar in Lagos. We got talking and after a few drinks he invited me to his room for a nightcap. I saw no harm in that, so off we toddled to his room. When we arrived he brought out a bottle of the *real* stuff, Aberfeldy, fifteen year-old single malt whisky. Well, as you can imagine the old tastebuds were in ecstasy and before we knew it we were over halfway through the bottle.' He was becoming more nervous and, taking his empty glass, returned to the decanter.

William watched with disgust as his brother almost filled the glass and started drinking it.

'I don't have an endless supply of whisky, so I would be grateful if you made that your last,' he said sharply.

Bernard returned to the desk and sat down. 'No need to be unpleasant, old man. You don't begrudge me a drop of Dutch courage, surely. Now, where was I?'

'Helping someone to empty a bottle of fine whisky in a Lagos hotel, I believe. Rather like you are doing now.'

Bernard cleared his throat once more, 'Yes, well, this young woman suddenly arrived and after another drink or two I passed out. Must have put something in my drink because I can hold my own with the best of 'em. Anyway, to cut a long story short, when I woke up I was back in *my* room again. By then it was morning. I took a shower, had some breakfast and didn't think of the previous evening until a note arrived.'

Judge Thornton was anticipating the worst as he frowned and asked, 'A note regarding the young woman?'

'Yes.'

'Tell me. Did you have sexual intercourse with her during that evening?

'Definitely not! And once I'd passed out, sex would have been impossible. A chap can't do anything in that condition, you know that.'

His brother got up and, looking out into the garden, became thoughtful. 'It would appear that you were the victim of some professional blackmailers. And I imagine the note was to demand payment for services the young woman claimed she gave, even though you have no recollection of those services being given.' He turned to Bernard and asked, 'Am I right?'

Bernard nodded.

'Did these people know that you were planning to leave Lagos and return to England?'

'I don't think I mentioned it, no.'

'Then I can't see that you have anything to worry about. I imagine they were annoyed at having wasted an evening and a good bottle of whisky on you, but no doubt they found another gullible male to extort money from. I really don't see any reason for you to lose any sleep over this matter. Unless there is something that you have omitted to tell me?'

Bernard became very edgy and uncomfortable as he reached into his jacket pocket and removed a brown envelope.

'Actually, it's a bit embarrassing, old man. You see, the thing is, I was set up.'

The judge looked at the envelope and, returning to his desk, sat down. Taking the envelope with apprehension, he asked, 'Before I look at the contents, are you absolutely sure that you want me to?'

Bernard nodded. 'As I say, I've been set up. Those photos are bloody fakes. But how do I prove it?'

His brother's expression remained unchanged as he looked at three photographs of Bernard and a young woman, naked on a bed and apparently having sexual intercourse. Each photograph had been cleverly staged, with Bernard on top of the woman to make it appear that intercourse was taking place. In each of the photographs the woman's face was contorted to give the impression that she was ecstatic, while Bernard's eyes were always closed, which could easily suggest that he was enjoying the young woman. The angle at which each photograph had been taken made it impossible to see whether or not intercourse was actually taking place.

'Well? What do you think? Bloody clever set-up, eh? Makes a chap look guilty as hell, wouldn't you say?' Bernard asked.

Judge Thornton put the photographs back into the envelope and pushed it across the desk to his brother.

'Did you happen to mention *me* by any chance?'

'I don't think so, old man. I mean, why should I?'

'But you do see the danger to me if you had?'

'For Christ's sake, it's me they photographed, not you! Why the bloody hell would you be in danger?' Bernard shouted.

His brother signalled him to keep his voice down. 'All right, all right. But you do see the potential if the blackmailer knew that your brother was a Crown Court judge. Imagine the damage your predicament could do to my reputation, to say nothing of my family.'

Bernard listened in disbelief. 'I thought I *was* your family, for Christ's sake! Why else would I come to you?' He picked up his empty glass and went to the decanter. 'If you don't mind. I really do need one.'

Judge Thornton gave a reluctant sigh. 'If you must. Just remember that it's alcohol that got you into this mess in the first place.'

'There you go, pontificating like a judge,' Bernard said, as he hurriedly filled his glass with the remainder of the decanted whisky. 'It's all right for you to be self-righteous, big brother. You ought to get out into the real world among real people, instead of sitting in your bloody stupid wig and robe, sending some poor sod to prison because he isn't one of your bloody golf club cronies.' He drank half his drink then picked up the envelope. 'Ever heard the expression "blood is thicker than water"?'

'Of course,' the judge answered quietly.

'Well, yours must be gnat's piss!' The alcohol was starting to take effect and his eyes became glazed as he said, 'I know what your trouble is. You need a bloody good woman. It's not natural for a man to live on his own the way you have since Angela died. Christ, man, it's nearly thirty years ago!'

His brother tried not to show his anger. 'Bernard, the way I choose to live is of no concern to anyone but myself. In any case, you are wrong. I do not live on my own.'

'Oh no, I forgot.' Bernard's tone became more unpleasant as he said with a sneer, 'You've got the ever loyal Emma to keep you company. I bet you've been giving her one on the quiet for years.'

Judge Thornton stood up and found difficulty controlling his fury. 'That was a disgusting thing to say and I find your company quite unpleasant, Bernard. I must ask you to go before I—'

'Pass sentence and have me locked away?' Bernard got to his feet and glared at his brother with contempt. 'You would, too, given half the chance, you sanctimonious sod.' He walked to the door with an unsteady step and opened it. Pushing it back against the wall with a bang, he put two fingers up to his brother and stormed out of the study.

For a brief moment Judge Thornton wanted to go after him but he hesitated, then heard the front door slam.

Alison came to the study, looking puzzled.

'Was that Uncle Bernie?'

'I'm afraid it was,' her father answered sadly.

'I was going to get him some tea.'

'I think *tea* was the last thing he wanted. As you can see by the empty decanter.'

'Good Lord!' she exclaimed. 'Did he drink all that?'

'He did.'

At that moment they heard a car start and drive away.

'He's in no state to drive!' declared Alison. 'Phone the police and get them to stop him before he kills someone.'

Reluctantly her father picked up the phone. 'You don't know his registration number, I suppose?'

'Sorry. Just tell them it's an old blue Jaguar.'

He dialled the local police station. 'What a stupid man he is. Nothing but trouble ... Hello ... This is Judge Thornton. An old-model blue Jaguar has just left my house, heading towards London, I believe. I'd appreciate it if you would stop it. The driver is well over the limit and may cause an accident. Thank you.' He hung up, looking dejected. 'No doubt he'll hate me even more now.'

Alison put her arm around him and kissed his cheek. 'A cup of tea will make you feel better,' she said with a smile.

He squeezed her hand and nodded. After she left the study he sat for a moment, then picked up the letter from the Prime Minister's office. He read the contents with shocked surprise. He read it again and was about to go to the door as Alison reappeared.

'Emma's bringing you some tea,' she informed him.

'Tea will be fine. Although I feel that champagne might be more appropriate on this occasion,' he said, sounding like an excited schoolboy.

'What do you mean? What's happened?'

He gave her the letter and waited for her reaction.

Alison looked up with pride and said, 'Father, darling! This is wonderful. They're offering you a knighthood!'

CHAPTER THREE

The weekend at his home in Guildford had been all too brief. Judge Thornton would have liked more time with Alison and Jody and wished he didn't have to keep the knighthood offer quiet until it had been officially accepted and announced in the birthday honours list. As it was, only Alison was aware of his accolade and after tea they celebrated secretly in his study with the two of them behaving like naughty children sharing a secret.

Having opened a bottle of Bollinger, he carefully poured out two glasses. His daughter gave him a tender kiss on the cheek.

'I'm so pleased for you, Father. Every girl dreams of her knight in shining armour but not many are lucky enough to get a *real* one.' She raised her glass to him. 'Cheers, darling.'

'Thank you.' He drank some champagne, then gave a smile. 'I wonder if they *give* me the shining armour or whether I buy that myself?'

Alison had always loved her father's quiet sense of humour and her face reflected the pride she felt for him.

'Getting nominated for this award just shows how much the help you have given to various charities over the years has been appreciated.' She put her arm around him and smiled. 'If it wasn't for people like you, giving money and getting your friends to put their hands in their pockets, think how worse off those children would be.'

Her words touched him and he kissed her cheek. 'You're somewhat biased, I think. But thank you.' Then thoughtfully he added, 'I really do enjoy helping those children. Despite my reputation for being a hard man.'

She gave his hand an affectionate squeeze. 'Every judge is hard at times. They have to be.'

'But some of us are harder than others, perhaps.'

Alison looked at him and said quietly, 'I can never think of you as being anything but fair.'

His reply was unrepentant. 'I believe in justice for the victim not the criminal. Being fair can often be mistaken for being weak, something one can never be when the accused are thugs and murderers.'

Alison suddenly thought of something she had been meaning to ask her father. 'Would you like your friend in Dorset to be at the party?'

'My friend?' he said with surprise.

'Yes. Only if you do, I need his name and address.'

'He's away at the moment, visiting relatives somewhere. So he wouldn't be able to come.' Then he gave her hand a tender squeeze. 'How nice of you to ask.'

'Well, I know you enjoy your short stays with him so I just wondered if you'd like him to come, that's all.'

'That's very thoughtful of you.'

'You'll have to invite him up another time.'

'Yes ... Yes, perhaps I will one day.'

'He was in the legal profession, wasn't he? A barrister or something. That's if my memory serves me correctly.'

'Your memory is excellent. Now let's not talk shop, eh?' he said, anxious to get off the subject of his friend. 'There are lots of my other friends coming to the party I imagine.'

Tapping the side of her nose, she grinned. 'That would be telling, wouldn't it? I think you'll find one or two people you know turning up. But you will just have to wait and see who they are, won't you?'

'All right. I shan't ask any more, I promise.'

Suddenly, out of the blue she asked, 'Why don't you write your autobiography?'

'Because my life is not for sale. Besides, my life is not over yet.'

He walked to the window and stared thoughtfully into the distance. Alison took the bottle to him and topped up their glasses.

'Penny for them,' she said.

'Oh, I was just thinking of your mother and how proud she would have been.' He continued staring into the garden.

Alison put down the champagne bottle and held his hand. 'I know,' she said with understanding.

A gentle smile came to him as he said, 'Just think. Your mother would have been Lady Thornton. Angela would have liked that.' He gave a sigh of regret. 'If only fate had been fair.'

He stood at the window, thinking how nice it would have been to have his friend from Dorset at the party. But he knew that wasn't possible.

The only thing that had almost ruined his time at home was his brother Bernard's unwelcome visit and subsequent arrest on the A3 for driving while over the legal alcohol limit. A phone call by the judge to his friend the chief constable had hopefully avoided any publicity that might connect Bernard to his brother. Judge Thornton was very much aware that any bad publicity at this time could result in the offer of his being elevated to the noble order of knights being withdrawn. These thoughts were in his mind that Monday morning as he arrived back in his chambers at court.

The journey to Winchester had been uneventful and because he had allowed plenty of time to get there, he was trying to relax and concentrate on the case before him. A case which he felt should only take two weeks at most, providing that Mr Phillip Burns, counsel for the defence, resisted his love of the theatrical, which had often turned the courtroom into a playhouse and angered Judge Thornton. Over the years the two men had become adversaries, with their dislike of each other common knowledge. After a while he changed into his robes and wondered just how much he would really miss wearing them once this case was over. His thoughts were interrupted when he was informed that it was time to make his way to the bench.

Thelma Davis was a twenty-seven-year-old woman accused of killing her husband Mark, who had discovered his wife with her lover, John Porter.

A neighbour had called the police when she heard raised voices and a woman screaming.

The first witness was Sergeant Daly, one of the two policemen who were called to the scene. After taking the oath, he was questioned by the prosecuting counsel Simon Reed, a tall man in his late fifties.

'When you arrived at the Davis residence, Sergeant, please tell the court what you found.'

'Mrs Davis let us in and was obviously in a terrible state with her husband lying there bleeding. I checked his pulse but it was obvious that he was dead,' said the sergeant.

'And what was Mrs Davis's explanation of this tragic and fatal occurrence?' He avoided the word *accident*, not wanting an objection so early in his questioning. 'I assume that she had one.'

'When we arrived, all she kept saying was that she hadn't meant to kill him.'

'So she admitted, quite freely, that it was through her own action that her husband had met his death?'

'Yes.'

Thelma Davis looked frail as she listened to the evidence. Occasionally she would appear to let her mind wander to other things.

'Apart from saying that she had not meant to kill Mr Davis, did she say anything else?'

'She said that her husband had returned home after having been drinking, and began pushing her around. She said that she had pushed him in retaliation which caused him to lose his balance. According to Mrs Davis, he fell backwards and struck his head on the corner of the hearth, which resulted in his death.'

'So there was nothing to suggest that Mr Davis had died from anything other than an unfortunate fall when he lost his balance due to a surfeit of alcohol in his body?'

The judge, curious as to why the prosecution was sounding more like the defence, awaited the reply with interest.

Sergeant Daly remained calm as he said, 'There were some blood-stains approximately four feet from the fireplace, which suggested that the victim had been moved from there to where we found him.'

Phillip Burns was quickly on his feet.

'I must object, m'lud. This witness is giving the court an opinion of what might or might not have taken place. As he is not a qualified medical man I ask that his last remark be struck from the record.'

Simon Reed was quick to reply. 'I should like to remind my learned friend that any police officer joining the force has to go through a training of first aid, and that when reaching the rank of sergeant would be experienced enough to know if an injured person had in fact been moved from the place where the injury had originally been inflicted.'

Judge Thornton enjoyed seeing Phillip Burns corrected and had difficulty hiding his pleasure as he made his ruling.

'Objection overruled.'

'Thank you, m'lud.' Simon Reed turned back to Sergeant Daly and asked, 'In your professional opinion, could a woman, even one as slight in build as the accused, be able to move a body weighing fourteen stone the distance of approximately four feet across a floor?'

'If she were to drag him, yes.'

'And were there any marks on the floor to suggest that he had been dragged from one area to another?'

'Despite what appeared to be efforts to remove such marks, yes, there were.'

'Thank you, Sergeant.' He turned to Phillip Burns and gave a courteous nod before sitting down.

Phillip Burns got to his feet and began to cross-examine. 'Sergeant, we have listened with interest to your *opinions* as to what may or may not have happened, and I would like to ask for your considered opinion as to this. Could Mr Davis have fallen and struck his head some four feet from the hearth and dragged *himself* towards the hearth where he then collapsed and died? Is that possible, Sergeant?'

Sergeant Daly was hesitant in answering. 'Well ... I suppose it would be possible but ...'

'Thank you, Sergeant. No further questions.'

The brevity of cross-examination took Judge Thornton and Simon Reed by surprise. As Phillip Burns sat down, Sergeant Daly was excused and Doctor Henderson the coroner was called to give evidence.

While the doctor was being sworn in, the judge glanced at his watch and was pleased with the pace at which his final case was moving along. Unless something unexpected happened, he concluded, he would be sitting at home enjoying his long-awaited retirement by this time next week. The sound of Simon Reed's voice brought his attention back to the case before him.

After establishing Doctor Henderson's official position at the coroner's office, Simon Reed began his examination of the witness.

'After your post mortem on Mark Davis, will you tell the court what conclusion you came to as to how he met his death, Doctor Henderson.'

The doctor spoke with the precise diction of a man used to giving evidence in a court of law.

'His skull was fractured, having made forceful contact with an object which had resulted in death.'

'This object. Could it have been the corner of a tiled hearth?'

Doctor Henderson was positive in his reply. 'There was a small amount of chalky substance in the wound which proved to be grouting, found between tiled surfaces. I would therefore have to say that it could have been the hearth, yes.'

'Is it possible that Mr Davis's fatal injury was caused by something *other* than the hearth, and that this grouting was added to the wound later to make it *appear* that he had fallen on to the hearth, in order to suggest an accident?'

Phillip Burns was unhappy and could see that Thelma Davis was beginning to panic as the court waited for the doctor to answer.

'Due to the angle of the blow that made contact with the victim's skull, it is quite possible that it was caused by him falling backwards and striking his head on the corner of the hearth.'

The doctor paused and Phillip Burns looked relieved until Doctor Henderson continued.

'However, it is equally possible that the victim could have been struck from behind by a heavy object then moved to the hearth as suggested in your hypothesis. In either case the wounds would be similar.'

Thelma Davis was shaking and Phillip Burns hoped that she would hold on until he cross-examined the doctor, which he was certain would be any minute now.

Simon Reed was looking confident and about to add another blow to Phillip Burns' defence.

'Finally, Doctor, let me ask you this. If there had been no tile grouting from the fire hearth in Mr Davis's wound, would your professional medical opinion be that he was killed in another area of the living room and *moved* to the position where the police found him? Namely, the tiled hearth of the fireplace?'

Thelma Davis became hysterical before the doctor was able to answer and her screaming echoed around the courtroom.

'We had to kill him before he killed me! The bastard was evil! Evil!' She burst into tears and sobbed as she said, 'Sorry, Johnny. I can't take any more.' She suddenly went limp and collapsed in a faint onto the lap of a WPC sitting next to her.

Phillip Burns quickly stood and looked at the judge. 'May the doctor be excused to attend to Mrs Davis, m'lud?'

Judge Thornton nodded his consent and while the doctor went to Thelma Davis, he banged his gavel and adjourned the court for thirty minutes. As he left the bench, he called the clerk to him.

'Inform both Mr Burns and Mr Reed that I wish to see them in my chambers. Also, instruct the officer that the witness John Porter is to be held in the building until permission is given by me that he may leave.'

Word of the incident inside the courtroom had quickly got to the ears of John Porter, who was waiting to be called as a witness. He sat nervously pushing his dark hair back from his strong features, where it kept falling each time he leaned forward in his seat.

He was a well-built man in his mid thirties and had the appearance of a strong manual worker. When he heard what had happened to Thelma Davis he tried to enter the courtroom, but was prevented from doing so by the policeman on duty. While he waited anxiously for news of his girlfriend, the judge's instructions were conveyed to him and he wished he knew what had been said inside the court. It was not knowing that worried him. Would it all work out the way he had planned? Had Thelma sat looking like a downtrodden, abused wife, the way they had agreed before the trial? Was she strong enough to stand up to all the questions she would be asked, and would he sound convincing when his turn came? These thoughts were starting to worry him. If only he could see Thelma, he could tell her not to be frightened and that everything was going to be all right. But he couldn't see Thelma. Not until he walked into that witness box. And knowing that she might get confused and become unstable under too much pressure, John Porter had every reason to be a worried man.

Both defence and prosecuting counsel arrived at the judge's chambers and closed the door behind them.

The judge had removed his wig and gown and was sitting at his desk as the two men entered and stood before him.

'Well, gentlemen, it appears that this case will soon come to its conclusion. Much earlier than even *I* had wished it to. I appreciate that neither of you could have anticipated what has taken place but

I am nevertheless interested to hear how you intend proceeding, Mr Reed?'

Simon Reed was confident as he replied, 'With the accused having implicated her lover as being involved in her husband's unfortunate death, I request that John Porter be detained and kept under—'

'I have already ordered that he be kept in the building,' the judge confirmed. 'Please continue, Mr Reed.'

'I was about to say that I shall read the transcript of her outburst back to her and hopefully get her to repeat her words, implicating John Porter as her accomplice in the death of her husband. Furthermore I shall ask that the charge of accidental death be changed to that of premeditated murder.'

The judge turned to Phillip Burns. 'No more than you would expect under the circumstances, I am sure, Mr Burns?'

Phillip Burns was slightly uncomfortable but tried to look confident as he spoke. 'I shall suggest in her defence that Mrs Davis was unwell, frightened and totally confused when she uttered the words she did. That the woman was under great mental strain and, as was seen by the way she collapsed, in no fit state to know what she was saying. And because she is in need of medical care, ask for a retrial when the results of a psychiatric examination are made known.'

Judge Thornton raised an eyebrow. 'And do you imagine that you would be granted one without proper medical evidence to show that the accused was in some way mentally unfit? No Mr Burns. I think you can rule out any retrial in this case. Now regarding John Porter, Mr Reed. In the event that you are successful in getting the accused to admit that he was indeed her accomplice, I cannot possibly allow him to be brought in as a witness on her behalf, while at the same time have him charged as an accomplice to murder. You do see the problem. Under the circumstances, I think we must deal with Mrs Davis now and hopefully get the jury to deliberate and return their verdict without too much delay. A subsequent trial for John Porter could then be held at a later date. I don't want this dragging on longer than is necessary.'

There was a hint of sarcasm in Phillip Burns' tone. 'Oh, I'd almost forgotten. You will be retiring after this case, won't you, m'lud?'

'Yes, Mr Burns. But not *until* then,' the judge retorted.

There was a knock at the door and the clerk of the court put his head in.

'Doctor Henderson, my lord.'

'Show him in.' The judge rose from his chair.

Doctor Henderson was ushered in and acknowledged the others as he went to the judge's desk. 'Mrs Davis is quite all right. She was under a lot of stress but has regained her composure. After some good old-fashioned smelling salts she is perfectly able to continue.'

Phillip Burns was not happy and showed it. 'But surely the lady is not stable? I may not be a doctor but it seems to me quite obvious that she should be examined by a psychiatrist before putting her through any further ordeal.'

Doctor Henderson shook his head. 'In my experience, women of her sort, in her position, try anything to convince a jury that they are sick or being hard done by. Having examined the lady I am of the opinion that she is playing for sympathy.'

'But surely—'

Phillip Burns was about to protest when Judge Thornton cut in, showing his aggravation.

'As you so correctly stated a few moments ago, Mr Burns, you are *not* a doctor!' Turning to Doctor Henderson he said, 'In your opinion then, Doctor, Mrs Davis is fit to continue?'

Phillip Burns was showing his displeasure as the doctor gave his answer.

'Certainly.'

'Thank you, Doctor. And now, gentlemen, I should like to proceed.' He scowled at Phillip Burns. 'Without any tedious theatricals, if you please.'

Phillip Burns and Simon Reed turned and left, with Doctor Henderson and the clerk following. The judge put on his robes and wig once more and left the room.

The court rose as Judge Thornton took his seat. Once he had settled and checked that his notes were in order, he asked Simon Reed to proceed.

Thelma Davis was called to the witness box and sworn in. She was still very pale and gave the outward impression of being mentally unstable.

Simon Reed surprised everyone by getting straight to the point.

'Mrs Davis, you have sworn to tell the truth and nothing but the truth, have you not?'

There was a nervous quiver in her voice as she answered quietly, 'Yes, sir.'

'Then please tell the court who Johnny is and why you were saying sorry to him prior to your becoming indisposed a short while ago.'

She sounded innocent as she answered, 'I don't know what you mean, sir. I didn't know what I was saying, you see.'

'Then I shall remind you what you were saying.' Simon Reed read from the transcript, imitating her inflection. '"We had to kill him before he killed me. The bastard was evil. Evil. Sorry, Johnny. I can't take any more."' Then looking at her with a half smile, he said, 'Do you remember saying that?'

'No. I must have been delirious if I said things like you say I did, cos I don't remember saying it!' she shouted back at him.

'So Johnny was just a name you picked out of the blue, was it? Or is Johnny what you call your lover, John Porter?'

Thelma Davis gave a threatening glare as she answered, 'You leave my personal life out of it. You've no right to make a remark like that about someone.'

Judge Thornton immediately cautioned her. 'You will answer the question or be in contempt of court.'

Realizing that she was making things worse for herself, she looked worried and then suddenly changed into hard-done-by little housewife. 'He's John Porter but to me he's always been Johnny. He's the only real friend that I've got.'

'I see.' Simon Reed became gentle in his approach. 'And it was when you realized that you had killed your husband that you turned to Mr Porter, was it?' He gave a benign smile and added, 'Is that what happened? You needed a strong man that you could trust and rely on, so you turned to John Porter.'

She hesitated before answering, as if uncertain as to what she should say. 'Yeah ... that's right.'

'And when he saw what you had done, he wanted to help you and comfort you, did he not?'

She was regaining her composure and becoming confident. 'Yeah, that's what happened.'

'And that's when he put the grouting onto the wound, wasn't it?' he asked casually.

'Yeah. I mean *no!*' she quickly corrected herself. 'No, he never did that!'

Raising his voice he asked, 'Then if it wasn't him, it was you! So which one of you did it, Mrs Davis? You or Johnny?'

She panicked and looked helplessly around for help, but Simon Reed pressured her by rapidly repeating his question. 'Well? Which one of you rubbed the grouting into the wound? You or John Porter? Which of you did it, Mrs Davis? Answer the question. Was it you or your lover?'

Phillip Burns was about to get up and object to her being harassed when Thelma Davis broke down and began crying as she spoke. 'It was an accident … An accident!' she shouted. 'Mark was drunk and when he saw Johnny was with me he set about me. Then he picked up the poker from the fireplace and was going to hit Johnny with it. Then I grabbed the stone vase off the mantelpiece and bashed him on the head.' She was trembling as she continued, 'He fell down and there was blood all over the carpet. And that's when Johnny said I'd killed him.' The WPC steadied her as she started crying. 'You see. I didn't mean to kill him. I just wanted to stop him hitting Johnny. It was an accident.' She wiped her eyes and held tightly on to the rail of the witness box.

Phillip Burns got to his feet. 'May I respectfully ask for a brief recess, m'lud, in order that my client might rest a few moments before continuing?'

Without answering directly, the judge looked at Thelma and enquired, 'Do you feel able to continue?'

She drank some water from a glass provided by the WPC. 'I'll be all right. I just want to get this over and go home. I want to go home.'

'As do we all,' said Judge Thornton with a sigh, 'but we must let things take their course before any of us can leave, I'm afraid.' He looked at Phillip Burns and said, 'Request denied,' then, turning to Simon Reed, asked, 'Do you wish to continue?'

'Thank you, m'lud.' Simon Reed took up where he had left off but in a less vigorous manner. Instead, he spoke as though he had been given all the facts and was simply recapping.

'Mrs Davis. You have told the court how your husband came home the worse for drink and on seeing John Porter there with you became violent and, to use your own words, set about you and then went to attack Mr Porter with a fire poker. Is that correct?'

'Yeah. That's what happened. He was mad drunk. He always got violent when he was drunk.'

'And so, to prevent your husband attacking Mr Porter, you took a heavy vase from the mantelpiece and struck him with it on the back of his head.'

'I had to do something.'

'And you *did*, Mrs Davis. That blow to the head killed Mr Davis and when you realized this you began to get frightened. It was then that John Porter saw a way of helping you and he moved your husband to the tiled hearth, placed some grouting powder into the wound to make it appear that he had fallen, striking his head on the hearth by accident. That is exactly what happened, isn't it? John Porter did what he did because of his love for you. Isn't that true?'

Giving a weak smile, she said, 'Johnny's a good man, sir. A kind man. Do anything for me, he would.'

'And he certainly did. It is precisely because of what he did that you are now standing in this court, charged with the unlawful killing of another human being!' Simon Reed shouted. 'In fact, when you struck your husband on the head it was with the knowledge that you would be ridding yourself of the man that you hated. Isn't that true?'

Her knuckles became white as she gripped the handrail and there was fear in her eyes as she realized the truth in his statement. Her voice was only just audible as she hung her head and said, 'Yes.'

'Can you speak up, please?' Simon Reed pressured her.

'Yes!' she shouted. 'Yes! I'm glad the bastard's dead. He should never have been born.' The bitterness in her voice was enough for Simon Reed. He knew that he would be wasting time to continue. Giving a momentary glance to the jury, he turned to the bench. 'I have no further questions.'

As he sat down, the judge gave an enquiring look towards the defence counsel.

'Mr Burns?'

Phillip Burns rose slowly to his feet, with none of his usual enthusiasm. He knew that he couldn't do himself justice by trying to defend a self-confessed killer, other than to try and convince the jury that she was not responsible for her action due to her mental condition. He was aware of the danger in trying to claim diminished responsibility but felt that it was the only course left open to him. As he glanced up at the clock, he saw the opportunity to gain some thinking time.

'My lord, as it is almost 12.30 might I request that we adjourn for lunch at this time? It would give both my client and the jury a much-needed break before I begin my cross-examination.'

The judge was pleased to grant his request and take an early lunch, especially if the defence counsel was to mount one of his long-winded cross-examinations in the afternoon.

Banging his gavel he announced, 'This court will adjourn and re-convene at two o'clock.'

The court rose as he left and Simon Reed wondered what his colleague Phillip Burns would be able to achieve after lunch – if indeed he could achieve anything in the way of defence now that Thelma Davis had admitted her guilt.

In the waiting area, John Porter was sitting, wondering when he might be called to give evidence. Then he heard that there had been an adjournment until two o'clock. Before he had a chance to move, two police officers approached him and asked that he accompany them to the detention room. It was then that he realized something had gone wrong.

Just as he was leaving with the policemen, Phillip Burns hurried towards them.

'I need to speak to this witness before you take him from the building. Would you please allow me a few moments alone with him in private?'

He took John Porter by the arm and led him to a nearby room.

'We shall have to stay with him, sir,' one of the policemen informed him.

Phillip Burns opened the door of a small room and turned to the policeman. 'As you can see, there is only one door. You can wait outside while I talk to this man.'

'But sir ...' the policeman protested.

Ignoring the protest, Phillip Burns ushered John Porter in and closed the door behind him.

The room was oak panelled with just a table and two chairs furnishing it. Mr Burns indicated a chair and both he and his witness sat down.

'What's going on in there? What's happening to Thelma?' John Porter showed his concern.

'Listen carefully and answer honestly, Mr Porter. We don't have much time. Now, firstly, Mrs Davis is under great strain and has made statements which implicate you as being involved in her husband's death.'

'But is she all right? Can't I see her even for a minute?'

'Out of the question, I'm afraid. You see, due to her claim that you were an accomplice in the killing of her husband, you can no longer be a witness in her defence. Unfortunately, she has now destroyed any chance of your making a statement that would help her. Instead, she has made it necessary for the law to charge you with being an accessory to the killing of Mark Davis.'

John Porter was stunned by this news and his mouth dropped open in disbelief. 'You mean, Thelma's gone and landed me in the shit!? I don't believe it. She'd never do that. Unless someone got her all twisted and confused and made her say things against her will.' He held his head in his hands. 'She must be in a right state, the poor little bitch. If only I'd have been there. She'd have felt safe if she'd seen me there. Now what's going to happen to her?'

'That all depends on whether I can convince the jury that she is mentally unstable and not responsible for her actions or what she says.' Phillip Burns sighed. 'But in any event it will not be an easy task with Judge Thornton against me.'

John Porter looked up in surprise. 'What do you mean?'

'The judge and I are not exactly on friendly terms. He will prevent me from getting Mrs Davis any psychiatric test which might prove her to be of unsound mind. That in turn prevents me proving that at the time of the accident she was suffering from diminished responsibility.'

'But you're a barrister. You must be able to do something, for Christ's sake!'

Phillip Burns tried to sound hopeful. 'I want you to tell me what really happened. And it has to be the truth so that I can use the facts to our advantage. Now, did Mrs Davis strike her husband with an object?'

John Porter became uncomfortable as he answered. 'Yeah.'

'And this object was what?'

'An old vase.'

'This vase. What became of it?'

'Nothing. I cleaned the blood off it under the tap, dried it with some kitchen roll and put it back on the mantelpiece where she got it from.'

'Why did you go to that trouble?'

'Because I didn't want the police or anyone to think she'd done it. That's why I thought of making it look like he'd had a fall and thumped his head on the hearth. I never dreamed it would turn out like this.' John Porter sounded despondent. 'I didn't want Thelma being accused of killing him. That's why I tried to cover up what she'd done. She can't take all this.'

'Unfortunately, your efforts to conceal the truth have put you *both* in jeopardy. I was hoping to convince the jury that Mark Davis met his death by accidentally falling, as Mrs Davis had originally stated. And that this story of the attempted attack on you with a poker and her hitting her husband with a vase to protect you from being beaten to death was simply a fantasy that she had created in her sick mind to give reason to what had *really* taken place. But now ...' He shrugged and shook his head despairingly.

'So what's going to happen to us?'

'You will no doubt be charged and brought to trial in due course, Mr Porter. I'm sorry I cannot be more hopeful but Mrs Davis has made the task of clearing you both very difficult. Very difficult indeed.'

'But if you can prove that Thelma wasn't responsible for what she did or what she said, because she's mentally sick, that would help me as well, wouldn't it?' John Porter asked hopefully.

'It certainly might. But as I told you before, the judge is not prepared to order a psychiatric report on her.'

John Porter became angry. 'Well, if the judge wants to play God with my Thelma, he'll find out that he's not the only one that can ruin people's lives. He'll live to regret it, and that's a promise.' His anger was increasing as he added, 'Not that she'd want to go through seeing all those shrinks again. But it's for her own good that she gets sorted out.'

'Again?' said Phillip Burns. 'What do you mean, *again*?'

The answer John Porter gave had the defence counsel on his feet and hurrying to the nearest telephone.

Judge Thornton had finished lunch and was sitting in his chambers drinking a cup of coffee. Although the case before him seemed to be coming to a conclusion, he was hoping that Mr Phillip Burns would not try to repudiate the evidence against his client with a time-wasting theatrical performance. To the judge, all that was now required was for the jury to decide the fate of Thelma Davis and thereby bring the case to a close.

He sat reflecting on how many people like Thelma Davis he had sent down over the years. He remembered them as being almost all the same type. People from working-class backgrounds with a low intelligence who turned to violence without considering the consequences. Why, he wondered, did they always seem to use brawn instead of their brain?

With the few minutes he had left before the court was to be reconvened, he let his thoughts wander to the days ahead. Days when he would no longer be Judge Thornton, or even Mr William Thornton. The letter from Downing Street had given him the opportunity to become *Sir* William Thornton and it was a title he intended to grab with both hands. On reflection he felt that he had earned the honour more than some actors and pop stars of whom he had never heard, and the thought of accepting the honour from Her Majesty filled him with great pride.

Suddenly it was time to get his robes on once more and he put all thoughts of his knighthood to one side and began to concentrate on the Thelma Davis case.

The court was reconvened and Thelma Davis stood facing Mr Phillip Burns, who knew that Judge Thornton would be watching his every move.

'Mrs Davis.' He smiled. 'This whole business has obviously been a great strain on you and I shall try not to keep you any longer than is necessary.'

Judge Thornton hoped this would be the case but was quite prepared to stop any delaying tactics by the defence counsel.

'Now tell me, Mrs Davis. Did you have an agreeable lunch in the cafeteria?'

'Yes, thank you, sir?'

'And you are now feeling much better than before the court adjourned? Well enough to answer the few questions I shall be putting to you?' His voice was kind and warm. 'Questions that I assure you will be easy for you to reply to.'

She smiled. 'I don't mind what you ask me, sir.'

'Good. Now, when my learned friend was asking you various

things this morning, you answered as best and honestly as you could, did you not?' He spoke softly as if to calm her.

'Yes, sir,' she whispered.

Judge Thornton was annoyed and showed it. 'We cannot hear you or the accused, Mr Burns.'

Phillip Burns was enjoying himself as he raised his voice to a considerable pitch. 'Sorry, m'lud. We will speak up. Can you hear me now?'

The judge hid his anger by forcing a smile. 'Perfectly.'

Phillip Burns was throwing caution to the wind but took a chance on his only way to get sympathy and possibly force the judge to order a psychiatric report. He smiled at Thelma as he asked, 'You told the court this morning that your husband came home drunk on the evening he died. How drunk was he? I mean, was he swaying and unsteady on his legs?'

'Yes. He always fell about when he'd been drinking.'

'And did he fall prior to receiving the blow that killed him?'

'Once. When he fell on the floor.'

'Was that the night of the accident or another time?'

She looked vague for a moment as if trying to remember.

'I think it was another time sir.'

'But you aren't certain?'

She struggled to remember and Phillip Burns allowed her to remain thoughtful before asking, 'Isn't it true that your husband would *often* return home the worse for drink and fall over, banging his head and spilling small amounts of blood on the carpet?'

Tears came into her eyes as she said, 'Yes.'

'And is it not a fact that because of his drinking and his threatening behaviour towards you that you were admitted to St Luke's Hospital in August 1998, where you received psychiatric treatment for ten weeks, in the care of Doctor Nealey?'

The court was silent as Thelma Davis sobbed, 'Yes. Yes.' As she broke down, Phillip Burns looked straight at the judge with a contemptuous stare.

'My lord, with this new evidence that has come to light in regard to Mrs Davis's mental condition at the time of her husband's death, I am sure the court will agree that this case should be halted until a full psychiatric examination of the accused can be made. If on the result of that examination it is decided that she was not responsible for her actions then I shall ask that all charges against her be dismissed on the grounds of diminished responsibility. If on the other hand the report shows otherwise, I shall call for a retrial.' Looking at Thelma Davis being comforted by a WPC, he added, 'I am sure that the sooner Mrs Davis is out of this courtroom, the better it will be for both her physical and mental state.'

Judge Thornton was aware of the press being present and did not want to blot his character with them at this time in his career. Even so, he was not pleased with the fact that Mr Phillip Burns had got his way after all. Reluctantly, he made his ruling.

'The accused will be released into psychiatric care until a final report on her mental condition is made.' Then turning to the WPC with Thelma Davis, he said, 'Escort Mrs Davis to a room where she can rest until transport is made available to take her to the hospital.'

Thelma Davis was helped from the witness box and left the court-room looking pale and confused.

Phillip Burns was enjoying being victorious and showed it.

'Thank you, m'lud. And there is one further request I wish to make.'

'And what is this further request?' asked the judge.

'It is that the detention order made by your lordship on the witness John Porter be lifted. I ask this on the grounds that his detention was ordered based on what we now know to be unreliable and confusing statements by the accused. And it would be most beneficial to her wellbeing to have him free to visit and comfort her during the traumatic weeks ahead.'

Judge Thornton was now in a difficult situation and he was well aware of the danger his reputation would face if he were to make an incorrect decision in this, his final case. After a moment's thought he spoke in a calm but firm manner.

'Because the evidence given by the accused so far may or may not be correct, and until it is confirmed one way or the other whether she was speaking the truth or not, it would be wrong of me to simply free John Porter at this time. However, I shall lift the detention order and put a conditional bail order in its place. This will require him to report to his local police station each day, at the same time allowing him to visit Mrs Davis whenever he wishes.'

'I'm obliged, m'lud,' said Phillip Burns with a regal bow.

The judge ignored the defence counsel's attempt to goad him and turned to the jury.

'The case against Thelma Davis will be held in abeyance until her psychiatric report is complete. In the event that a retrial is ordered, a new jury would be called. This jury is excused.'

The court rose and Judge Thornton left the bench for the last time.

As he went from the courtroom, Simon Reed complimented his learned colleague.

'I've got to hand it to you. I was sure that I would get a conviction.' He shrugged. 'Ah well. Win some, lose some. So here's to the next time.'

'I don't think there will be a next time for *this* case. My money is on the doctors finding Thelma Davis was not of sound mind when she killed her husband.' Putting his papers away in a briefcase, he looked around the almost empty courtroom. 'Must be strange for old Thornton to know that he won't be sitting on that bench again. Can't say I'm sorry though. If he'd had his way, Thelma Davis would be on her way to Holloway by now, and for a long time. Hard old devil.'

'You enjoyed rubbing him up the wrong way, didn't you? For one moment there I thought he was going to lose his cool with you. I don't suppose you'll be saying goodbye to him?' Simon Reed said with an air of sarcasm.

'Not bloody likely,' laughed Phillip Burns as he walked to the main doors. 'See you in court,' he called as he went out.

Phillip Burns left with the jaunty step of a man who had won. He was pleased to have got his way and felt a glow of self-satisfaction at getting his client psychiatric help, despite Judge Thornton's determination to deny her that right. And now he looked forward to giving John Porter the good news.

As he sat in the taxi on his way to the police station he remembered John Porter's comment about the judge playing God with people's lives and the threatening way he had promised that Judge Thornton would live to regret it. Despite hearing criminals make wild threats on various occasions, there was something about the way John Porter had said it that made Mr Phillip Burns feel rather uncomfortable.

CHAPTER FOUR

A little over a week had passed since Judge Thornton had sat on the bench at Winchester Crown Court, and although he was pleased to be home, he would have preferred the Thelma Davis case to have been concluded satisfactorily rather than be left as it was, in limbo. But it was no longer any concern of his, he told himself. His time could now be spent doing what he wanted and he intended to enjoy his remaining years to the full.

His birthday was just over one week away, as was the party that Alison had organized for him. He had already received a few cards wishing him well on his retirement and the mail on this Saturday morning also included some birthday greetings.

He enjoyed receiving funny cards but most of the ones he opened were the traditional, non-offensive type. One card, however, was different to the rest. On the outside were the words 'On Your Retirement' and the message inside read 'Wishing You Many Years Of Happiness'. But the word 'Happiness' had been crossed out and replaced with 'Hell'.

As it had been sent to his private address, he assumed that one of his friends had intended it as a joke, but he didn't find it particularly amusing. The postmark showed that it had been sent from Glasgow on the previous day. The only person he could think of who lived near Glasgow was a cousin who had been dead for six years.

Looking at the card again he realized that the sender had neglected to sign it, even with a *silly* name. He thought this rather strange, as even his friend the chief constable would have signed it with a funny name like PC Plod had he sent such a card. But he wasn't going to waste time worrying, so he dropped the card in his litter bin and continued opening the rest of his mail.

It was just after ten o'clock when Emma Roberts brought in his morning coffee. His eyes lit up when he saw that she had included his favourite chocolate biscuits on the tray.

'Ah, thank you, Emma. You're spoiling me, you know. I shall be putting on weight before long.'

Emma smiled as she poured him a cup of coffee. 'You could do with some extra meat on you. All those years of stress and strain on the bench didn't allow you to put on any weight. I bet you didn't have many good meals while you were at court.'

'Why, of course I did,' he said, unconvincingly.

'A quick sandwich more like it,' she said reproachfully.

'Yes, well ... those days are gone now. So I shall rely on your culinary skills from now on.'

She gave a warm smile. 'I shall look after you properly now that you've retired.'

'You always have.' He gave her hand a grateful pat and as she turned to leave he took a biscuit and enquired, 'And what is for lunch today?'

'You'll get *nothing* if you fill yourself with biscuits.' She went to the door and with a smile announced, 'Fresh Dover sole, new potatoes and peas.'

As Emma left, he smiled and wondered what he would ever do without her.

Emma Roberts had not only been the Thorntons' housekeeper, she had also proved herself to be a very capable surrogate mother to Alison and was now looked upon as a member of the family. An attractive woman of fifty-eight, Emma had always admired Judge Thornton for the way he had cared for and protected his young daughter, and she was grateful for the kindness and respect he had always shown her.

Her thoughts often went back to the days when a young girl from a working-class background was employed by a man who treated her with patience and consideration. She had been the first applicant the agency had sent and Judge Thornton chose to give her a month's trial. But all that was so long ago. Now he had retired and she was spending more time in his company than she had ever done before.

It hurt her to think that he had a reputation for being severe and heartless when he presided in court. This was the man who had shown nothing but a caring nature to Alison, Jody and to her.

As each day passed, she became aware that the fondness she had felt for him was growing into something much deeper.

Bernard Thornton was sitting in the living room of his flat in Clapham Common, south-east London, when the summons arrived. It was to notify him that he was to appear at the Guildford County Court in fourteen days' time if he wished to defend the charge of driving while under the influence of alcohol. Or he could plead guilty by signing the summons and sending a cheque for the fine and his licence for endorsement.

Bernard had been embarrassed at being stopped and breathalyzed on the A3, but what had really angered him was the humiliation of having to spend the night in a cell at Guildford police station like a common criminal. It was an experience that he hoped would never be repeated.

He had no intention of going to court and being humiliated for a second time. Suddenly, a thought entered his head. Was it just bad luck that he had been stopped that afternoon on the A3. Or could it be that somebody had informed the police that he was driving whilst over the limit? And if so, who else other than his brother knew that he had drunk more than he should? After a moment's hesitation he picked up the telephone and dialled.

It was Emma that answered.

'Hello, it's Bernard.'

'Oh, hello. What happened when you called the other day? I didn't get a chance to see you before you rushed off.'

'No. Sorry about that. Is my brother there?'

'He's in the garden. I'll give him a shout. Hang on.'

'Thanks.'

Bernard wondered if he had done the right thing in ringing but felt that he had to know if it *was* William who had called the police that day. After a few moments he heard his brother pick up the receiver.

'Hello, Bernard,' William said, trying to sound pleasant. 'This is a surprise. Everything all right?'

'No, it isn't. After I left you the other day I got stopped by the police and breathalyzed. Ended up spending the night in a bloody police cell. I was driving carefully so there was no reason for the boys in blue to pull me over. Somebody must have put them on to me. Was it you?'

His brother saw no point in hiding the truth. 'You were in no fit state to drive. You could have killed somebody in the condition you were in. My conscience would not allow me to let that happen. You must understand that, Bernard.'

'The only thing I understand is that you've probably cost me my licence, to say nothing of the fine. I was perfectly able to drive. Unlike some people, I can hold my liquor. Why did you have to do it? I'm your brother, for Christ's sake!'

William paused before answering, 'And if you had killed a child or been killed yourself, how do you think your brother would feel, knowing that he could have prevented it?'

Bernard knew that he couldn't win and that annoyed him. 'I can't make you understand, can I? Well, now that you've done your duty and put me in the shit, thanks a lot, big brother. I hope you can sleep at night!' He slammed the receiver down. 'Bastard!'

It was to be the first real family lunch at Four Oaks for some time, with Alison, Gary and Jody all together, and Emma joining them as she had done for the past few years. She still got up between each course to clear away and get the next one on the table, though; she liked to be in charge of the kitchen and allowed no one to trespass on her domain.

Usually on a Saturday Alison would cook lunch for Jody and herself at the flat, while her husband was either on his way home from a northern venue or on his way to another town. Her father normally played golf on a Saturday and would be at the clubhouse getting a sandwich at lunchtime. But today was to be different.

Judge Thornton was pleased to have his family together at the dining table, a tradition that he felt was an important part of family life and one that was becoming non-existent in most people's homes.

Emma had cooked the Dover sole to perfection and William Thornton made no secret of his delight when she got up from her chair to clear the plates away.

'That was utterly delicious,' he said, wiping his napkin over his lips.

'It certainly was,' Alison agreed.

'I couldn't eat another thing, Emma,' said Gary Hanley as he patted his stomach with a contented smile.

Emma was amused at the way Jody had said nothing about the sole but sat with a look of expectancy on her face.

'I don't suppose you have any room for apple crumble with home-made custard?' Emma asked her.

The little girl's face broke into a wide grin. 'I think I might be able to force myself, Emma.'

'Then I'll go and see if I remembered to make some.' Emma winked and went out of the room with the dirty dishes.

Gary Hanley waited for her to go and then said, 'I wonder why some man never snapped her up?'

'What a funny thing to say,' Alison remarked.

'Well, she's so competent. I've never understood why she didn't marry, that's all.'

'Too busy looking after us, wasn't she, Father?' said Alison.

William Thornton said thoughtfully, 'I used to wonder if there had ever been someone in her life, but I never brought the subject up. As long as she is happy with us we should all be very grateful that she *didn't* run off and get married.'

Jody became anxious. 'Emma wouldn't leave us, would she, Grandpa?'

'Of course not,' he reassured her. 'Now let's have no more silly talk like that. Emma would never leave. She's part of the family.'

'Why didn't you play golf today, Pops?' Gary asked in an attempt to change the subject.

'James MacCormack had a meeting at police headquarters, so we shall do battle in the morning.'

'Unusual for you to play on a Sunday, isn't it?'

'Not really. We've often had to rearrange a game because some business or other had cropped up.'

'You always beat him, don't you Grandpa?' Jody said with a proud smile.

'Not *always*, dear.' He winked. 'I let him win sometimes.'

Alison was curious and asked, 'Why on earth do you want to keep playing with someone you nearly always beat? Doesn't it become boring?'

Her father smiled as he replied, 'James is never a bore, Alison. He simply isn't a very good golfer, that's all. But he's good company and a good friend to have.' Changing the subject once more, he said to Gary, 'You're doing a show near home this evening, I understand.'

'Yes. A private cabaret in Basingstoke so I shall be coming home tonight.'

'It will make a nice change for Alison to have you home on a Saturday night. I never understand why you're always going up north to do these shows of yours.'

'I have to go where the work is and most of the clubs are up north.'

'I suppose so,' agreed the judge. Not wanting to spoil the family get-together, he refrained from adding, 'Why on earth don't you get a decent job?'

As Emma returned with a tray containing apple crumble and a jug of custard, Jody's eyes lit up. The others watched Emma spooning the crumble into a dessert plate and adding custard to it. The plate was passed to Jody, who sat looking at it with longing while she waited for the others to be served.

'Who else would like some?' asked Emma.

'I'm sure we all would,' said Alison, staring at Jody's dish. 'If there's any left, that is.'

Jody giggled at her mother's comment.

Emma served Alison and her father and then herself. As she sat down, Gary Hanley looked slightly hurt at being left out.

'You said that you hadn't room for anything else,' Emma teased, 'So I didn't give you any. Changed your mind, have you, Gary?'

Without waiting for his answer, she served another portion of crumble and passed it to him.

'Thanks, Emma.' Gary smiled gratefully.

'And now I suggest we eat before it gets cold,' said Emma.

Jody didn't need telling twice and started tucking into her dessert.

Alison tapped her daughter's arm and warned, 'Not too fast or you'll get indigestion.'

After everyone had finished, Emma suggested that they all retire to the sitting room to have their coffee in comfort.

Once the coffee had arrived, Jody wanted to leave and go back to the flat to play a computer game, and with her mother giving her permission to leave, the little girl thanked Emma for the lovely meal and hurried out of the room.

Suddenly, Alison broached the subject of holidays and made the suggestion that her father should get away now that he had retired from the legal profession.

'What do you mean by "get away"?' asked her father. 'Can I be looking in ill health and not noticed?' The sarcasm in his voice made Gary laugh.

'You sounded just like a judge then,' said Gary.

'That's because I am a judge.' Then he corrected himself. 'I mean *was* a judge.'

'You know what I mean, Father. You haven't taken time off for a proper holiday for ages. All you ever do is spend the odd weekend with your friend in Dorset. But now that you are free, why don't you get away for a week and recharge the old batteries?'

'Are you suggesting that I go away on my own?'

'Why not?'

'Because I would be bored with my own company after a few days and long to get home again. It may be difficult for you to understand, but I have spent so little time here over the past years that to be here now that I have retired is as good as any holiday to me. Besides, I can always visit my friend in Dorset when I want to.'

'When are we going to meet your mysterious Dorset friend, Pops?'

'What makes you think my friend is mysterious?' the judge asked.

Gary laughed as he said, 'Everyone who lives in Dorset is mysterious, aren't they? It's all that cider they drink.'

'I think you're referring to Somerset, not Dorset,' Emma corrected him.

'Never mind Dorset,' said Alison. 'Don't you ever want to go somewhere exciting, Father?'

Taking her hand in his, he replied, 'Alison, being able to spend more time with you and Jody is all the excitement I ask for. I was away so much while you were growing up and I have always regretted that. Emma saw more of you than I ever did, and all I need to recharge my batteries, as you put it, is to be with my family here at Four Oaks.'

'Come to think of it, Emma, I've never known you to have a holiday either,' said Alison.

'No ... well, I never felt the need,' Emma replied. 'I visit my sister in Somerset every year and that's all the holiday I want. Like your father, I'm happy being here.'

She picked up the coffee pot and offered everyone a second cup.

As the others declined her offer, the judge said, 'I think I'd like another one. With a brandy, please, Emma.'

Emma was refilling his cup when the doorbell rang.

'I'll go,' said Alison.

She walked into the hall and glancing at herself in the mirror automatically ran a hand over her hair to put it in place. She opened the front door to discover their neighbour, Gerald Turvey, standing on the doorstep.

'Hello, Gerald. Did you have a good holiday?'

'Terrific. Couldn't fault the weather. Sunshine every day except one,' he said with enthusiasm.

'When did you get back?'

'Just arrived,' said the huge ex-rugby player.

'Coming in for a minute?'

'Some other time. Haven't even unpacked yet. This letter was waiting on the mat with our mail so I thought I'd better drop it round.' He handed her the envelope.

Alison took it from him and smiled. 'Thank you, Gerald. You are coming to the party next Saturday, aren't you?'

'Of course. I must dash. Say hello to everyone for me.'

Gerald hurried back down the drive as Alison closed the door and took the envelope to her father in the sitting room.

'That was Gerald,' she announced. 'This letter was dropped through his letterbox by mistake.' Looking at the postmark, she said, 'It was only posted four days ago, so at least it hasn't been sitting on his mat for two weeks.'

Her father took the letter and looked at the postmark. It had been sent from Glasgow. He opened the envelope and took out a piece of paper. It was obvious by the expression on his face that he was troubled by the message it contained.

Gary was intrigued. 'What is it, Pops? Bad news?'

'No no,' the judge replied. 'It's just a silly joke.' He smiled and laughed it off as he put the paper in his pocket.

'Well, aren't you going to let us in on it?' asked Alison.

Her father tried to appear amused as he replied, 'It's one of those cryptic clues one gets in a crossword. No doubt from my old friend James MacCormack. If you'll excuse me a moment, I shall go to the study and solve the puzzle.'

He left the sitting room and made his way to the study, as if he was enjoying a childish prank. Emma watched him thoughtfully, not wholly convinced.

Once out of the room, Judge Thornton took the paper from his pocket and read it again. All that was printed on it was 'Matthew 7, verses 1 & 2.'

He arrived at the study and went straight to the bookcase. Taking a Bible from the shelf, he opened it at Matthew 7 and read verses 1 and 2.

Do not judge, or you too will be judged. For in the same way as you judge others, you will be judged, and the measure you give, will be the measure you get.

He read it twice and then closed the Bible and put it back on the shelf. He sat at his desk, looking again at the note. Who, he wondered, would send such a note? And why?

There was a gentle knock at the door and Emma entered with a glass of brandy.

'I thought you might like your brandy in here,' she said, putting the glass down on his desk. Then she walked to the door but instead of leaving made sure that it was closed and in a soft, gentle voice said, 'Something's worrying you. Do you want to talk about it?'

'What on earth makes you think something's wrong, Emma?' he asked casually.

She smiled and said, 'You don't fool me. I've known you a long time, remember? Was that letter sent by the same person that sent the retirement card?'

He looked surprised. 'How did you know about the card?'

'I saw it when I emptied the litter bin that day. At first I thought you might have thrown it away by accident so I took it out and looked at it,' she said. 'I didn't think it was in very good taste.'

'Quite honestly, I had forgotten that card until this note arrived.'

'Is it from the same person?' Emma asked. 'I assume you've an idea who sent it, even though it wasn't signed.'

He knew that Emma was too perceptive to fool and he wanted to discuss it with someone, especially now that this note had been sent.

Passing it to her he said, 'Perhaps someone thinks I might find it amusing, but I'm afraid I don't.'

She took the note and read it with confusion. 'But what is it supposed to mean?'

'It's a quotation from the New Testament. In a nutshell it says not to judge others or you yourself will be judged. And that you will receive as good as you give. That's the gist of it. You can read the actual quote for yourself.' He pointed to the bookcase. 'It's on the second shelf.'

Emma took the Bible down and opened it at Matthew 7. She read verses 1 and 2 and said thoughtfully, 'But if the same person sent both this and the card, it doesn't look as though they meant them as a joke.' She gave the note back to him. 'Unless this person in Glasgow has a warped sense of humour.'

'Please don't mention this to Alison,' he pleaded. 'She'll only worry herself about it.'

Emma smiled and said, 'We'll let the others go on thinking that it's a friend of yours having a joke. But if you take my advice, I would let the chief constable know what's happened when you meet him tomorrow. Promise you will, please?'

Taking her hand, he replied, 'I promise. Now I think you should go back to the others and tell them I shall be along in a few moments.'

Realizing he was still holding her hand, he released it. Emma gave him a warm smile and without saying anything left the room.

He stood for a moment, staring anxiously at the note, then opened his desk drawer and placed it inside. He removed the letter from the Prime Minister's office and sat down at his desk.

Looking at the official letter, he realized that he had to accept the offer within a few days. Sitting thoughtfully for a moment, he made his decision. Taking a sheet of his headed notepaper, he wrote his reply.

Judge Thornton waited until they had finished playing and were back at the clubhouse bar before bringing up the subject of the card and note.

'I know this is your day off, James, but I would like your advice on a matter that concerns me somewhat.'

James MacCormack sipped his whisky and joked, 'I see. Not content with thrashing me at golf, you want to spoil my day even further. Go on then. Ruin my Sunday for me.'

They were sitting at their usual corner table where it was quiet and they couldn't easily be overheard. The judge took the two envelopes and passed them to his friend.

The chief constable picked them up and opened the one containing the card. He read it and smiled. 'You've got some strange friends, haven't you?'

The judge said nothing and simply pointed to the second of the two envelopes. James opened it, took out the note and read it without understanding the significance. 'I'm afraid I don't quite follow. What does it mean?'

'It's a quote from the Bible,' he explained, keeping his voice low. 'I copied this from it.' He took a piece of paper from his pocket and passed it across the table.

James read the quote from Matthew 7 and shrugged as he gave it back. 'Some sort of nutter, I imagine. I wouldn't let it bother you too much. You must have had dozens of things like this over the years, surely?'

'Actually, no. Oh, I've been shouted at by some of the accused when I've handed down a stiff sentence. But I cannot recall receiving two such communications from the same person before.'

'How do you know it's the same person?'

'They were both posted from Glasgow.'

James looked thoughtfully at the postmarks. 'Oh yes. Mind you, that doesn't mean the sender is a resident there. In any case I wouldn't let them worry you. I'd forget about them.'

'Would you really?'

'Yes.' And with a grin he added, 'One of these cranks who constantly send religious literature to people. There's lots of them about. Just forget it.'

Despite James MacCormack's attempt to put his mind at rest, William Thornton knew that for the next few days he would be anxiously looking for a Glasgow postmark on all the letters that arrived at Four Oaks.

John Porter had remembered how Thelma Davis always laughed when she saw anyone arrive at a hospital ward with grapes for the patient. So today he decided to be the typical visitor, walking into her room with a bunch of the seedless variety.

She had been in the psychiatric ward for more than a week but had not shown any improvement. If anything, John thought she was slightly more depressed each time he saw her. All he wanted was for things to work out the way he had planned, and for her to take her tablets every day.

He walked into the main hospital entrance and passed the desk where a nurse was talking to an orderly. He went to the lift and pushed the call button. As he waited for the lift to arrive he wondered how long Thelma's illness would linger on. All John Porter wanted was to lead a normal life again.

When he arrived at her room he cautiously opened the door, only to see an empty bed where Thelma had been the last time he had visited her.

As he stood looking into the room, a nurse approached him. 'Can I help you?'

'The lady that was here, Thelma Davis. Where is she?'

'Are you a relative?'

'I'm her boyfriend.'

'We can only give out information about patients to their relatives, I'm afraid.'

'All I want to know is where she is now,' he explained with frustration. 'Surely you can tell me that?'

The nurse gave an apologetic look and said, 'I'm sorry.'

At that moment a doctor came from one of the private rooms and John approached him.

'Excuse me. I'm looking for my girlfriend but no one will tell me what's happened to her.'

The doctor could obviously see that John Porter was disturbed. 'Who is it that you are enquiring after?'

'Thelma Davis. I know I'm not a relative but I must find her. She'll be wondering why I haven't come to visit her.'

'What is your name?' asked the doctor.

'Porter. John Porter.'

'Come with me, please.' The doctor led him to an office and opened the door. 'After you.'

John Porter entered the office. It was a small room with a wooden desk and metal filing cabinet being its only furnishing.

The doctor closed the door. 'I take it you're the Johnny she referred to?'

'Yes.'

'When Mrs Davis was admitted she told the nurse that she had no family. Do you know if that's true?'

'The only relative she had was her husband and you know what happened to him. That's why she's in here. I'm the only person who cares about her. Why wouldn't the nurse tell me where she is? Has something happened to her?' His frustration was obvious as he asked, 'What have you done with her? Where is she?'

The doctor saw no point in concealing the truth from him.

'I'm afraid Mrs Davis died during the night. I'm sorry.'

John Porter leaned against the desk to steady himself and in a weak voice repeated, 'No ... No ... She can't be dead.'

The doctor rested a sympathetic hand on John Porter's arm and said, 'I'm afraid she is, Mr Porter.'

'It's not true ... Not Thelma.'

John Porter became weak at the knees as he shook his head in disbelief.

'I'm very sorry. Let me get you a chair.'

The doctor opened the door and called for a nurse to bring a chair and a glass of water. John Porter was staring at the floor and shaking his head as the doctor steadied him.

A nurse carried in a chair while a second nurse brought a glass of water. They helped John to sit and as he sipped the water the doctor signalled the nurses to leave.

Gradually accepting the reality of Thelma's death, John asked, 'Was it her heart?'

'We're waiting for the autopsy report now. Until then we won't know for certain.'

John's face screwed up as he said, 'Autopsy? You mean they have to cut her open?'

The doctor tried to sound sympathetic as he explained, 'When the cause of death is uncertain, an autopsy is required by law.'

John Porter was confused, 'But you're a doctor. You must have *some* idea of how she died.'

The doctor hesitated and then explained. 'She was found in the bathroom by one of the other patients. We believe she had a heart attack.'

'Heart attack?!' John said with disbelief.

'Yes. But as I said, we won't know for certain until the autopsy report.'

'I can't believe it. I never knew she had a weak ticker.'

'She was suffering from heart fibrillation when she was admitted.'

'What does that mean?'

'Irregular twitching of the heart muscles. It's quite a common problem and she was given Digoxin to correct it. In a patient that suffers from mental stress it can be difficult to treat until they are calm. Unfortunately Mrs Davis appears to have suffered a fatal attack before the treatment had the desired effect. The autopsy result will tell us whether or not it was just her heart giving up,' the doctor told him.

John Porter looked the doctor straight in the eye. 'Tell me the truth, Doctor. If she hadn't had to go through all that pressure of the court case, would she have been all right? What I mean is, if she could have had medical treatment instead of having to go to trial, would she have been alive now?'

The doctor shrugged. 'No one can be sure. But the mental trauma of going to court would certainly have had an adverse affect on her condition.' Seeing that John was feeling better, he asked, 'Do you feel well enough to go now?'

John looked at the bag of grapes and gave a sad smile. 'I brought these to make Thelma laugh.' Then, fighting back the tears, he said, 'Give these to somebody who likes grapes, will you? It might cheer them up.'

Without saying any more he gave the grapes to the doctor. As he walked to the lift the doctor asked where Mrs Davis's personal effects should go, but John Porter was too absorbed in his thoughts to hear. The doctor decided to leave him in his grief, convinced that he would come back to collect them at a later time.

CHAPTER FIVE

Anne Lawrence had just finished the housework at her country cottage in Sherborne, Dorset, and was relaxing with a cup of coffee when the postman arrived.

There were two letters, one from her sister in Wales, and one addressed to Lawrence Anne from a firm advertising handmade shirts for men. As her husband had died fifteen years earlier and only once had his shirts handmade, she concluded that the firm's computer had the surname first and that one of their staff had assumed they were contacting a man. Throwing the communication into the wastebin, she began reading her sister's letter.

Apart from a reference to the weather and the rising price of petrol, it was mainly about Anne's gentleman friend. There were questions about his intentions and advice on how Anne would be better off reaping the benefits of marriage rather than live the rest of her life alone, especially now that she was almost fifty-four years old.

Anne smiled to herself as she read her sister's advice, knowing that it was because she really cared for Anne that she had written. As she put down the letter she wondered what her sister would say if she knew the truth about the man who enjoyed his weekends with her, the man she introduced as her brother to the locals, whenever he came to stay.

She looked up at the clock on the mantelpiece which showed the time to be almost 10.30. She wondered whether he would be able to telephone her as often now that he was spending more time at home. She finished her coffee and went out into the garden.

She was cutting back some ivy that had got out of hand when she heard the telephone ringing. She ran to the kitchen and lifted the receiver from the wall phone.

'Hello,' she said, hoping it was him.

'Hello.' His voice was quiet but sounded warm. 'I can't be talking to you for long but I had to hear your voice and know that you're all right.'

'I'm fine, now that I've heard from you … I take it you're calling from home and that your minder's about,' she said.

'Yes. She's very astute and I don't want her knowing about you. She could make things very difficult if she did.'

'I understand. I wish you were here now.'

'So do I. I'm sorry I can't make it this weekend.' His voice became a whisper. 'But I'll make it up to you.'

'I know. I understand, really I do. Next weekend you can tell me all about the horrible time you had this weekend because you missed me.'

'I shall look forward to that. And then I can tell you of my plan. I think you'll like it.'

'I'm a woman. How can I wait a whole week now that you've teased me? Can't you give me a tiny clue?'

He gave a light chuckle as he said, 'Only that to make the plan work you may have to pretend to be someone else.'

'What do you mean?'

'Didn't you tell me that you were in an amateur dramatic group at one time?'

'That was when I was younger.'

'I'm sure you can play the person I have in mind without any problem. It'll be fun because I shall be playing a part as well.'

'Please explain what you mean,' she pleaded.

'I'll explain when I see you. And I'm sending you a letter of reference that I want you to copy in your own hand and put in the stamped addressed envelope I'll enclose. Post it when you've written it. OK?'

'But …'

'I must go now,' he whispered. 'I can hear her coming. Bye for now.'

He hung up, leaving Anne curious as to what he meant by playing a part. But she was happy that she would see more of him now: she hated not being able to see him while he had had to spend so much time in court.

*

Judge Morrison Holloway was enjoying his evening in the company of three friends from the legal profession. He always made an effort to meet his colleagues at least twice a year, to catch up on events and swap stories.

Those present were Charles Verney, a retired QC in his early seventies, Elwyn David, a circuit judge in his middle sixties, and Donald Hubbard QC the youngest of the group at fifty-seven, who had become one of the top criminal lawyers.

The Pilgrims Club was ideal for such meetings, not only in respect of the good food they served but because there were four private dining rooms in which guests could relax. Despite the solid walls, staff would often hear the laughter of Judge Holloway during his visits. Known as 'the jolly judge', his large frame would shake vigorously when something amused him. The only thing he disliked about himself was the Christian name that his parents had forced upon him and among family and close friends he preferred to be called Maurice.

After dinner, Charles Verney commented on a conversation he'd had with Phillip Burns, defence counsel in the Thelma Davis case.

'I hear old Thornton's swansong was rather unpleasant.'

'So is he,' said Donald Hubbard with acerbity.

'At least he had the decency to retire early,' Elwyn David said with sarcasm.

Judge Holloway tried not to show his amusement as he asked Charles Verney, 'What did your informant have to say about my colleague, Charles?'

'Well, apparently the case was suspended while the woman on trial underwent psychiatric examination. According to Phillip, the woman should never have been put through her ordeal. But Thornton refused to order any psychiatric examination until it was too late.'

'Typical,' said Elwyn David.

'So what happened?' asked Donald Hubbard, helping himself to the cheeseboard.

Charles Verney took a sip of port before answering, 'Heart attack, they say. But if the truth's known she probably topped herself.'

'Good grief!' exclaimed Elwyn David. 'What a horrible way for Thornton to end his career. Not that I can see him losing any sleep over it.'

'I wonder why he never remarried?' asked Donald Hubbard.

'I can't imagine any woman wanting to live with Thornton,' Charles Verney said with a sneer.

'Actually a woman *does* live with him,' Judge Holloway said quietly, as he refilled his glass with port. 'Apart from his delightful daughter, he's had a housekeeper living with them for a number of years now.'

'Really?' Elwyn David said with surprise.

'I met her once when I had to call on him,' Judge Holloway informed them. 'A very good-looking woman too. I can remember him telling me that she had been employed soon after his wife died, so she's been with him a very long time. Proving that there is at least one woman who wants to live with him,' he said, addressing his remark to Charles Verney.

Charles Verney thought for a moment and then asked, 'She's not his mistress, surely?'

Donald Hubbard burst out laughing. 'Oh, come now, Charles! You can't be serious? Old Thornton with a mistress! Can you imagine anything more ludicrous?'

'I shouldn't think he could still manage it these days,' remarked Elwyn David.

'Why? Can't *you* manage it these days, Elwyn?' asked Judge Holloway, keeping a straight face.

'What are you trying to imply?' Elwyn David enquired with embarrassment.

Judge Holloway smiled as he replied, 'Only that Thornton and your good self are about the same age, that was all.'

Elwyn David looked uncomfortable as Donald Hubbard and Charles Verney laughed.

Judge Holloway changed the subject by looking at his watch and commenting, '*Tempus fugit*, gentlemen. I think we should go soon.'

The others agreed that it was time to leave and the four men finished their port and said their farewells.

It was gone 2 a.m. when Judge Thornton woke up with a start. He had been dreaming that someone was breaking into the study just below his bedroom.

He sat up, his heart racing. He seldom had a dream but this one seemed particularly realistic. The light from the moon made it unnecessary to switch his bedside lamp on. He could see the illuminous hands of his clock showing it to be 2.16 a.m. and began to settle down once more.

A sudden noise from below made him sit up again. This time it was not a dream. Someone was in his study.

The only other person in the house was Emma, though what she would be doing down there at this time in the morning he couldn't imagine. The only way to satisfy his curiosity was to find out for himself who it was downstairs.

He quietly got out of bed and put on his dressing gown. Then, taking a torch from his bedside cabinet, he walked slowly towards the door, careful to avoid the floorboard that he knew creaked. When he opened the door he could see along the hall to Emma's bedroom. Her door was closed and there was no light showing from under it. He knew that if Emma was downstairs she would have left the door ajar and the light on.

He crept quietly along to the landing, where he paused and listened. Although the sound was faint, he had no doubt that someone had gained entry to the house.

Despite feeling nervous, he was determined to confront the intruder, whoever it was. He carefully opened the door of a storage cupboard and removed a broom. Leaving the cupboard door open, he went slowly down the stairs, holding the broom as if it were a weapon.

He got to the bottom of the stairs and stopped, trying to remember which section of the hall floor creaked. Unable to be certain which area to avoid, he took a chance and stepped around the edge of the hallway towards the study. From under the door he could see an occasional light and he knew someone was using a torch to find whatever it was they were looking for. As he moved towards the door, his foot found the creaking floorboard.

There was a sudden noise from the study and, taking a firm grip on the broom, Judge Thornton opened the door and quickly switched on the light.

The intruder was just leaving by the window. Although the judge was unable to reach him, he could clearly see that he was wearing a woollen balaclava, a dark bomber jacket and light-coloured trainers. As he got to the open window he saw his visitor run down the drive and disappear into the distance. The judge waited for a moment and listened for the sound of a car. When no car was heard he went to his desk and telephoned the police.

As he hung up, he heard Emma calling anxiously from the landing.

'Is somebody down there?'

The judge went to the door and called up as he switched a hall light on.

'It's me, Emma.'

'Oh … I thought I heard a noise and then someone talking.'

'That was me speaking to the police. We've had an intruder, I'm afraid.'

'An intruder? Let me get my dressing gown and I'll make us some tea.'

'While we're waiting for the police, a cup of tea would be most welcome,' he replied.

He walked back to the study and stood looking at the open window, wondering who would want to break in, and why. Then he looked at the desk and realized that the middle drawer had been opened, as if someone was looking for something. After a few moments he went through to the living room, hoping that the arrival of the police wouldn't disturb Jody and her parents at this unearthly hour of the morning.

The speed and efficiency of the Surrey police force in the capture of Barry Feldman surprised even the chief constable and he couldn't wait to telephone Judge Thornton personally.

'I thought you'd like to know that we've got your burglar in custody,' he informed his friend.

Judge Thornton was quite shocked by the news. Looking at his watch, he said, 'But it was only half an hour ago that I watched him running down the drive! Are you sure you've got the right man?'

'Oh yes. One of our patrol cars picked him up soon after you telephoned. He was taking a short cut over the green. He admitted breaking in once they got him back to headquarters. He's a lad with form apparently. Mostly burglary and he's on probation at the moment so they'll throw the book at him this time.'

'Not hard enough, I fear,' said the judge. Then realizing the time, he sounded concerned as he asked, 'I hope they didn't wake you up just because it was *my* house that was broken into James?'

James MacCormack laughed as he replied, 'They didn't wake me up. I was on my way back from a conference in Manchester when they called me on the hands-free. Knowing I was a friend of yours they thought I might like to let you know that we've got chummy tucked away for the night.'

'Well, I do appreciate it. Where are you now?'

'Almost home. You get back to bed and get some sleep. I'll see you tomorrow sometime. And try not to worry. You won't be having any more trouble tonight.'

'I'll get back to bed as soon as your fingerprint chap has finished. Thank you again for letting me know that you've got the man. Good night, James.'

'You mean good morning,' James laughed as he hung up.

Judge Thornton turned to Emma, who was sitting on the sofa, listening with interest to his conversation.

'They've got the fellow, Emma.'

'Yes. So I gathered. They didn't waste any time.'

'At least he won't be breaking into anyone else's home for a while. It seems he has a record of breaking and entering.'

'Well, I hope he gets his just deserts,' said Emma.

'He'll probably get sent to a Spanish resort at the tax payer's expense for what the do-gooders call rehabilitation. Our legal system has gone completely mad,' he said bitterly.

'If only you'd switched on the alarm,' said Emma. 'I don't know why you had it fitted if you never put it on.'

He became irritated as he replied, 'Because I cannot come downstairs if I want a cup of tea during the night without setting the blasted thing off, that's why. Besides, I do not see why I should turn my home into a prison just because our intruder isn't *in* one.' Then in anger he added, 'That's where his sort should *all* be.'

The scenes of crimes officer came to the living room and knocked on the open door.

'I've finished dusting the study, sir. But I shall need the lady's and your fingerprints so that we can eliminate them from the others.'

'Yes, of course,' the judge said with reluctance. 'Did you know that your people have the man in custody at Guildford?'

'That was quick. Even so, I shall need your prints.'

'I quite understand. Perhaps you could do my housekeeper's first. Then she can get back to bed.'

As Emma followed the officer to the study, Judge Thornton

wondered why his intruder had chosen Four Oaks, and why he had remained in the study rather than go to the living room where there were valuable paintings and china. The whole business struck the judge as being most odd.

At breakfast the only topic of conversation was the events of the previous evening.

Alison and Gary had heard nothing in the rear bedroom but Jody, whose bedroom overlooked the front drive, was furious because she had slept through till morning without seeing any of the excitement. She was particularly disappointed not to have seen the police arrive.

'Oh, Grandpa! Why didn't you come and wake me up? I might have seen the burglar from my window.' Then a thought crossed her mind and she asked hopefully, 'Will we be in the papers?'

'I don't think so,' her grandfather replied. 'At least, I certainly hope not.'

'Pity you didn't have the alarm on, Father,' said Alison.

Gary buttered a slice toast and said, 'I bet you'll put it on after this, eh, Pops?'

The judge looked uncomfortable but said nothing as he took a slice of toast from the toast rack and waited for Gary to finish with the butter.

'Did the man come and see you about the alarm, Grandpa?' Jody asked.

'What man?' Emma enquired.

'The man who was checking that all the alarms were working in the area,' Jody replied, before taking another mouthful of cereal.

The others looked at each other with curiosity.

'This man. When did you see him, dear?' asked Alison.

'When I came home from school the other day.'

'And where was he, Jody?' her father asked.

'At the bottom of the drive. He was standing there writing in his book,' Jody said. 'He was very nice.'

Her grandfather smiled, so as not to worry the child. 'And this man. What was he like, dear?'

'How do you mean, Grandpa?'

'Well, was he young, old, tall, short, thin, fat?'

Jody thought for a moment and then said, 'He was the same size as Daddy but older. Oh, and he had a funny moustache.'

'What was funny about it?'

'Well, it looked as though it was going to fall off on one side,' giggled Jody.

Her grandfather pretended that he too was amused and then casually asked, 'You said he was checking the alarms. Did he say anything particular about this house?'

Jody swallowed a mouthful of cereal before replying, 'As a matter of fact, Grandpa, he thought you were naughty for not putting yours on at night. He said he would have to talk to you about it.'

'And how did he know that Grandpa didn't put his alarm on at night?' Alison asked.

'I must have told him.' Then wiping her mouth, she put down her napkin and asked Emma, 'May I leave the table, please?'

'You may,' said Emma. 'Now run along. And don't forget to brush your teeth.'

Jody kissed her grandpa and parents before hurrying from the dining room to get ready for school.

As soon as Jody had gone, Judge Thornton got up from the table.

'I think I'll walk her to school this morning,' he said in a quiet voice, 'just in case the gentleman who was interested in our alarm happens to be about.'

'I thought he was in custody,' said Alison with surprise.

The judge shook his head and said, 'I think not. The man they have arrested is young. James MacCormack referred to him as "a lad with form". According to Jody, the man she saw was older than her father. I think they are two different people. And both appear to be interested in this house, which I think might be more than just a coincidence. I won't be long.'

As he left the room, Emma began clearing the table, unable to hide the concern she was beginning to feel.

'I didn't say anything at the time but I did think it was strange that someone would break in when they must have seen the alarm box on the wall,' she said. Then thinking aloud she asked, 'I wonder if any of our neighbours were broken into?'

'Yes,' Gary said, thoughtfully. 'That's a good point.'

'This man that Jody saw must have lined up the places that were safe for his friend to break into,' said Alison. 'They were obviously working together.'

Emma took a trayful of crockery to the kitchen. As she went

through the hall she saw the judge picking up the mail that had just been delivered. When she returned from the kitchen to the hall, she saw that one particular envelope was causing him some concern.

'Glasgow?' she asked anxiously.

He nodded and opened the envelope. As he was about to read the contents, Jody came running down the stairs. He quickly put the letter back into its envelope and, putting it with the rest of the mail, handed it to Emma.

'Put these on my desk, please.' He smiled at Jody. 'I shall walk with you as far as the school gates. I need to stretch my legs.'

Jody's face lit up with a smile. 'Will you come and meet my friends? I've told them that you send people to prison but I don't think they believe me.'

He was taken aback by her remark. 'You make me sound like some sort of monster. I shall just walk as far as the end of the school gates and then come home.'

Jody took his hand and looked apologetic. 'I only told my friends that you were a judge, Grandpa. I would never make you sound like a monster.'

Giving her hand a squeeze he said, 'Of course you wouldn't, Jody. That was a silly thing for me to say. Come on or you'll be late.'

They said their goodbyes to Emma, who waved them off. She then took the letters to the study and put them on his desk. She was about to leave when her curiosity got the better of her.

She removed the sheet of paper from the envelope that he had opened and read the note enclosed. On it was printed two Bible references: Proverbs 22.8 and Isaiah 47.11.

Emma went straight to the bookshelf and, taking the Bible, looked up both references. Together they read:

Whoever sows injustice will reap calamity, I and the rod of anger will fall.

But evil will come upon you, which you cannot charm away; disaster shall fall upon you, which you will not be able to ward off; and ruin shall come upon you suddenly, of which you know nothing.

A shiver ran down her back and Emma felt that whoever was sending these was either very sick, very dangerous, or both.

It was just before lunch that James MacCormack arrived and was shown straight to the study. As Emma announced him, Judge Thornton got up from his desk to greet his friend.

'Thank you so much for coming round. Please sit down.'

'I wanted you to know about this lad that we're holding.' James sat as he continued, 'According to his story, someone paid him to simply break in, throw a few papers about and get out without anyone seeing him. That's why he wore a balaclava, just in case. And that's why you didn't find anything missing from the room. Strange business altogether.'

The judge frowned and asked, 'Did he say who paid him to do it?'

'Claims he didn't know the man. He was approached in a pub and told that it was a practical joke on a friend. He said he was offered fifty pounds for his effort.'

'Would he recognize this man again?'

'Possibly. But he thinks he had on a disguise. A man about fifty with a ginger moustache and gold-rimmed spectacles. He believed the moustache was false because it didn't match the man's brown hair.'

'But why did he want my house broken into without anything being taken? And how did he know that this young man had the ability to do it? He must have been aware of the young chap's criminal record. And how did he know about that, I wonder?'

The two men looked puzzled.

'And how did this man know that your alarm wouldn't be on last night?' James asked.

Judge Thornton showed some discomfort as he said, 'I think my granddaughter was responsible for that.'

James MacCormack looked surprised. 'Jody?'

'Yes. I'm afraid so,' the judge said reluctantly, 'She met a man who said he was checking on the local alarms and during their conversation she let it slip that mine was never put on at night.'

'Oh dear.'

'But of course she had no idea what this man was up to,' Judge Thornton said in her defence.

'No, no. Of course not. Did she describe him?'

'Only that he was older than her father and was obviously

wearing a false moustache. Apparently the sight of it falling off on one side amused the child. I walked her to school this morning just in case he might be about but no sign of him.' The judge shook his head and said, 'I find it extremely odd. And very worrying.'

'I understand that the only damage done during the break-in was to the window lock,' said James as he got up to look at the window for himself.

'Yes. I'm having a new one fitted this afternoon. There is something else,' Judge Thornton added. 'I've received one of those biblical references again today.'

'From the same person?'

'From Glasgow, yes.'

He took the envelope from his desk drawer and passed it to James, who looked confused until the judge gave him a paper on which he had written the quotes.

James finished reading them and looked concerned.

'Getting beyond a joke, isn't it?' he said

The judge nodded in agreement. 'I know you told me not to worry about the previous card and letter but this latest one is much more threatening. And I am beginning to wonder whether these letters and the break-in are somehow connected.'

James MacCormack re-read the quotations and frowned. 'But why? I mean, what's the point of breaking into your study but not taking anything? It just doesn't make sense.'

'I know.' Judge Thornton sighed. 'No sense at all.'

'Unless, of course,' James said thoughtfully, 'someone is getting revenge by carrying out a vendetta against you.'

'You're not serious?'

'Oh but I am,' James said. 'You've sent a few people away during your years as a judge. Any one of them could want some sort of revenge when they got out.'

'But that's ridiculous. It's true that some people make a stupid threat when they're sentenced but that's only because they have been found guilty. A criminal is always under the illusion that they won't get caught, and it hurts their pride when they are. You of all people know that's true, James.'

James hesitated before saying, 'But that's what I mean. If they're serving a long sentence, they've got time to build up a grudge against the people who put them there. The policeman who arrested them, or the judge. Especially if the judge gave them a longer sentence than they expected.'

His comment only aggravated the judge. 'My dear James, you and I always believed in ridding society of the criminal who causes pain and grief to the decent people. But unfortunately our laws prevented *me* from putting them away for longer! Had this young man been given a longer sentence when he first started to burglarize, he would not be free to cause the sort of distress that he has to this household.'

'Oh, I agree with you,' said James, realizing his friend was more upset than he had previously shown. 'As you know, if I had my way, these little buggers would all be locked away. We're far too lenient, I'm afraid.'

'Not lenient, James. The word is *soft*.'

James MacCormack put the letter carefully back into its envelope. 'I'll take this with me and see if our young friend knows anything about it. It's a long shot but you never know. He just might.'

'Find out if he has any contacts in Glasgow,' the judge said, as if giving instructions, 'and you might be able to find out who the man is that paid him to break in here.' Then with a scowl he said, 'I would very much like to have that man standing before me in a court.'

'Yes, well, you won't get a chance now that you've retired, will you? Never mind. I shall see what I can find out.' James walked to the door. 'Cheer up. After I've thrashed you on the fairway in the morning, you'll have the party to look forward to.'

Judge Thornton scratched his head and forced a smile. 'I'd completely forgotten about the party.'

James gave his friend a gentle pat on the shoulder. 'You mustn't let a silly note from a crackpot upset you. I'll see you tomorrow.'

The judge walked with him to the front door and opened it.

'Thank you for coming.' Then quietly he said, 'Remember, not a word of this to Alison or Gary. We mustn't worry them.'

'Mum's the word,' James whispered, then left the house.

The judge closed the front door and turned to see Emma as she came from the kitchen into the hall.

'James will do what he can,' he informed her, 'although I don't hold out much hope of him discovering who our religious correspondent is.'

Emma watched him as he walked slowly to his study and shut the door behind him. For the first time, she could see that he was looking old and vulnerable, and it upset her.

The man watching Jody coming home from school looked much different today. Gone was the false moustache. He now wore a trilby hat and tinted spectacles in gold frames as a means of concealing his identity.

He looked at his watch and made a note of the time she had left school. He watched her walk happily along with a friend, unaware of being followed.

Jody was excited about something and when the man heard her grandfather's birthday party mentioned, he took an extra long stride to get closer. He smiled to himself when he heard Jody mention birthday presents and wondered what surprise he could arrange for her grandfather.

When the girls reached the entrance to the drive of Four Oaks, Jody and her friend parted company.

He waited for the friend to go and then walked slowly past the driveway of Four Oaks. Glancing up towards the house, he saw Jody being greeted by her grandfather, who embraced the child with obvious affection.

The man continued on to where his car was parked and got in. He sat for a moment, going over his original plan in his mind. He had to be sure it would succeed before setting it in motion. He finally drove away, convinced that if all went as planned, Judge Thornton would be made to suffer as others had suffered because of him. And that in his twilight years, this judge would come to know the meaning of retribution.

CHAPTER SIX

Bernard Thornton was at the home of a woman in Esher, Surrey. He had been drinking heavily and fallen into a deep sleep on her bed.

Sheila Munroe had met Bernard in a public house in London that lunchtime and accepted his offer of a lift home. After a few more drinks, Bernard suggested that they went upstairs to make love. Despite Sheila's eagerness, once Bernard had got on the bed he was unable to perform and promptly fell asleep. Sheila went back downstairs and had two more glasses of red wine before getting onto the settee and going into a deep sleep herself.

It was Bernard who woke first. As his eyes opened and they tried focusing, he looked around, hoping to remember where he was. He vaguely recalled a lady and wanting to get her into bed. Then he suddenly realized that he was only wearing underpants. He got up and sat on the edge of the bed, looking at the rest of his clothes on the floor. It was then that he remembered Sheila and wondered where she was. He got dressed and found the bathroom, where he threw cold water on his face before quietly venturing downstairs.

Sheila was still asleep and when he saw her he realized that she wasn't as young or attractive as she had appeared in the pub.

He was about to open the front door and leave but turning the lock made a noise that disturbed her.

'Bernard?' she croaked. Clearing her throat, she sat up and asked, 'Were you just going to sod off without even a goodbye?'

'No, no,' he said, trying to sound convincing. 'Just making sure the car's still there, old love, that's all.'

'And is it?'

Bernard opened the door and looked out. 'No problem. Can't be too careful, though.' He gave a nervous laugh.

Sheila stood up and held her head. 'I think a strong black coffee is needed. Want one?'

'Hair of the dog would be welcome. If you don't mind, that is?'

'Oh God.' She cringed. 'How can you, after all the booze you've put away?'

She went to the kitchen while Bernard took the glass he'd used earlier and half filled it with whisky. He took a large mouthful and gave a gratified sigh as if it were nectar.

'Ahh. That's more like it. Cheers, old love.'

'You were telling me earlier that you might lose your licence,' she called from the kitchen, 'I must say I'm not surprised if you drink like you do and then drive. Didn't you say it was near here that you got stopped?'

Bernard became bitter. 'Just outside Guildford it was. There was no need to stop me. I was driving perfectly.'

Sheila came from the kitchen with her cup of coffee.

'You mean you *think* you were driving perfectly.'

'I tell you I *was*,' he said angrily.

'Then why did the police stop you? They must have had some reason,' she argued.

'I'll tell you why they bloody well stopped me. Because my sanctimonious brother tipped them off that I'd been drinking, that's why.'

'Why on earth would he do that?'

'Because he's an upholder of the law, old love,' he said with malevolence.

'You mean he's a policeman?' Sheila asked in surprise.

'Worse.' Bernard scowled. 'He's a judge. Thanks to him I was arrested and locked up for the night.'

'What a horrible thing to do to your own brother. Sounds a right bastard.'

'You've got him in one, Sheila, old girl. Nasty bastard and that's a fact.' He finished his whisky then added, 'It's the old bugger's birthday tomorrow and guess who wasn't invited to the party?'

'You're kidding!'

Bernard started to giggle and helped himself to another drink.

'What are you laughing at?' she asked, smiling.

'Just had a thought.'

'What's that?'

'Why don't we go out to a local restaurant tonight? Then I could stay here and we could both go and gatecrash his party tomorrow. What do you say?'

'I don't think that would be such a good idea,' she said reprovingly.

'Come on. It would ruin his day,' laughed Bernard.

'If you don't go easy on that whisky you'll be in no state to drive. And I don't want you staying here another night.'

'Why not? We've got last night to make up for.' He grinned as he pinched her bottom. 'I could give you a bloody good time, my old lovely. They don't call me the stud for nothing, you know.'

As he went to pull her towards him she pushed him away, went to the front door, opened it and smiled.

'Time to go home, dear. And if you go now like a good boy I promise I won't put the police onto you. All right?'

Bernard could see that she meant it and didn't want any trouble. He pulled himself up to his full height and walked to the front door.

'Why are women such bitches?'

'Because men are such bastards. Drive carefully. And thank you for the lift home,' she said with a benign smile.

She shut the door, leaving Bernard feeling angry. Pushing the letter box open he called into the house, 'No wonder your husband pissed off with a younger bird!'

He went to his car and got in, wishing he hadn't been such a useless lover the previous night. As he drove onto the A3, he saw the sign to Guildford and the memory of his night in jail became vivid in his mind. He knew that he would never be happy until he had avenged his brother's action.

Kenneth Matthews had been clerk of the court during many of Judge Thornton's cases. Like so many people, he believed the judge had been harsh with many of his sentences, but had personally found him a tolerable man. He had even felt sorry for him when they said their goodbyes after the Thelma Davis case had been suspended. Defence counsel Phillip Burns was conspicuous by his absence when other court officials said their farewells, and Kenneth Matthews thought his behaviour was uncalled for.

He looked at the official notification from the hospital giving details of Thelma Davis's death. It had been sitting on his desk for some time and he wondered if he should send a copy to Judge Thornton. In the normal course of events, a case was concluded before a judge retired from the bench. But this was different, Kenneth Matthews told himself. This case had not had a satisfactory conclusion and he was sure the judge would be interested to know what had happened.

Without further hesitation, he made a copy of the report and put it in an envelope with a compliments slip. On it he wrote, 'I thought you might be interested in this. Regards.' He signed it and put it in the postbag.

Jody was up early and couldn't wait to take the birthday present to her grandfather. After a quick bowl of cereal, she hurried downstairs with the gift that she had bought and wrapped herself. A silk tie with a subtle motif of golf clubs.

She crossed the courtyard from the apartment to the house and noticed her grandfather's garage door open. Although he seldom locked it, Jody knew that he would never leave the door open unless he was in there. Then she noticed that both rear tyres were completely flat. Her first thought was to run and tell her grandfather but not wanting to upset him on his birthday, decided to go and inform her parents instead.

As they listened to her describe what she had seen, Gary became concerned.

'They can't *both* be flat, surely? Punctures don't usually happen in pairs.'

'But they are, honestly they are,' Jody insisted.

'You'd better take a look,' Alison advised her husband. 'I don't want Father having to worry himself over a stupid thing like a puncture. Not today.'

Gary got up from his chair and beckoned to Jody. 'Come on. Let's go and have a look.'

When they got to the garage Gary was surprised to see that the back tyres were sitting flat on the wheel rims, just the way Jody had described. As he examined them closer, he could see that both tyres had been deliberately cut.

'I told you they were flat,' Jody said.

'Yes, darling, you did,' said Gary, looking worried. 'Now listen, Jody.

72

Don't mention anything about the tyres to your grandpa. Mustn't start his birthday morning with bad news or it will spoil his day.'

'I won't say anything, I promise,' she said, 'but he's sure to see them when he goes to play golf.'

Gary looked at his watch. 'Yes. Well, he can borrow my car this morning. I'll ring National Tyres when they open. Let's hope they've got this size in stock. Run along now. And don't forget, say nothing about this for the moment. I shall come along later and explain to Grandpa what's happened.'

'OK,' she said and hurried away.

As she ran off, Jody's main concern was not the tyres but whether her grandfather would like the present she had chosen for him.

James MacCormack was just getting the clubs out of his car when he saw his friend arrive in a Ford Mondeo. Surprised at not seeing the Bentley, he walked over to the Ford and watched William Thornton get out from behind the wheel.

'What's this?'

'I had to borrow Gary's car. Someone slashed the tyres on mine.'

'You're joking!'

'I'm afraid not, James. Somehow, somebody has managed to get to the car and deliberately cut both the rear tyres. Gary and Alison insisted I borrow his Ford while they try and get new tyres fitted. But being Saturday it might be difficult, of course. I just hope someone has them in stock.'

'Look, would you rather call our game off?' James asked.

'No, no,' the judge replied, taking his clubs and putting them on a trolley. 'I shall feel better once I get going. No point in sitting at home and moping.'

'I suppose not. It may sound like a contradiction in terms under the circumstances but happy birthday.'

'Thank you. I shall do my damnedest to enjoy it, despite the incident with my car.'

The chief constable tried to cheer his friend up.

'Come on. You'll feel better when you've thrashed me.'

The judge was not feeling very humorous. 'But I'll feel a lot happier when I know who's behind these incidents. Why are they doing this to me? The biblical quotations. The burglary and now this deliberate attack on my car. Why?'

James was more worried than he wanted to appear. 'It could be that all these things are unrelated, you know. These tyres, for instance. They could simply be the work of a young vandal.'

'I think not,' said the judge. 'I just wish I knew who was doing it. I'm beginning to wonder what else they have in mind for me.'

'Had any more letters from Glasgow?' asked James.

'No, but I haven't had this morning's mail yet. It's always late on Saturday for some reason.' The judge gave a sigh and said, 'I don't normally worry about things but this business is beginning to get me down, I'm afraid.'

'You'll cheer up and forget all about it at the party this evening,' James said. 'I'm afraid you'll have to wait for my present till then.'

'Thank you.' The judge managed a smile. 'This tie is my present from Jody. I had to wear it or she would have been most upset. It has little golf clubs on it.'

James admired the tie. 'Most appropriate. She's very fond of you, that young lady.'

'No more than I am of her, I can assure you.' Tying up his golf shoes, the judge said, 'Let's go.'

The two men left the changing room and set off for the first tee.

It was 12.15 by the time the fitter had replaced the new tyres. Gary gave him a cheque and was relieved to see the car in good order before his father-in-law returned from the golf course.

Alison was busy with Emma, moving the furniture around to get the living room ready for the party, while Jody was busy polishing and generally making herself useful. She, more than anyone, was already getting excited at the thought of all the people arriving. And the prospect of being allowed to stay up late made her more enthusiastic to help prepare for this very special evening.

When she had finished polishing, she went to the front door to shake the duster. As she stood on the front step she saw a man looking up the driveway towards the house. On seeing her, the man quickly turned his head and moved away. For a moment, Jody thought it was the same man she had seen wearing the funny moustache, but as she went back into the house all thoughts of the man disappeared, insignificant compared to the party and all the lovely food she would be eating.

*

When he arrived home, the judge was pleased to see his car back to normal and after inspecting the new tyres thanked Gary for his efforts and went straight to his study to make out a cheque.

The post had been placed on his desk and as he picked up each envelope he was relieved that none had been posted from Glasgow.

Most of the envelopes contained birthday and retirement cards, wishing him good luck. There was one official envelope from Winchester Court, which he opened with curiosity. As he sat reading the report of Thelma Davis's death he remembered how he had obstructed Phillip Burns in his attempt to have the woman placed in psychiatric care. He replaced the report in its envelope and sat thinking of Phillip Burns and how the two men had always disliked each other. And then a feeling of unease came over him as he remembered. Phillip Burns was from Scotland.

CHAPTER SEVEN

By the time James MacCormack arrived, the party was under way, with everyone in groups, talking and enjoying themselves.

Alison had made sure that most of the invited guests knew each other and had something in common to talk about. She had local caterers to provide and serve the food, which had given Emma the freedom to relax. But being Emma, she couldn't rest while the caterers were using her kitchen to prepare and heat up the various quiche and vol-au-vent dishes.

James walked through the room, acknowledging the large number of guests he recognized. He saw the judge, deep in conversation with Councillor Jim Morris, the mayor, and made his way over to them.

'I agree. The roads are in need of repair and should have been done ages ago,' said Jim Morris. 'The problem is, with all the cutbacks we've had from the government, we just don't have the money I'm afraid.'

'Well, now that I have two new tyres that have cost me a fortune, I should like to be able to drive them on a decent surface instead of trying to avoid potholes,' the judge said with emphasis.

'Couldn't agree more,' James said as he joined them. 'I'm sure you could sue the council for the damage the roads have done to your tyres, William,' he added with a wink.

'Just what I was thinking,' said the judge, playing along.

'Now hold on,' protested Jim Morris, 'I don't think you can do that. Not unless you can prove that it was the condition of a road that did the damage.'

'Oh, I think a good lawyer could win a claim for new tyres, plus inconvenience and out-off-pocket expense,' the judge said with a straight face. 'Oh yes. If I were on the bench I would probably award compensation of several thousand pounds.'

'You're not serious!'

For a moment Jim Norris was taken in but then the smile on James MacCormack's face made him realize he was the butt of a joke. Not wanting to appear foolish, he laughed as if enjoying it and went to join another group in the room.

'We had him going there for a minute,' James giggled.

The judge smiled. 'Yes, I think we did.'

Taking his arm, James asked, 'Could we go into the hall for a moment?'

'Yes, of course.'

James walked through the crowd and into the hall, where he produced a bottle of whisky from behind the coat stand.

'Couldn't very well march into the party with this. One of your friends might have got you to open it,' he laughed. Then handing it to the judge, he said, 'Here's to many more happy years, old friend.'

'My favourite malt! Thank you. I shall hide this away in the study. Make yourself at home and help yourself to any food or drink. There's plenty of it. I'll be along shortly.'

As the judge walked to the study, Emma came down the long staircase wearing a very attractive blue dress. James could see that she had gone to a lot of trouble with her appearance for the party. She always looked nice but today she was even more lovely, he thought. She returned his wave, then followed the judge into the study while James went to the living room to get a drink and something to eat.

The judge was about to put the bottle of whisky into the cupboard below the bookshelves as Emma knocked and entered.

'Oh, Emma. Come in. Look what James gave me. Wasn't that kind of him?' He held up the fifteen-year-old single malt as if it were a trophy, then put it in the cupboard.

'Very kind. I hope you're enjoying the party. Alison was so anxious to make it a day to remember and invite the people you like.'

'It's a wonderful party. Oh, and thank you for the lovely dressing gown.' Taking her hand he said, 'If you'll forgive an old cliché, it's just what I wanted. But you should not go spending your money on me.'

Giving his hand a gentle pat, she smiled and asked, 'Who else would I spend it on?'

He was touched by the sincerity of her question and found himself asking one of his own, a question he had never felt the right to ask before. 'Has there never been *anyone*? It's none of my business, of course,' he added hastily. And as if excusing his inquiry, he said, 'But you are a very attractive woman. And, if I may say so, never more so than you are this evening.'

Emma, completely surprised by his compliment, responded by giving a grateful curtsy. 'Well, thank you.'

He smiled at her for a moment, then as if embarrassed by the subject said, 'I'm sorry. I didn't mean to pry into your private affairs. Look, why don't you and I try a glass of my birthday present from James?' He went to the cupboard and retrieved the bottle of whisky.

'Are you sure you want to open it?' Emma asked.

'Certainly. After all, it's my birthday.'

'Yes. But wouldn't you rather be with your guests?'

'No.' He poured two glasses of whisky. 'Would you prefer a splash of soda?'

'Water's fine.'

He saw that something had amused her and asked, 'What is it?'

'It's just the fact that my employer is waiting on me when normally it is *I* that wait on him.' She smiled.

He paused for a moment, as if something had just occurred to him. 'My dear Emma. Are you telling me that in all these years you have thought of yourself as simply an employee? I cannot believe that to be true. Why, you are the best friend this family could possibly have.' Taking her hand again he said, 'I don't know what I would do without you. You're part of the family. Surely you know that?'

Emma looked down at his hand holding hers and smiled. 'What would people think if they saw you holding my hand, I wonder? And twice in one day.'

Releasing her hand he apologized. 'Forgive me, Emma. I didn't mean to embarrass you.'

'You didn't embarrass me. But I think we might have given the policeman dusting for fingerprints confused signals the other night,' she said with a gentle laugh.

He gave a quizzical look. 'I don't quite follow.'

Emma smiled and explained, 'Well, there we were. Just the two of us sitting together on the settee in our night attire like a Darby and Joan.'

'Oh, yes,' he said with slight embarrassment. 'The thought hadn't occurred to me until you mentioned it. But I see your point. He no doubt wondered what a woman like yourself was doing with an old fuddy-duddy like me.'

He took two glasses from the silver decanter tray and put a good measure of whisky in each. He added water from a jug and offered Emma her glass. 'Your very good health,' he said as his glass clinked against hers.

'Happy birthday,' said Emma. 'And you are definitely *not* a fuddy-duddy. You're what this country is rather short of, as a matter of fact.'

'And what is that, may I ask?'

'A gentleman.'

Becoming a little coy, he said, 'Well, I sincerely hope that I *am* a gentleman.'

'But you are. A gentleman who took a young girl on trust those many years ago and for whom I have nothing but respect, admiration and affection.'

Emma quickly sipped her drink, leaving the judge feeling slightly nonplussed by her statement. After taking a moment to collect his thoughts he said kindly, 'My dear Emma. I have always believed myself to be a very lucky man in having your complete loyalty and friendship. Without you I cannot imagine what life at Four Oaks would be like. You have taken care of my family and myself in an exemplary way for more years than I can remember. And perhaps we have all taken you too much for granted. I do hope we haven't.'

Emma gave a warm smile and said, 'Don't be silly. To be honest with you, there were times when I bossed you about as though I were the mistress of Four Oaks.' Then jokingly she said, 'Not that you didn't deserve it, mark you.'

Smiling in acknowledgement, he said, 'I'm sure I did.'

Emma finished her drink and put the empty glass down. 'You asked me just now if there had ever been anyone.'

'It was impertinent of me to ask. Please forget that I did so.'

'Oh, I don't mind. There was a boy that I was very fond of when I was nineteen. I used to dream that he would ask me to marry him one day. But then my mother died and I couldn't see my father without someone to look after him. And so I stayed at home, the dutiful daughter.' She shrugged and said, 'After he passed away you offered me the position here and the rest, as they say, is history.'

He sipped his drink and asked, 'But in all these years, has there been no one else?'

'There's enough love in this house for me to share. And—' She stopped before she made a fool of herself '—I think we should be getting back to the others,' she said softly.

'I suppose we should. But before we do, there is something I should like to confide in you.'

'Oh?' She waited for him to continue.

He appeared troubled, and hesitated before explaining, 'It is regarding these biblical quotes that were sent to me from Glasgow.'

'You've not received another one?' she asked anxiously.

'No. But I've had a thought as to who might have sent them. Just a thought, you understand. Nothing more.'

'Have you told the chief constable?'

'Not yet.'

'Hadn't you better do so?'

'The person I suspect is not, and never has been, one of my favourite men. But what if he is innocent and became aware of being investigated because of me? You see the difficulty I find myself in. I really don't know what to do.'

'Either a person is guilty of a crime or they're not. And if this man is guilty he should be punished. Isn't that what the law states?'

'Oh yes. That's exactly right,' he replied. 'But this man is also a member of the legal profession.'

'Good Lord!' she exclaimed.

Judge Thornton nodded solemnly as he said, 'A barrister, in fact. Which only adds to my dilemma.'

Alison was relieved to see Emma come into the living room and, excusing herself from the guests, went over to her.

'Emma, have you seen Father?'

'He went to the study. He'll be out in a moment.'

'Good. The Martindales have just arrived and were asking where he was hiding himself,' Alison said as she caught sight of her father entering the room. 'Ah, there he is.'

As Alison went over to her father, Emma saw Gary Hanley with a tray of assorted drinks heading her way.

'You've not got a drink, Emma. Can't have that. What would you like? Gin, whisky or bucks fizz?' he asked.

Emma studied the glasses thoughtfully.

'Hurry up and take one,' Gary begged her. 'These drinks are damned heavy.'

Emma grinned and took a bucks fizz from the tray. 'Crystal glasses are always heavier than plastic ones, Gary.'

Gary winced disapprovingly at her attempt to be humorous and continued to circulate.

Emma saw Jody in conversation with neighbours Gerald and Patricia Turvey and was about to join them when the telephone rang. She hurried to the hall and picked up the receiver.

'Hello.'

'Aah. The lovely Emma, I believe.'

There was no mistaking Bernard Thornton's voice and it was obvious that he had been drinking heavily.

Trying to sound friendly, Emma said, 'Hello, Mr Thornton. How are you?'

'All the better for hearing you, old love. Anyone ever told you that you have a sexy voice on the telephone? Eh?'

Ignoring his remark she asked, 'Do you want to speak to your brother?'

'Did you hear what I said?' he whispered. 'You could turn a chap on with that voice of yours. Is that what you do to my brother, is it? Use your voice to work him up to a lather, do you?'

Resisting the temptation to hang up, Emma said in a firm tone, 'I think you've had too much to drink.'

'Want to spank me, do you?' he giggled. 'I bet we could do more than spanking if we had the chance, eh? God, I bet you could go through the card without having to study a reference book, eh?'

'I'll see if your brother's about,' she said sharply. 'Hang on a moment.'

'I'd hang on to you any time, old love,' he said lecherously.

She put the receiver down and went to the living-room door, signalling to the judge that he was wanted on the phone.

He left the room and joined Emma in the hall.

'Who is it?' he asked.

'You may prefer taking this call in the study,' Emma said quietly. 'It's your brother. And he's been drinking.'

The judge gave a despondent sigh. 'Oh dear.'

'It could be worse,' Emma said drily. 'At least he's on the phone and not at the door.' Then picking up the telephone receiver she said to Bernard, 'He's just coming.'

As she held the receiver while the judge made his way to the study, she heard Bernard's drunken voice again. 'What do you wear in bed, Emma? Jamas, nightie or does he prefer you in the raw, eh?'

Hearing the study receiver being lifted, she quickly hung up, wondering how many other people might think she shared a bed with her employer.

'Yes, Bernard. What is it?'

'Bloody awful timing, big brother. Emma and I were just in the middle of arranging a sexy night together.' His drunken laugh made his brother cringe. 'I bet you'll be getting a good seeing to tonight, eh? Birthday present from the lovely Emma, what?' He sniggered then said, 'I envy you, old man.'

'Apart from being obscene, is there any other reason for this call, Bernard?' the judge said angrily.

'Aah … yes … Thought you'd like to know that I didn't lose my licence, despite your efforts to keep me off the road. The fine's three hundred quid. And to me three hundred quid's a fortune. Thought you might like to cover me with a cheque to tide me over. Bit short of funds, you understand. Besides, it was you that landed me in the shit, old man.'

Judge Thornton hesitated before replying. 'I will not send you a cheque, Bernard. You would only drink yourself to death. No. You send me the summons and I'll see that it's paid,' he said abruptly and hung up. As he did so, he hoped it would be a long time before he heard from his brother again.

Jody was holding her grandfather's hand and pleading with him to let her stay up a little longer. 'I don't want to go yet, Grandpa. I'm not tired, really I'm not. Can't I wait up until everyone's gone?'

'Well, I—'

'Please! Mummy will listen to you.'

The judge sighed reluctantly and said, 'It is past your bedtime and if your mother says you must go …'

'But it's your birthday and it's Saturday. Please!'

He could never resist his granddaughter when she looked at him with moist eyes. He patted her cheek and whispered, 'I'll see what I can do.'

Suddenly, Jody's eyes began to shine again as he wandered over to where Alison was in conversation with their next-door neighbours, the Turveys.

'Hello, Father. Gerald was just telling me about the work he's having done.'

'I was saying to Alison that I hope the workman knocking down our walls won't disturb you too much,' said Gerald.

Judge Thornton shook his head. 'Good Lord, you mustn't let that bother you, Gerald. You and Patricia are the ones having to put up with the mess. I must say I don't envy you, though.'

Alison noticed Jody staring at her with anticipation. 'I have a feeling that my father has been sent over here on an errand,' she said to Gerald with a knowing smile. 'Is that right, Father?'

Her father nodded. 'It is. She would like to stay up for a little longer as it's Saturday. And as I haven't seen much of her this evening, I would like her to. With your permission, of course.'

'That child can twist you round her little finger whenever she wants to, Father.'

'Rather like a little girl named Alison used to, I seem to recall,' he said pointedly.

Alison threw up her hands and sighed. 'All right. I give in. Tell her she can stay up for another half hour.' Then turning to Gerald, she said, 'See what I have to put up with? How can I win against the pair of them?'

The judge winked at Gerald and went back to Jody.

'What did she say?' Jody asked impatiently.

Taking her hand, he replied, 'You can stay up for another half an hour.' Then in confidence he added, 'Which, if we are lucky, might turn into forty minutes. Come on. Let's mingle with the guests.'

Alison watched her daughter's face beaming in triumph and said to Gerald, 'Just look at them. They simply adore each other.'

Gerald nodded in agreement. 'It's lovely to see a child so happy with her grandfather. Difficult to think of him sending people to prison when you see him with Jody.'

'I know,' said Alison. 'If anything happened to separate them, I hate to think what life here would be like.'

Suddenly Alison felt a cold chill run down her back. It was as if she had had a premonition that something unpleasant might happen.

'Are you all right?' Patricia asked, noticing the sudden change in her hostess.

'Someone just walked over my grave, that's all,' Alison said, nervously laughing it off. 'If you'll excuse me, I shall go and get a drink.'

'Make it a stiff one,' said Gerald. 'Something to put the colour back in your cheeks.'

As she caught sight of herself in a mirror, Alison was shocked by how pale she looked. She went to the drinks table, poured a large brandy and gulped it down. She took a deep breath and turned to see Emma looking concerned.

'Are you not feeling well? You look as though you've seen a ghost.'

'I'm fine,' Alison said, forcing a smile. 'Needed a drink, that's all.'

'You've certainly earned one,' said Emma. 'The party is a great success.'

'Yes. I think everyone's enjoying themseves,' said Alison, trying to pull herself together. 'Thanks for all your help. I think Father's having a good time.'

'I'm sure he is,' said Emma. Then taking Alison's arm, she asked quietly, 'Do you want to tell me?'

'Tell you what?' Alison asked.

'What it is that's troubling you.'

Alison knew that she couldn't hide anything from Emma and with a half smile she said, 'It's silly really but all of a sudden just now, I felt that something was going to happen to Father or Jody. Something unpleasant. It made me go all cold and clammy.'

'Probably something you ate,' said Emma, managing to sound unconcerned. 'Go outside and get some fresh air for a moment. It'll make you feel better.'

'I think I will,' said Alison, only too pleased to have an opportunity to compose herself again.

As Alison left by the front door, Emma could see Jody and her grandfather happily together in the living room. As she watched them talking to the guests, Emma wondered if Alison's anxiety over her father and daughter's wellbeing was simply an irrational emotion or something more serious.

Her thoughts were quickly interrupted by James MacCormack.

'Ah, Emma. There you are,' he said, guiding her further into the hall and out of Judge Thornton's sightline. 'Can I have a word?'

'Yes, of course,' said Emma with curiosity. 'Do you want to speak to me in private?'

'If I may.'

'The dining room should be quiet,' she said, ushering him through the hall.

They entered the dining room and found it deserted. Emma closed the door and waited for him to explain the need for secrecy.

'It's about William,' said James.

'Yes?'

'How worried is he about these Bible quotations? I mean, is he really concerned?'

Emma was surprised by the question, 'Of course he is. They don't appear to be a joke. In fact, quite the opposite. Each of them is obviously meant as a threat. And it worries me. I don't like him being upset.'

'To be perfectly honest with you, I didn't think the card was anything more than a silly prank,' he said. 'But then this Bible business started and quite frankly I don't know what to make of it.'

'Isn't there something you can do?' Emma pleaded.

'Well,' he said thoughtfully, 'perhaps there won't be any more posted to him. In my experience, these people get tired of their little game and stop playing it eventually.'

'But what if this lunatic doesn't stop? You'll *have* to do something then, surely?'

'If he receives any more, I shall certainly do something, I promise you.' Seeing the relief on Emma's face, he said, 'You're very fond of him, aren't you?'

A gentle smile appeared as she replied, 'I think you could say that, yes.'

He put his hand gently on her shoulder and said in a soft, kindly voice, 'You mustn't worry. He'll be just fine, believe me.'

'I hope so,' she said with a sigh. 'I don't know what I'd do if anything happened to him.' Then suddenly remembering, she said, 'You know that Alison and Gary are unaware of these letters, don't you? They mustn't know or they will worry.'

He nodded and was about to speak as the front door opened and Alison came in.

'Hello! What are you two plotting?' she asked jokingly.

'That would be telling,' said Emma with a laugh. 'You look better now the colour's back in your cheeks. I told you the fresh air would do you good.'

'Feeling poorly, were you?' enquired James.

'A bit queasy, that's all. I'm OK now though.'

'Come on,' said Emma. 'Let's get back to the party before they wonder what's happened to us.'

CHAPTER EIGHT

Anne Lawrence had spent the afternoon at an antiques fair in Sherborne. This was the first weekend for some time that her gentleman friend had not visited but she knew that it was impossible for him to get away. Although she hadn't purchased anything, she had enjoyed her afternoon. There was something exciting to her about articles that were a part of another era. Things that had belonged to people who had been unable to outlive their treasured possessions. Objects that were part of a family history.

As she arrived at the cottage gate, her elderly neighbour, Joyce Walters, called out from her garden. 'Anne, dear, I've got a parcel for you. Hang on a moment and I'll fetch it.'

Anne was curious as to who this unexpected parcel was from and what it would contain.

Joyce duly arrived with a package in the shape of a box one normally associated with clothing of some kind.

'There we are, dear,' said Joyce as she handed it to Anne. 'The postman arrived soon after you went out so I took it in.'

'Thank you, Joyce.'

'No trouble, dear. I thought it might be something special that you have been waiting for.'

'No, it isn't actually,' said Anne, trying to make out the postmark. 'I wasn't expecting anything.'

'Oh well, it's a nice surprise then. I hope it's something lovely,' Joyce said as she walked to her door. 'Bye, dear.'

As Joyce went into her cottage, Anne took the parcel into the living room and gave it a gentle shake before tearing off the brown paper. She was surprised to see a cardboard box on which was a note saying, 'Can't wait to see you in this. I will be in touch and let you know where and when. Miss you.'

Her curiosity increased as she removed the lid and saw the black and white uniform that had been carefully packed inside the box. She removed the contents and lay them out on the oak table. There was a black skirt with matching top, a white cap and apron and black stockings. She could see that it was a complete maid's outfit and she started laughing to herself. 'So he wants me to play the part of a maid, does he?' Then holding the clothing against herself, she looked at her reflection in the mirror and chuckled, 'I wonder what the old devil's up to?'

Having spent Sunday clearing up after the party and getting meals prepared, Emma was glad when Monday arrived.

Gary had gone to a meeting with an agent in Reading, Jody was back at school and, with Alison gone to visit a girlfriend for lunch, Emma had the judge and the house to herself.

When the mail dropped through the letterbox, it was Emma who picked it up and sorted it. There were two letters for Alison, one for Gary and four addressed to the judge – one of them with a Glasgow postmark.

Her first instinct was to destroy it so as not to have the judge get upset, but she knew that she would have to satisfy her curiosity and be with him when he opened it. Reluctantly, she took all four letters to the study.

'Ah. I thought I heard the postman,' he said as Emma took the letters to him.

'I'm afraid there's another one from Glasgow,' she said.

He took the envelope and removed a sheet of paper that was identical to the previous communication. He read the contents, which said simply 'Job 19.29'. He was about to rise when he saw that Emma had already removed the Bible from its shelf. He took it from her and neither of them spoke as he opened it and found the page. He read the quotation, unable to conceal his anxiety:

> *Be afraid of the sword, for wrath*
> *brings the punishment of the sword,*
> *so that you may know there is a*
> *judgment.*

Emma waited impatiently for him to tell her what it said as he put the Bible down, still open at Job 19.

'Well?' she asked. 'What does it say?'

He closed the Bible and in a determined voice said, 'That it's time I called my friend the chief constable. That's what it says, Emma. And I hope he can do something to stop whoever this person is that's sending these letters. They really are becoming quite annoying.'

As he picked up the telephone receiver and tapped in the numbers, Emma knew that deep down the judge was becoming more worried than he would admit.

Detective Inspector Trevor Buckley was given a brief summary of the situation by the chief constable as they drove from police headquarters to Four Oaks.

They were greeted by Emma and shown immediately into the study, where Judge Thornton was waiting.

'James, thank you for coming,' he said. 'This business has gone beyond that of a practical joke, I fear.'

'Let me introduce you to DI Buckley,' said James. 'I am putting him in charge of this matter.'

The two men shook hands and Judge Thornton offered both his visitors a seat.

'I can't stay I'm afraid,' James said apologetically. 'I'm due at a meeting in half an hour.'

'Oh,' said the judge, disappointed.

'Don't worry, old friend,' James said. 'Trevor's a good man and you can rely on his discretion. You can confide in him as you would me, in complete confidence. Now I really must dash. I'll be in touch with you later.'

James MacCormack hurried from the room with a wave of his hand, leaving Judge Thornton calling, 'Thank you for coming,' as he closed the study door behind him.

DI Buckley sat in the chair facing the large mahogany desk and waited for the judge to sit before speaking.

'Before we do anything else, can I see the most recent letter, sir? And I believe there was a greetings card that had been turned into a suggestion that you meet Lucifer.'

Judge Thornton was surprised at the inspector's choice of phrase and wondered if he really was a man of intelligence or just trying to impress. He was in his early fifties and by his general appearance looked like someone who had a lot of experience but, for whatever reason, had never become a superintendent. Yet he had the complete confidence of his chief constable, which was reason enough for the judge to put his trust in the man.

'I have it here,' he said, opening the desk drawer. He passed the envelope across to the inspector, who said nothing as he studied it carefully. He then held it up to the light of the window. Finally, he put it back on the desk and said, 'It was much easier with the old typewriters. Each machine had its own story to tell in those days.'

'Pardon?'

'The type was quite distinctive no matter what the make. It was always possible to match the type to the machine that had been used. Now, with computers, it takes longer for our chaps to find a match. So many use an identical typeface. But none are without their own idiosyncrasy,' said Inspector Buckley with conviction. 'Once we have a lead we'll be able to pin down the computer that chummy used to send you these. It may take a while but with a bit of luck we shall be able to nail him. Or her, as the case may be.'

Judge Thornton showed surprise at the last remark. 'I must say, I had never thought of the sender being a woman.'

'Have you *any* idea at all as to who might be sending these to you, sir?'

The judge became uncomfortable as he answered, 'There is only one person I can think of that comes from Scotland. But I find it hard to imagine that he would do such a thing.'

'From Glasgow, is he?'

'I believe so, yes.'

'His name?'

Judge Thornton hesitated before saying, 'The man happens to be a barrister.'

DI Buckley gave a quizzical look and asked, 'You believe that a barrister sent these letters?'

'I think it possible. Unlikely perhaps. But possible. He certainly never hid his dislike of me.'

Inspector Buckley was intrigued. 'Is this man religious, do you know?'

'I have no idea.'

'Well, this person would have to know his Bible to be able to pick out these quotations with such accuracy, wouldn't you say?'

'I think that is a fair assumption, yes. But as I said, I find it hard to imagine someone of his intelligence sending such things.'

'If you will tell me his name I can do a discreet check on him.'

'Burns. Phillip Burns. But he mustn't know that I suspect him, you understand,' he said anxiously.

DI Buckley wrote the name in his notebook. 'This Burns gentleman will be quite unaware of my investigation, sir, that I can assure you.' He finished writing, then asked, 'Is there anyone apart from this Mr Burns that might dislike you enough to threaten you this way?'

'Inspector, I have only just retired from spending years punishing criminals by sending them to prison. No doubt there are hundreds of men and women who are, or have been, locked up and would like to see me rot in hell. However, it has been my experience that few judges have ever felt their wrath. I am of the opinion that this person, whoever it is, is not one of those unfortunates, but someone far more calculating and clever.'

'Clever?'

'Oh yes. Clever because they know that their efforts to wear me down will finally do just that, if they are allowed to continue.'

'I shall do everything I can to bring this person to book. You can rely on that, sir,' Inspector Buckley assured him.

'I wish you luck, Inspector. I sincerely do. And by the way, my daughter and her husband know nothing of this matter. And so I must ask you to be discreet in their presence.'

'Certainly. I'll check on this Phillip Burns as quickly as possible. Then at least we shall know one way or the other if he's our man. Do you happen to know his address?'

'I'm afraid not. I assume he has a flat somewhere in the south of England but where, I have no idea. I think he goes home to Scotland at weekends whenever possible.'

'Is there a Mrs Burns?'

'I believe so. But I'm not certain of that.'

It surprised the inspector that Judge Thornton appeared to know so little of the man he suspected of sending this mail. He rose from the chair and put the letters and card into his pocket. 'I shall take these with me, sir. Our forensic people may find something, you never know.'

The judge stood up and opened the study door. 'Thank you for coming, Inspector. I do hope you will get to the bottom of this business fairly soon.'

'I'll do my best, sir.'

They walked to the front door and as the judge opened it he realized that James MacCormack had driven DI Buckley to the house and taken the car when he left.

'You have no car, Inspector. Do you wish to phone for one?'

'No, thank you, sir. The walk will do me good and give me a chance to think. I'll report back as soon as I have anything. Good day, sir.'

He walked briskly down the drive, leaving the judge hoping that the chief constable's faith in this Detective Inspector Buckley did not prove to be mistaken. As he closed the door he remembered his car tyres and wondered why he had neglected to mention it, but suddenly the thought of a man like Phillip Burns coming to the house and deliberately cutting tyres seemed quite preposterous. Gradually, the judge began to feel that he was making a fool of himself by ever suggesting that the barrister could be his adversary. But if it wasn't Phillip Burns, he wondered, then who else could it possibly be?

When James MacCormack returned from his meeting he made a call to DI Buckley's office in the hope that he was there.

'Hello, Buckley. How did you get on with Judge Thornton?'

'I got on all right with *him*, sir. But it looks as though he is wrong about the man he suspects of sending these letters.'

'Oh?'

'Yes. This Phillip Burns has not been back to Scotland for over a month. And he doesn't have a home in Glasgow. He has a place in Haddington, which is between Glasgow and Edinburgh.'

'You're certain of this?'

'Positive. I got Glasgow and Edinburgh police to check him out and they both came up with the same info.'

James MacCormack was not happy at the news. 'So what's the next move?'

DI Buckley paused before answering, 'Quite frankly, sir, unless forensic come up with something, there's not much that I can do. With Phillip Burns in the clear and no one else in the frame, we've nothing to go on.'

After a moment's thought the chief constable said, 'I know it's a long shot, but if we can get some copy paper from this fellow Burns' office and check it against the paper the Bible quotations were printed on, we would know for certain whether he's involved or not. We mustn't overlook the possibility of him sending them to someone in Glasgow to post for him.'

'Mmm. Possible, I suppose,' said the inspector.

'As I said, it's a long shot. But I want you to do it. We mustn't write this barrister off just because he hasn't been to Scotland lately,' James MacCormack said impatiently. 'Get on to it as soon as you can.' He hung up, wishing that there was something more tangible to go on.

Emma had never interfered in any quarrel between Bernard Thornton and his brother. Despite hating Bernard for the way he womanized and drank, she had always tried to avoid making an issue of it, but now she felt anger and resentment at the way he had treated the judge and spoken to her on the phone. No man had ever said filthy, suggestive things to her before and the more she thought about it, the more convinced she was that it could be Bernard who was sending the religious notes. His way of getting revenge on his brother for telephoning the police and having him arrested, she reasoned. After giving it some thought, she decided to share her suspicion.

William listened to her without interruption. When she had said her piece he looked towards the window of his study and stared at the garden. After a few moments, he looked back at Emma.

'Yes, the possibility of Bernard being responsible for all these unpleasant happenings had crossed my mind earlier. But I discarded the idea some time ago.'

'May I ask why?'

'Because my brother is a womanizer, a drunkard and a waster. Yes, he is all these things. But there is one thing Bernard is above all others. Bernard is a coward. I cannot believe he would have the courage to do these things.'

'Perhaps you're right,' said Emma with reluctance. 'I just wish you could enjoy your retirement the way you deserve to. You of all people shouldn't have to contend with this nasty, vindictive sort of thing.'

'You make it sound as though I were an angel,' he said, smiling.

'Not an angel, perhaps, but certainly not a man who should have these nasty things happening to him.'

He gave her a warm smile. 'My dear Emma, I have recently had cause to look back at certain moments with some regret. I fear that I was not always fair in my judgement. And that is something I am forced to admit, no matter how unpleasant that it may be.'

Emma jumped to his defence and said, 'I don't believe you would ever be unfair to anyone. Certainly not deliberately.'

'Oh but I'm afraid I was,' he said regretfully. 'I wish I could say otherwise.'

'You mean in court?'

'Yes.'

'In what way were you unfair?'

He thought for a moment before speaking. 'Because of my own contempt for a colleague, I was myself contemptuous by having unforgivable disregard for a young woman's rights. I refused to allow her the medical attention she so obviously required, until it was too late.'

Emma looked perturbed as she asked, 'How do you mean?'

He spoke awkwardly as he explained. 'I wanted my final case to be a clean finish to my career. No loose ends. Everything tidy. But I totally disregarded my obligation to be fair and impartial. I allowed my personal dislike of Phillip Burns to affect my decision. And through that momentary, unforgivable lack of professional judgement, a young woman is now dead.'

Emma held a hand to her mouth. 'Oh no!'

'I'm afraid so,' he said sadly.

Emma was apprehensive as she asked, 'How did she die?'

'The hospital report said it was a massive heart attack. It seems the poor woman had a weak heart. She had apparently been taking tablets that had not been officially prescribed and they had helped to precipitate her death. Together with her mental condition, the trauma of the trial proved too much it seems.' With guilt he added, 'Her death might have been avoided had I acted differently.' Closing his eyes, he sighed and whispered, 'Oh Emma, I've been so wrong.'

Instinctively she reached out and held his hand to comfort him. 'You mustn't blame yourself for what happened.' Then in a quiet voice she asked, 'What had this woman done?'

'She killed her husband. She claimed that she did so to protect her lover and herself from a violent attack by him. I have to say that thinking back on the evidence, there was a doubt as to her mental condition at the time. But I committed an unforgivable sin myself. I refused the request of defence counsel to order her psychological examination.' With remorse he added, 'And all because I allowed my personal animosity to take over. A terrible thing to do. Quite unforgivable.'

He placed his hand on hers and gave it a gentle pat, as if thanking her for being there.

'Try and forget about it,' she said softly as she squeezed his hand. 'I'll make us a cup of tea.'

As Emma let go his hand and left the room, he realized how much closer they had become since he had retired. These past few days she had shown a warmth and understanding that made him feel different towards her. Throughout the years he had allowed her to run the house and bring up Alison with all the expertise at her command. But never had he thought of her as anything other than good reliable Emma. Until now he felt only gratitude for her loyalty, especially during his years at court. Now, for the first time, he was seeing her for what she really was – an attractive woman with whom he felt safe, a woman who was able to show him affection in a way he had not experienced since his wife had died. Her very presence had and now become more important to him, and was now fond of her in a way he had not thought possible before. He prayed that whoever was behind these letters would soon be apprehended and that life at Four Oaks would be pleasant once more.

Judge Thornton was deep in thought when Emma returned with the tea tray and it was only her voice that made him aware of her being there.

'I had a sudden thought while I was making the tea,' she said. 'Could it be the boyfriend of the woman who killed her husband that's sending you these quotations?'

He looked surprised as he answered her. 'There is an old proverb which says, "Two minds with but a single thought." And it was that thought that was going through my mind just prior to your coming into the room.'

'Perhaps it's an omen?' Emma said hopefully.

'Perhaps it is,' Judge Thornton replied with optimism. 'Why didn't I think of him before!'

He picked up the telephone and decided that after he had spoken to the chief constable's office, he would phone to see if it was convenient to pay an old friend a visit. Someone he could discuss his problem with. Someone whose advice he would more than welcome.

Reginald Byers-Wheatley had been a close friend of William Thornton ever since they had first met. Thirty years earlier they had walked into a courtroom as legal adversaries, William as the prosecuting counsel, Reginald as counsel for the defence.

The case appeared to be an easy one for William to win – as far as he was concerned, it was an open and shut case. A woman had been pushed to her death over a cliff in front of several witnesses. All he had to do was call each witness in turn and the accused would be found guilty. End of case.

But he hadn't bargained on his opponent's skill in court. Reginald tore the witnesses' evidence to shreds. He carefully, cleverly confused them regarding their description of the man they *thought* they saw commit the offence. They had described the accused as heavily built and scruffy in appearance with long hair. But the man Reginald had dressed in a black suit, clean shaven with neatly groomed hair, bore no resemblance to the man they had described to the police. And when the jury, through lack of evidence, returned a not guilty verdict, it was the beginning of William Thornton's admiration for the man he was on his way to visit.

As he drove towards Poole in Dorset, he remembered the way Reginald would stand with his back to a witness, then quickly turn and surprise them with a question which threw them off guard, and how he had become the most sought after QC of his day.

But now he was in a wheelchair, unable to move from the waist down. The victim of a car crash twenty years earlier, he was still, however, kept up to date on legal matters and was still one of the brightest legal brains alive. A man William had always been mentally stimulated by, a man that even a judge could learn from.

As he turned into the drive he saw the front door open and Reginald's wife, Katherine, giving a welcoming wave.

Parking carefully in the small driveway, he got out of the car and greeted his hostess.

'Katherine,' he said, kissing her cheek, 'how nice to see you.'

'It's been too long, William. Reggie is so looking forward to seeing you. He thinks about you often. Pity you can't stay the night,' Katherine said with sincerity. 'He so loves your company.'

'I know. Another time perhaps.' The judge smiled. Then he asked, 'How is he?'

'Just the same,' she said.

'Still putting the world to rights?'

'Oh yes,' she laughed. 'Especially the legal world. Come on in.'

Katherine was a woman of sixty, with auburn hair that was only now showing some grey. Her petite frame gave her the look of a younger woman and her freckled face made her appear to possess a healthy tan.

As they entered the hall William saw Reggie at the drawing-room door, grinning from ear to ear. He held out a hand to welcome his guest. 'My dear friend. It's lovely to see you.'

'Lovely to see you, Reggie. You're looking well.'

Reggie gave his old friend a brisk handshake.

'I'm *feeling* well. Thanks to my ever-loving nurse,' Reggie said, as he blew a kiss to his wife.

Katherine gave him a suspicious look. 'Whenever he flatters me I know he's after something.'

'Two glasses of that new Chilean red would be welcome, my love.' He winked at William. 'You'll like this wine. It was discovered by my neighbour at the local supermarket. Jolly good it is too, eh, Katherine?'

'Yes, dear. But perhaps William would prefer a cup of tea after his long drive.'

'Rubbish!' said Reggie. 'He can have a cup after he's had a glass of wine. Pour it out, there's a love.' Positioning his wheelchair opposite a comfortable armchair he said, 'Sit down and tell me what it is that's bothering you.'

'What makes you think that something is bothering me?' the judge asked, making himself comfortable in the armchair.

'Because you sounded just a little too cheerful when you telephoned me,' said Reginald as he raised an eyebrow and gave a look of suspicion. 'And that suggested to me that you had a problem that you wished to discuss. Am I right?'

Judge Thornton gave a quiet laugh as he answered, 'You are

without doubt the most perceptive devil I ever knew.' Then looking at Katherine, who had just finished pouring the wine, he asked, 'Are you ever able to keep anything from this man?'

'Only my affair with the milkman,' she joked as she passed each of the men a glass of wine.

'Oh, come now, Katherine, I have known about it for ages but was being discreet,' Reginald laughed as he held his glass up to the judge. 'To us. Them like us. Damned few and they're all dead. Cheers.'

'Cheers,' responded the judge. Then seeing Katherine with no glass, asked, 'Not joining us, Katherine?'

'No,' she said, smiling. 'I've got things to do and wine makes me sleepy. I'll leave you two to catch up on all the scandal. If you will forgive me.'

The judge got up as she left the room then, resuming his seat, said, 'You have a lovely lady there, Reggie. You're a very lucky man.'

'I am. Very lucky. What do you think of the wine?'

Taking a sip from his glass, the judge said, 'Mmm. It has a nice dry but fruity flavour.'

'Glad you like it,' said Reginald. Then putting his glass down on the side table, he asked, 'So what *is* the problem?'

'Difficult to explain really. It sounds like a practical joke that students play during rag week. But it isn't a joke, I'm afraid,' the judge sighed.

Reginald could see that his friend was troubled as he said philosophically, 'Every problem has a solution. If it hasn't got a solution it isn't a problem, it's a fact. And if it's a fact we must accept and live with it. Now. Tell me about it, my friend. If I can help, I will.'

Judge Thornton explained, 'It all began with a retirement card that had the message, "Wishing You Many Years Of Happiness" but "happiness" had been crossed out and replaced with "Hell". This I assumed to be someone's idea of a joke and dismissed it.'

'I take it there was no signature.'

'None.'

'Go on.'

'Soon afterwards I began to receive envelopes containing a quote from the Bible. Or rather the book and verse that these quotes were from. The envelopes had all been posted from the city of Glasgow. I made copies of them for you to see. The originals are with the police.'

Passing a sheet of paper to Reginald, he sat back, waiting for his reaction.

'Mmm. And the retirement card was also posted from Glasgow, I assume?'

'It was.'

Looking at the quotes again, Reginald said thoughtfully, 'And you have informed the police?'

'Oh yes. As a matter of fact the chief constable is a good friend. He's looking into it. But with discretion, of course.'

Sounding sceptical, Reginald said, 'Yes. Well, let's hope he knows what he's doing. I always preferred to use a private detective myself. I found the police too busy with red tape.'

'I didn't want to have anyone other than my friend looking into this matter. I couldn't afford to have this leaked to a member of the press,' the judge said uneasily.

Reginald was intrigued and asked, 'But my dear friend, what reason do you have to keep it hushed up? You are now retired, so it wouldn't hurt your career in any way. Not only that, it might scare this person off if he thought the press were on to his nasty little game.'

'I must ask you not to mention to anyone anything I am about to tell you. Not even Katherine,' the judge begged.

'You have my word.'

Judge Thornton hesitated a moment before saying, 'I've had a letter from Downing Street offering me a knighthood.'

'My dear fellow, how wonderful!' exclaimed Reginald. 'May I offer you my sincere congratulations.'

'Thank you.'

'You must be thrilled to pieces.'

'Yes. But you see the problem if the press got onto these letters. They could ruin my chance of ever having this honour bestowed on me.'

Reginald was thoughtful for a moment. 'Nothing else came with the Bible references? I mean, no demands or anything?'

'No. Nothing else.'

'So they are purely threats of something that might be going to happen, something that has not yet taken place but according to these quotations will be swift and hurtful when it does.' He closed his eyes and reflected for a moment. 'I suppose you wouldn't consider a sudden illness, would you?'

The judge was surprised by the suggestion. 'What on earth do you mean?'

'Well, a heart attack, for instance. Or a fall downstairs. Something that would make you bedridden for a while.'

'You aren't serious!'

'Oh but I am,' said Reginald. 'Very serious.'

'But what would be the point?'

'The point, my dear fellow, would be to create an illusion that would probably bring this letter sender out in the open and end this bloody business once and for all.'

Looking confused, the judge said, 'I'm afraid you've lost me.'

Reginald wheeled his chair around and positioned it nearer to his guest. 'If this chap thinks you are ill, there isn't any point in him threatening that something unpleasant will happen to you. Because it already will have. In which case he will have no reason to send any more of those quotes. On the other hand, his sick mind will probably want to confirm your being incapacitated. That is when he may be tempted to come out into the open. Even pay you a visit. Pretend to be from the gas board or a telephone engineer. Anything that would give him a legitimate entry to your home. Do you follow me?'

'Yes,' the judge reluctantly agreed, 'but the idea of the press being informed of a fake illness and then friends and relatives telephoning and sending flowers, well, that would be too much. And besides, if it were known that *I* had been party to a fraud, I could certainly kiss the knighthood goodbye.'

Reginald sighed. 'Yes. Well, it depends what you consider more important. Your peace of mind and sanity to enjoy your remaining years, or a tap on the shoulder with a sword.'

Judge Thornton looked perplexed and said, 'If only I knew who was doing this to me, who it is that hates me so much.'

'Well, I know what I would do,' said Reginald.

'Then tell me.'

'To be frank. I'd let your policeman friend carry on with his effort to help, but I would also employ the services of a good private investigator. Someone discreet who can usually, by fair means or foul, use methods the police either won't or cannot apply. And I know just the man. Raymond Farraday would probably get quicker results than your boys in blue. No paperwork or red tape to go through.'

The judge was unconvinced and shook his head. 'But Reggie, how can he be better than the police, with all their computers and other advanced equipment?'

'You trust me, don't you?'

'Yes, yes, of course. But—'

'And you can trust Farraday. I'll give you his number in case you change your mind. Tell him I suggested that you call and that will get him cracking. Oh, and he's not one of your "sitting in a tree taking photographs of some poor fool having it off with his mistress" investigators. He's top drawer.'

The judge was still not convinced. 'I'll certainly give it some consideration, Reggie. But thank you anyway.'

'Your choice,' said Reginald, 'Now, changing the subject,' he said, getting confidential, 'how's your love life?'

The judge became embarrassed. 'What on earth do you mean?' he asked, unable to prevent a blush.

'Oh, come on, William. I can remember the way you used to go dashing off to have a dirty weekend,' Reginald said. 'Was it with your housekeeper? Come on. You can tell me.'

Judge Thornton said awkwardly, 'Nonsense. Why do people assume that there's a sexual relationship between myself and my housekeeper? Just because we live under the same roof?'

'Let's be realistic,' said Reginald. 'She is rather lovely, old man. Good-looking too. Yet you insist you don't fancy her, eh? Must be something wrong with you, that's all I can say.' He began to chuckle.

'What's so funny?' the judge asked.

'I was just thinking about the way you used to nip off to London to see whoever it was. You were like a rabbit on heat in those days. If it wasn't your Emma, who the devil was she, eh?'

The judge was unable to hide his embarrassment as he said in his defence, 'That was a moment of weakness on my part and you are the only person who knew about it.'

'Oh, it was weakness all right,' laughed Reginald. 'Weakness of the flesh.'

'Please, Reggie, I don't like harping back on that period of my life and I wish *you* wouldn't. It was wrong and I still regret it.'

Reginald frowned thoughtfully and said, 'I bet *that's* why you've never invited me to Four Oaks, you old reprobate! You are afraid I might let the cat out of the bag in front of the family. And your Emma in particular.'

'Don't be ridiculous,' the judge said unconvincingly. 'I haven't invited you because, well …'

'Yes?' Reginald teased.

'Well, with you being in a wheelchair and my house having steps and, er.…' Annoyed at his poor effort to create a real excuse, he said angrily, 'Oh all right. The reason I haven't invited you is just as you surmised. I would hate my family to learn of my improper behaviour so soon after Angela's untimely death.'

'You don't really believe that I would do that to an old friend and colleague, surely?'

Hesitating before answering, the judge said, 'I thought that after a few drinks you might have said something. And I couldn't take that risk. You do see that?'

Reginald laughed. 'Fair enough. I suppose I might have put you in the old fertilizer without thinking.' Then he quickly added, 'But not deliberately, old man. I'd never do that.'

Trying to regain his composure, the judge explained, 'It was a difficult time for me, Reggie. I needed female company. But in many ways it was unfair to the woman in question. You see, while I was making love to her it was Angela that I was thinking of.'

'A natural way of excusing a sexual need. Quite a common thing for someone to have sex while thinking of someone else. Even women do that, old man,' Reginald stated. 'But what I'm damned if I understand is why you nipped off to London for a bit of naughties when you've got that lovely Emma woman on your doorstep! Doesn't make sense to me.'

The judge showed his discomfort again. 'Let us change the subject, Reggie. We've talked enough about my sex life.'

After reminiscing about their earlier days together when they were both barristers, it was time for the judge to take his leave. He said goodbye to Katherine and Reginald and as he walked to his car, promised to stay overnight on his next visit. They both waved as the car went down the drive and out of sight.

As Reginald wheeled himself back into the house and into the living room, he felt guilty at the way he had goaded his friend regarding his sex life. Even so, he was curious as to whether William was still in touch with the lady he secretly met in London all those years ago. If so, where did they now go for their secret meetings? The thought of the tyrannical Judge Thornton having an affair with anyone amused Reginald. Even so, he wished his friend well and looked forward to his becoming *Sir* William. His only worry was that something was going to happen that might stop that dream from becoming a reality.

It was early on Tuesday morning that James MacCormack rang to arrange a meeting with Judge Thornton.

Just after 9.30, Emma opened the front door and let the chief constable in.

'He's in the living room,' she informed him. 'You go on in and I'll bring some coffee.'

As he entered the room he didn't relish giving his friend the news he had brought with him.

'Well?' said the judge hopefully, offering James a seat.

'What would you like first?' asked James. 'The bad news or the bad news?'

'Oh. Like that, is it?' said the judge despondently.

'Afraid so. Your Phillip Burns isn't responsible for those letters. DI Buckley did a thorough check on him and he's in the clear.'

'Strangely enough, in a way I'm relieved,' said the judge. 'I should have hated it to be a colleague, even one that I had always disliked.'

'Well, we even managed to do a check on his copy paper and the test was negative. Sorry.'

'Thank you anyway. I do appreciate your efforts.'

'Now for the other bad news. The woman's boyfriend, John Porter. We traced him to the address he gave the court but it turned out to be a bed and breakfast place. The hospital had expected him to return to collect Thelma Davis's things but he didn't ever go back there.'

The judge was silent for a moment. 'I see. So John Porter may have believed that I was responsible for her death and decided to take his revenge.'

Emma entered the room and, hearing him make the comment, was unable to hide her feelings. 'You aren't responsible for this person's actions so let's hear no more of that talk.'

She put down the tray and began pouring the coffee as if nothing was wrong. James was already taken aback by the way she had admonished her employer.

'But Emma, that poor woman's boyfriend must have hated me on learning of her death,' the judge explained. 'Don't you see? If I had acted differently she might still be alive.'

Unmoved by his supposition, she said, 'And he could have spent his days visiting her in prison or a secure hospital, where she would be locked away for the murder of her husband. Isn't that the truth?'

Judge Thornton held his hands out in submission. 'You see what I have to put up with, James?'

Not allowing James to reply, Emma said, 'And you can see what *I* have to put up with!' As she gave him his coffee she begged him, 'Tell him he's wrong to blame himself for the woman's death.'

James gave a half smile to his friend and said, 'Emma is right. You mustn't hold yourself responsible. A criminal is a criminal, no matter what sex they are.'

'Quite right,' Emma said as she poured the judge's coffee.

Judge Thornton gave a shrug and was about to speak when the doorbell rang.

'Now who can that be?' said Emma as she hurried from the room to find out.

'Perhaps it's that chap from the premium bonds to tell you that you've won a million,' James joked.

'Now that would be most acceptable,' the judge replied. 'I might even buy you a drink if it is.' He smiled.

'I should expect a case of champagne at the very least,' James informed him, keeping a straight face.

Emma re-entered the room and announced the visitor. 'It's Mrs Harper from the school.' Then she quietly added, 'She seems worried about something and wants a word with you.'

'Jody's head teacher?' The judge enquired.

'Yes. May I show her in?'

'Yes. Yes, of course,' Judge Thornton answered. He stood to greet his visitor, wondering what on earth had happened to bring the head teacher to his house.

James got up to leave, 'I'll go, shall I?'

'No. Don't go,' the judge insisted as he stared anxiously at the door.

Mrs Harper, a woman in her fifties, was ushered into the room by Emma. Judge Thornton greeted her and introduced her to James MacCormack.

'I'm pleased to meet you, Chief Constable,' she said with a certain unease. 'Are you here because of this business about Jody?'

'Business? What business is that?' James asked. Before she could answer, the judge became frightened. 'Has something happened to Jody?'

Mrs Harper looked perturbed as she said, 'I had a note to tell me that Jody was staying in bed with a fever for a day or two. But there was something about it that troubled me. Do you mind if I sit down?'

'Please do.' The judge indicated a chair.

Mrs Harper gratefully took a seat, producing a note as she did so. 'This was given to me by Marion Cleave, one of Jody's schoolfriends. She said that a man gave it to her.'

'Man? What man?' asked Emma, becoming concerned.

'May I see that note, please?' The judge held out his hand and read the note aloud:

Jody will not be at school for a day or two. She has a slight fever
and I am keeping her in bed.
   Alison Hanley.

Unable to hide his distress, he exclaimed, 'This is a forgery, of course! It is not her mother's handwriting and Jody is not in bed with a fever. So where *is* she?!'

James MacCormack took the note from the judge and spoke as a police official. 'The man that gave the girl this note, Mrs Harper. Did she say whether he had a car?'

'No. All she said was that a man gave her the note. When I asked who the man was she said she didn't know,' Mrs Harper replied.

James stood up and spoke directly to the head teacher. 'I should like to speak to this Marion girl as soon as possible, Mrs Harper.'

'Yes, of course,' she said, getting to her feet.

The judge stood up. 'I'll come with you.'

'No,' said the chief constable, 'I want you to stay here just in case this man should telephone. And I'd like a photo of Jody to circulate. What about her parents, by the way?'

'They went on a shopping trip to London,' Emma explained. 'I expect them home around teatime.'

'I'll collect the photograph after I've spoken to Marion Cleave.' Then with a sense of urgency he turned to Mrs Harper, 'Let's go.'

Emma left the room to see them out, leaving the judge in a state of shock. He poured himself a glass of whisky and tried to come to terms with what had happened. His hands were trembling. Then, as Emma returned, a sudden thought occurred to him.

'Alison! How am I going to tell Alison that Jody has been abducted?'

He rubbed his forehead as if searching for an answer. Emma rested a consolatory hand on his shoulder, trying hard not to show the anguish she too was feeling.

'Jody will be all right,' Emma tried to convince him. 'This man wants to frighten you, that's all. Like he did with the letters and those silly quotes. She'll be home before you know it, you'll see. By the time Alison gets back from London this afternoon the police will have found her, I'm sure.'

'If anything should happen to her I should never be able to forgive myself,' he said with self-reproach. 'Oh God, Emma, what is happening? Why would someone want to take Jody?'

Emma was unable to answer, and knowing that she could not control her tears, patted him on the shoulder and left him in his chair, hands clasped together, as if in silent prayer.

Marion Cleave had been nervous when she was first called to the head teacher's office and told that the chief constable wanted to ask her some questions, but after a few moments his tactful approach had the girl feeling relaxed and prepared to answer his questions.

'When I was at school we used to play Kim's game. I don't know if it's played today,' James MacCormack said, smiling. 'It's a game where you have twenty articles on a tray that you study for one minute. Then you cover them up and try and remember as many of them as you can.'

'Yes. We play that sometimes,' said Marion.

'Ah, but are you good at it?' He grinned.

'Pretty good,' she said proudly.

'So was I,' he said. 'I think that's why they made me the chief constable.' He laughed.

Mrs Harper sat at her desk and chuckled. 'Oh, I don't think that's true.'

James wished she was somewhere else as he continued asking his questions. 'Tell me, Marion. Do you think you'd be able to remember twenty things that you saw this morning on your way to school?'

Marion raised a quizzical eyebrow. 'What sort of things?'

'Anything,' he said casually. 'This man who asked you to deliver the note to Mrs Harper, for instance. What did he look like? Do you remember what he was wearing?'

Marion was thoughtful for a moment. 'He had a blue jacket with something in gold on the top pocket.'

'Excellent. Then it was a blazer, was it?' James asked.

'Yes. It must have been because it had gold buttons and no flaps on the side pockets,' she said.

James was surprised at the accuracy of her description and encouraged her to continue. 'Tell me what else you remember about him, Marion. What about his height, face, colour of his eyes and hair, age? Imagine I was going to draw him and you are describing him for me.'

'Like a police picture that we see on television?'

'Exactly.'

Again she became thoughtful before speaking. 'He was a bit taller than you, with brown hair and a moustache that was a funny kind of ginger colour.'

'Ginger? Are you sure about the colour?'

'Yes, I remember thinking it looked funny.'

James was pleased with the information and hoped for more. 'What else did you notice about him?'

'That he seemed very nice,' she replied. 'I remember he'd got a kind smile.'

James gave a friendly smile of his own and asked, 'Apart from his blazer and ginger moustache, not forgetting his kind smile, is there anything else you can tell me about him?'

A thoughtful frown appeared on her forehead and she closed her eyes to concentrate. 'He had brown eyes. And a tooth was missing about here.' She pointed to her upper right canine. 'And he was wearing a wedding ring, I think.' She opened her eyes. 'I'm sorry. I can't think of anything else.'

'You've been a great help, young lady. A great help. How old would you say he was?'

'About the same as my father, I would say. Fifty-ish.'

'Did this man have a car?'

Marion was uncertain for the first time, 'I'm not really sure. But when he left me he walked away as if he was in a hurry, so perhaps he didn't have a car. Perhaps he lived in the area and didn't need one.'

From the mouths of babes and sucklings, James thought as he stood up. 'Thank you, Mrs Harper, for allowing me to use the office.'

'Not at all. I hope Marion has been of some help in finding the person you're looking for,' said Mrs Harper, trying to be discreet and not show her own anxiety.

'This man,' said Marion. 'Has he done something awful?'

'We hope not,' said James. 'Thank you again, young lady.' He walked to the door and opened it. 'I'll see myself out.'

As he left to hurry back to Four Oaks, his main priority was to get Jody's description circulated as soon as possible, before this man could do her any harm.

CHAPTER NINE

.

She winced as the small needle of the hypodermic pierced her arm. Within seconds she fell into unconsciousness and all her anxieties vanished.

Doctor Holden placed the syringe back in his case and felt her pulse. Satisfied that she would sleep safely for a few hours, he left Alison to rest.

Pulling the bedroom door closed behind him, he signalled Gary to follow him down the stairs and went into the living room of the flat.

'She'll be fine now,' the doctor said. 'Probably sleep for five or six hours.'

Gary was obviously on edge as he said, 'This whole thing has been a terrible shock. I just wish we knew where and how Jody is.'

'Might I suggest that you go and join your father-in-law and have a stiff drink. I think he needs your company right now just as much as you need his,' the doctor said.

Gary became fidgety. 'I don't like leaving Alison alone.'

Doctor Holden gave a reassuring smile as he said, 'She's not going to need company for quite a while, Mr Hanley. You'll do no good moping about here. Do as I say and go over to the house, there's a good chap.' Then jokingly he added, 'Unless you would like me to give you an injection too?'

Gary managed a smile and replied, 'No thanks.'

'Then off you go. As soon as there's any news of your Jody the police are sure to contact the house, don't you think?'

Reluctantly, Gary nodded in agreement.

As they went to the front door the doctor said, 'You can pop back every once in a while just to reassure yourself that your wife is all right. But try not to wake her. She needs to rest right now.'

Doctor Holden left, leaving Gary uncertain as to whether he should leave Alison alone or not.

He stood watching the doctor walk to the house to give the judge his report. Then after hesitating for a few moments, he decided to take the doctor's advice. Closing the door quietly behind him, Gary left the flat.

Emma had not cooked a meal that evening. Neither she, Gary or Judge Thornton could have eaten much. While the two men sat with a drink, Emma produced thinly cut ham sandwiches for them, insisting they had something other than alcohol inside their stomachs.

Gary had been back to check on Alison twice in the first hour after the doctor had left, each time he returned giving the same report, that she was sleeping.

It was almost 7.30 when the phone rang and Gary leapt to his feet and answered it.

'Hello. Yes?'

'Ah. That sounds like my nephew-in-law. How are you, old lad?' asked the unmistakable voice of Bernard Thornton. 'You don't normally answer the phone, Gary-boy. Everything all right there, is it?'

'No. No, it isn't, as a matter of fact, Bernard. Jody's gone missing. I thought you might be the police with some news.'

At hearing Bernard's name the judge signalled Gary to get his brother off the line.

'Christ!' shouted Bernard. 'When you say gone missing, do you mean run away?'

'Er, no. Look, we don't know for sure but we think she was abducted. Now I really must hang up in case the police try to get through. Sorry, Bernard.' Gary hung up before Bernard was able to say any more.

'Always managed to call at the most inconvenient time, did my brother,' said the judge. 'I wonder what he wanted?'

'To annoy you, probably,' Emma said curtly.

Gary began to pace the living-room floor.

'Please sit down,' said his father-in-law. 'Pour yourself another drink and try to relax.'

'How can I relax, for God's sake? How can anyone relax?' Gary said with a raised voice. 'Where's Jody? Where have they taken her?' Gary poured another drink and took a gulp. 'I'll kill the bastard if he hurts her.'

Emma walked over and put her arm around him. 'Calm down, Gary. Come and sit over here.' She led him to the sofa and sat with him. 'We mustn't get ourselves in such a state. That's just what this person wants us to do.'

'You speak as though you know who he is,' Gary said with surprise.

'Not *who* he is. Only that he wants to upset the family as much as he can,' said Emma.

'What do you mean?' Gary asked.

Judge Thornton felt unable to remain silent. 'I think it's me that this person wishes to hurt,' he said remorsefully. 'In fact I *know* it is.'

Emma gave a reproachful glance and could sense even more trouble in the air.

'I don't understand,' said Gary, looking confused. 'If this person wanted to hurt you, why would he do this to Alison and me?'

Before the judge could answer, the telephone rang and this time Emma answered it. 'Hello.'

'Judge Thornton, please,' said a man's voice.

'Just a moment,' said Emma and signalled the judge to come to the phone.

William gave her an enquiring look but Emma shrugged and passed him the receiver.

'Hello?' he said with curiosity.

The man's voice became quiet as he said, 'Now you know how it feels to have someone you love taken from *you*.'

The judge began shaking as he asked, 'Who is this?'

'Timothy,' the voice said in a sinister tone.

'Timothy who?'

'Timothy three, verse one.'

Judge Thornton tried not to sound troubled as he asked the caller, 'What do you mean, Timothy three, verse one?'

The caller's voice sounded sinister as he said, 'You will soon find out.'

Suddenly the judge shouted down the receiver, 'I warn you, it's only a matter of time before you're caught and then ...' He realized that the caller had hung up and that he was talking to himself. He stood holding the telephone for a moment, angry and breathless.

'Glasgow?' Emma asked apprehensively.

Judge Thornton simply nodded as he replaced the receiver.

'Well?' Gary was becoming impatient. 'Will somebody tell me what's going on? And who's Timothy?'

Judge Thornton sat back in his chair. Reluctantly he said to Emma, 'I'll have to tell him, won't I?'

Emma nodded.

'Would you fetch the Bible from the study, please, Emma?' he asked quietly.

'Of course,' she replied, and left the room.

Gary sat looking confused, waiting for an explanation.

Emma got the Bible down from the shelf but before taking it to the living room, she opened it at Timothy 3. She looked at verse 1, and felt a shiver as she read:

You must understand this,
that in the last days
distressing times will come.

Emma's thoughts turned to that earlier conversation with her employer. Could the man she loved and admired have ever been so inhuman as to deserve the pain that had now fallen on him and his family? She took the Bible and returned to the living room, desperately afraid of what the future held.

Bernard Thornton was concerned at the news his nephew had given him. He didn't know Jody Hanley very well but the idea of anyone abducting a child filled him with revulsion.

As he poured himself a whisky, he thought of his brother and the way he had behaved towards him. He was now regretting his vengeful behaviour just a few nights before. He tried to convince himself that it was the alcohol that had encouraged him to take his revenge but his conscience reminded him that it was his vindictive nature that had made him seek out and pay a complete stranger to do his dirty work for him.

And now, Bernard Thornton sat drinking alone, unhappy in the knowledge that he was too cowardly to ever be a *real* man. Without the aid of alcohol to boost his confidence, he was not a man at all. That same alcohol that had made him a failure as a lover and a laughing stock among several women. With the truth too painful to accept, Bernard poured himself another whisky and wished he was rich.

After hearing the biblical quotes, Gary agreed with his father-in-law and Emma that Alison should be spared the worry of knowing about them. He now understood why he had also been kept ignorant of their existence.

'But if this man only wants to hurt you, why has he taken Jody?' asked Gary.

'Because he knows how much she means to me,' replied the judge. 'We are dealing with a sick mind, I'm afraid.' Becoming impatient, he stood up and looked at the telephone. 'Why doesn't James call?'

'He will,' Emma assured him, trying to keep the atmosphere calm.

'I'll just go and make sure Alison is all right,' Gary said, and got up and left the room.

Emma went to the window and watched him hurry nervously to the flat. As Gary entered his front door, Emma was about to turn away from the window when she saw a girl appear from the road and hurry up the drive towards the house. She could see that the girl was carrying an envelope.

'I'll be back in a moment,' Emma said.

She walked quickly to the front door and opened it just as the girl was about to put the envelope through the letterbox. When she saw Emma standing there, she looked startled.

'Hello,' said Emma with a smile. 'What brings you here?'

The girl offered Emma the envelope. 'A man asked me to put this through your letterbox,' she explained.

Emma took the letter and seeing that it was addressed to the judge, asked casually, 'And what man was this, dear?'

'I don't know who he was,' said the girl. 'I'd never seen him before.'

'I see,' said Emma in a friendly voice. 'You're not one of the girls from St John's School, are you?'

'No, miss. I go to Morgan Street Comprehensive.'

'Well, thank you, er, what's your name, dear?'

'Mandy Calloway, miss.'

'Well, thank you again for bringing this to me, Mandy. This man. What did he look like?'

The girl thought for a moment before answering, 'He had one leg that was stiff.'

'You mean he had a limp?'

'Yes.'

'Anything else? Did he have glasses or a moustache?'

'Glasses but not a moustache. He was tallish though. And he had brown hair.'

'Oh, yes,' said Emma convincingly. 'I know who it was now. Well, thank you again, dear. Goodbye.'

'Goodbye.'

As Mandy went hurrying off down the drive, Judge Thornton came from the living room and into the hall. When he saw the girl leaving, he asked hopefully, 'Who was that, Emma? One of Jody's friends?'

'No. Just a girl delivering this.'

She gave him the envelope, which he opened impatiently and removed a newspaper cutting. As he read it he became cold and breathless. He sat quickly on a chair, the colour draining from his face.

'What is it? What's happened?' Emma took the cutting from his hand. It was a small headline and part of a story from a newspaper:

GIRL'S BODY FOUND BY WOMAN WALKING HER DOG

The body of a young girl was discovered by a woman who was walking her dog in a local park this morning. The discovery was made when the woman, a retired dinner lady at

The rest of the story had been cut out by the sender.

Emma fought back the tears and rushed to the kitchen. She returned with a glass of cold water, which she put into the judge's hand.

After a few sips he looked up helplessly at Emma and, trying not to tremble, said, 'It can't be Jody ... Emma. It can't be her, can it? What are we going to do?'

Emma wiped her eyes and said bravely, 'We're going to pull ourselves together, that's what we're going to do. This could be about anyone. It doesn't say how old this girl is or even what actually happened.' Trying to convince herself as much as the judge, she said, 'This could be from any newspaper. There isn't a date or anything. It could be days or even weeks old, couldn't it?'

Weakly, Judge Thornton took her hand and said, 'Oh Emma, I would give anything that you're right.' Then closing his eyes he whispered, 'Please God. Don't let it be Jody.'

Emma was trying to think clearly. 'We must let the police know about this immediately. I'll telephone them now before Gary gets back. At least then we'll know if anyone *was* found in a local park this morning.'

'Yes. You're right,' the judge said, trying to control his fears. 'Pass me the phone, please.'

Suddenly Emma said, 'But wait a minute. If this girl had been Jody, we would have been told long before the story got to print, wouldn't we?'

William tried to clear his mind and think logically. 'That's right! Of course! I should have thought of that. Even so, I think we should make that call. Just to put our minds at rest, eh?'

Emma managed a smile as she nodded and went to the phone. She passed the telephone to him and watched as he tapped in the direct number of James MacCormack's office.

'Come on. Come on,' he said impatiently.

After a few moments, a woman answered, 'Surrey police. Can I help you?'

'This is Judge Thornton speaking. Can you put me through to the chief constable, please? It's most urgent.'

'I'm afraid he isn't here at the moment, your honour.'

'Then put me through to central control, please.'

'Hold the line.'

Within seconds a man answered. 'Central control. Sergeant Baker speaking.'

'This is Judge Thornton.'

'Yes, your honour.'

'I need information. Can you tell me if a girl's body was reported being found in a local park this morning?' His hand shook nervously as he waited for an answer.

'I haven't heard of anything. This morning, you say?'

'Yes. You see, I received a newspaper cutting regarding a girl being found in a local park this morning. And I'm trying to establish whether this is true or simply a hoax.' He spoke with impatience as he added, 'Can you confirm whether this is true or not?'

'I'll check with the incident room, sir. If you'll hold on a moment.'

'Yes, yes, I'll hold.' He turned to Emma, who was trying to remain calm. 'He's finding out now.'

Despite her efforts, Emma was unable to hide her anxiety. After what seemed like an eternity, the judge heard the phone click at the other end.

'I've checked with our people here, your honour. There has not been any girl found at any time during the past months, let alone this morning. It looks as though you've been the victim of a sick joke, sir.'

'Thank you,' said the judge with relief. 'Thank you very much. You'll let the chief constable know I called.'

'Of course, sir.'

The judge hung up. He looked relieved but was unable to hold back a tear. 'It was a sick joke, Emma. A horrible sick joke.'

She put an arm around him and he responded by holding her closer to him. For the next few moments they just sat there, saying nothing.

The silence was broken when they heard Gary coming through the door from the kitchen. Instinctively, they released their hold on each other as Gary entered the room, looking tense.

'Alison is still out to the world,' he informed them. 'You obviously haven't heard anything.'

'Not yet,' said Emma. 'But you know what they say. No news is good news.'

Emma's effort to relieve the tension with the old proverb had little effect.

Gary paced the floor then suddenly stopped as a thought occurred to him. 'Suppose this man wants money. And that's why he's taken Jody. For a ransom!'

Judge Thornton shook his head. 'I don't think that is his motive,' he said sadly. 'I wish it was. I would willingly pay to have her back with us.'

'And anyway,' said Emma, 'if that were the case we would have surely heard from this man by now?'

The judge nodded in agreement. 'Emma is right. Reluctantly I have to agree with her.'

The telephone rang and the judge quickly picked up the receiver. 'Judge Thornton.'

'Hello, William,' said James MacCormack. 'I understand you called. Any news?'

'I've received a newspaper cutting.'

'About a girl's body being found in a park?'

'Yes.' Judge Thornton said with surprise. 'Your people are certainly efficient at keeping you informed of events.'

'That's their job,' said James. 'How did this cutting get to you?'

'A schoolgirl delivered it. Have a word with Emma. She was the one that spoke to the girl.'

Emma took the receiver from him. 'Hello, Mr MacCormack.'

'Hello, Emma. This schoolgirl. Do you know who she was and how she came by the newspaper cutting?'

'She said that her name was Mandy Calloway, from Morgan Street Comprehensive. And that she was asked to deliver it to this address by a man she described as having brown hair and glasses.'

'Moustache?'

'No. I asked but she said he hadn't got one. Apparently he did have a limp though. Mandy described it as a stiff leg.'

'Well, that's something,' said James. 'I'll get that sent out straight-away. What with Jody's photograph and this girl's description of the man, we should get a result soon.' James was trying to sound confident. 'Don't worry, Emma. Just keep William as cheerful as you can.'

'I will,' Emma replied.

'I know you will. Chin up.'

As Emma replaced the receiver she said to the others, 'He sounds fairly confident that they'll find this man.'

'As long as they find my little girl, and find her soon!' Gary cried impatiently.

It was gone 7.30 when Doctor Holden returned to see Alison. Gary hovered over him while he was checking her pulse, irritating the doctor with his nervousness.

'Your wife is still sleeping comfortably, Mr Hanley. And I don't anticipate her waking for at least two hours. So there really isn't any point in your coming and possibly disturbing her until then. Meantime, I should like you to take one of these.' He took a pill box from his bag and opened it.

'What are they?' asked Gary.

'Tranquillizers,' replied the doctor. 'They will help you to stay calm and be of help to your wife when she wakes.' He took two tablets from the box and gave them to Gary. 'Mustn't let her think that you're losing your nerve, now must we?'

'I don't need tranquillizers.'

'I really think you do.'

'I don't like taking pills,' he said adamantly. 'I'll be OK.'

'I really feel that under the circumstances, you would be much more relaxed and able to think better if you took the tablets.'

Gary went to the kitchen and poured some water in a glass. Holding one of the tablets up to show the doctor he was about to take it, he popped it in his mouth. Drinking the water and swallowing hard, he put the remaining tablet in his pocket.

'I assume you only meant me to take one of them, Doctor?' Gary said sarcastically.

'One is fine,' said Doctor Holden. 'You might want the other one before you go to bed.' Then looking at his watch he said, 'I must be off. Please give Judge Thornton my regards. If you should need me you only have to call. I'll see myself out.'

Gary let him make his own way to the front door and went back to the bedroom. He stood gazing down at his wife, lying there looking tranquil. The doctor had not said whether he would return that evening and Gary wondered what he would do when Alison woke up.

With every hour that passed the tension was becoming more unbearable. What was his daughter going through? Had she been ill treated? Had the man who took her physically abused her? With these thoughts going round and round in his head, he decided to go downstairs and have just one drink before returning to the house. As he sat alone in the small living room with a glass of whisky, one agonizing question kept coming to mind. Was Jody still alive?

Anne Lawrence knew who the letter was from as soon as she opened the front door and saw it on the mat. She had been out since mid morning and had hoped to find a message from him on her answerphone. It was unusual for him to write and she tore open the envelope, impatient to read its contents.

Hello sexy,

Everything is going as planned. In fact it couldn't be better. By the time you receive this I will have the whole family worried. There is nothing like the loss of something precious to have an effect. And what could be more precious than the family treasure I have arranged to go missing? It was a last-minute idea that should really cause anguish and set the scene for the final act.

Because of this additional plan, our original one will have to remain on hold for a while. I'll be in touch regarding where and when.

She watches my every move so I have to be very careful and simply play along with things here.

Miss you.

Can't wait for some you know what!

Love,

Me XXX

Anne finished the letter, wondering what precious treasure he was referring to.

She wished he had telephoned rather than written. She was tempted to call his number but knew his female minder would probably answer and that could prove too dangerous. Instead, she decided to be patient, hoping he would call her in the morning.

CHAPTER TEN

Emma had brought the judge a glass of his favourite brandy to the living room, where he was anxiously waiting for a call from James MacCormack. As each hour passed he became more and more frightened that Jody would not be seen alive again. He would give anything to be able to put his arms around her and hear her laughter. And he was desperately worried about Alison. And all because somebody was taking revenge? But who and why? If only he knew the answer it might make things easier to endure.

Emma sat in an armchair with a mug of hot chocolate, still trying to hide her fears for the little girl's safety. Putting on a brave face was all she felt able to do, but silently she was praying that the telephone would ring before the night had passed and that the news would be good.

Gary came in from the kitchen, looking tired and restless. Unable to sit still he paced back and forth. 'Why don't they find her?' he shouted. 'Oh, they're quick enough when it's a motorist they want to find for some stupid parking offence!'

'Calm down, Gary,' Emma said quietly. 'It won't help things by getting angry.'

'Emma's right,' the judge agreed. 'No good will come of losing control of your emotions.'

'Then what am I supposed to do, for Christ's sake? Jody's out there somewhere, though God knows where, in the hands of some perverted nutter! How the hell can I calm down?' He sat with his head in his hands.

Emma got up from her chair and put her arm around him. 'We'll hear something soon. You'll see,' she said in a comforting voice.

The three of them sat, feeling helpless and saying nothing for several minutes.

Suddenly Gary looked at his wristwatch, which said four minutes past nine. Checking it with the French marble clock standing proudly on the mahogany mantelpiece, he stood up and announced, 'I'm going to phone the police and find out if they have any news.'

'If they had any news they would have told us,' the judge said. 'Now please try and calm down, Gary. You are making Emma and myself nervous with your jumping up and down.'

'It isn't your daughter that's gone missing, is it!' Gary snapped.

'That was totally uncalled for,' Emma reprimanded.

Gary realized that she was right and apologized immediately. 'Sorry. I shouldn't have said that, Pops.'

'It's all right. I'm afraid we are all rather on edge,' the judge said, as he toyed nervously with his whisky glass.

Unable to remain calm, Gary continued to pace up and down, while Emma fiddled restlessly with an earring.

A few moments of silence was broken by the doorbell ringing.

'That might be the police!' said Emma, jumping to her feet and hurrying to the hall. Gary quickly followed her and when they reached the front door it was Gary who reached out and opened it. They were surprised to see not the police but Mrs Harper, Jody's headmistress, standing there.

'I happened to be passing and wondered if you had had any news of Jody?' she said. 'Only I've naturally been worried` and as I was near I had to ask. I hope you don't mind?'

Despite his disappointment at the caller not being someone with news, Gary managed to be polite. 'No news, I'm afraid, Mrs Harper. But thank you for your concern.'

'Yes. Nice of you to call,' added Emma with a half smile. 'I shall inform the judge that you called.'

'You'll let me know the moment you hear anything? I won't rest until I know that she's safe and well,' Mrs Harper said.

'Yes, of course,' said Emma.

'Thanks again for calling,' Gary said.

They waited for Mrs Harper to turn and start walking down the drive before closing the front door.

Gary and Emma returned to the living room and were about to

inform the judge who had called when he held up his hand and stopped them. 'I heard,' he said dejectedly.

Emma watched him sitting there, looking frail and tired. She wanted more than anything to wake up from this terrible nightmare and for the house to be a happy, normal one again. But the longer Jody was missing, the more she became aware that the child might not be alive. Fighting back the tears, she turned and walked towards the hall, keeping her back to the men as she said, 'I'll go and make us a hot drink.'

When she reached the hall she hurried to the kitchen, where she sat and cried. 'Oh please. If there's a God, give us back our Jody.'

James MacCormack was in his dress uniform along with other senior police officers at Mount Browne, the headquarters of the Surrey police in Guildford. Traditionally, the all-male dinner had a distinguished guest speaker and this year it was the home secretary.

On display in the oak-panelled senior officers' bar was a varied assortment of trophies. Impressive silver cups dating back over many years stood proudly alongside plaques and shields. As the home secretary inspected them, it was the task of the chief constable to explain their history, and despite playing the perfect host to his visitor, James MacCormack had something other than trophies on his mind tonight. Apart from having to make a speech and introduce his guest, his thoughts kept going to the missing little granddaughter of his friend. More than anything he was hoping for news of her whereabouts and to hear that she was safe, rather than the alternative.

By the time they sat down to dinner, the home secretary was in a jovial mood. Having enjoyed the hospitality he had been offered earlier, his amusing conversation during the meal managed to keep James's mind occupied.

At 9.15 the master of ceremonies rang the bell and called the room to order.

'Please be upstanding.' Once everyone had stood, he called in an official voice, 'Pray silence for the chief constable, who will give the loyal toast.'

James MacCormack raised his glass and said, 'Her Majesty the Queen.'

'The toast is Her Majesty the Queen,' repeated the master of ceremonies, shouting like an army sergeant.

Everyone repeated 'the Queen', had a drink and resumed their places.

As the chief constable took his speech from his pocket in preparation for the ordeal, he noticed a uniformed policeman enter the room and walk towards the top table. As the officer got nearer, James tried to guess from his expression whether he was the bearer of good or bad news. The officer walked up behind his superior and leaned down to him.

'Sorry to bother you, sir,' he whispered.

'What is it?' James asked.

'You wanted to be told immediately if there was any news regarding a young girl.'

'And?' said James with apprehension.

The officer gave a piece of paper to him. 'Sergeant Baker thought you would want to see this. Just came in, sir.'

James read the message and, obviously perturbed by it, got up and turned to the home secretary.

'Forgive me a moment, will you, sir? Something has just come in that I need to check. I'll be back in a moment.'

'Yes, of course. Carry on,' the home secretary said, as his glass was topped up by an efficient wine steward.

As the chief constable left the table, it fell to a chief superintendent sitting on the home secretary's left to keep him entertained.

James reached the telephone in a small unoccupied office and got through to Sergeant Baker at central control. 'This is the Chief Constable. Tell me about this girl that's been found.'

'Yes, sir,' said the sergeant. 'She was found lying on the roadside of the A3 south of Liphook. A passing motorist saw her and called an ambulance. They think she might have been the victim of a hit and run. There was bruising to the side of her head and body.'

'Do we know her condition?' James asked anxiously.

'Only that she was unconscious.'

'No name or identification?'

'No, sir. But I've got a description and it fits the girl Jody Hanley. Same colour hair and eyes. About the same age as well.'

'At least she's still alive,' James said with a sigh. 'We need a positive ID. Did they describe her clothing?'

'They're sending it through to us ASAP, sir.'

'Well, you've got details of what Jody Hanley was wearing. As soon as you know one way or the other, *I* want to know. Is that understood?'

'Yes, sir.'

James MacCormack hung up, wondering how he would tell his friend the judge if this girl was his granddaughter. But now he had to compose himself and go back to the dinner, not only to make a speech of his own but to listen to the home secretary waffle on about how proud he was of the Surrey police force, and what good chaps they were, et cetera. It was this thought, plus having to wait for news of the little girl's identification that made James wish he was anywhere but where he was.

It was just after 9.20 when Gary went back to the flat to check on Alison once again.

He could think of nothing but his daughter. He imagined her tied up in a darkened room or cellar, perhaps being ill treated and in pain. He longed to get his hands on whoever had taken his daughter and beat them mercilessly until they begged him to stop. But he would keep beating them and break every bone in their body, he decided. That was what he wanted to do more than anything.

He opened the door to the flat and went quietly up to the bedroom, wondering if Alison had stirred at all. His wife was still sleeping and he watched her looking peaceful, as though nothing traumatic had happened. He sat in the bedroom armchair and after a few minutes his eyelids grew heavy. Try as he may, he couldn't stay awake. The combination of whisky and anxiety was taking its toll. Within minutes his head fell slowly to one side until it gently rested on the back of the armchair. Soon he was in a deep sleep.

The doctor at the hospital had X-rayed the girl but found no broken bones. Who the child was would remain a mystery until she regained consciousness but his examination of the injuries she had received suggested that she had suffered an epileptic fit. Her tongue had been bitten and the bruises on her body and arms were consistent with those caused by uncontrollable convulsions.

He administered an injection and waited for the child to respond. Within seconds her eyes flickered and opened.

*

The chief constable was keeping his speech short and as he was winding up he noticed the police constable who had given him the earlier message from Sergeant Baker. He was standing at the door with a piece of paper in his hand, waiting for his superior to finish speaking.

'And so we thank you, Home Secretary, for honouring us on this special occasion.' Then addressing his officers he said, 'Gentlemen, I ask you to stand and drink the health of our distinguished guest.' Taking his glass and raising it, he said in a respectful voice, 'The Home Secretary.'

Once more the master of ceremonies repeated in a loud and precise manner, 'The toast is our honoured guest the Home Secretary.'

While everyone stood and drank the toast, James nodded to the constable, who came hurrying to the top table.

As they began to get seated again, James took the message and anxiously read it:

Girl found on A 3 is NOT Jody Hanley.
Girl is Sylvia Turner from Liphook and is now recovering after an epileptic fit.
Sgt Baker

With a sigh of relief, the chief constable put the message in his pocket. As the master of ceremonies began to introduce the home secretary, James felt better able to listen to the speech he was about to make. As he politely laughed in all the right places, he still found his thoughts constantly returning to Jody Hanley. Despite hoping for good news, there was the reality that had to be faced. Jody Hanley might never be seen alive again.

The dream was a mixture of fantasy and reality. One minute Gary was at home, the next he was in the car with Alison and then the car became a space capsule and they were driving out through the clouds on their way to the planet Mars. Within a short time they had arrived on the surface to be welcomed by the judge and Emma who, for no logical reason, had arrived on an earlier spaceship. A Martian creature with big green hands appeared and was holding Jody. Gary and the judge threw rocks at the creature to try and make it let go of the child, whose cries for help had Emma in tears. And then the creature left in a small rocket which took off with Jody looking through a window pleading for help.

Suddenly, Gary was in the spaceship trying to release Jody from the creature's grip. A grille on the wall expelled lethal gas and the creature laughed as Gary slowly weakened and fell into a heap on the floor. Trying in vain to stay conscious, he could feel himself at death's door as Jody cried out for her father to stay alive and save her.

Gary became restless as he heard Jody calling to him. Then he felt a hand pushing at his arm in an effort to wake him.

'Daddy ... Daddy.'

As Gary awoke from the dream, he felt his heart pounding at a rate that frightened him. Then he opened his eyes and heard Jody's voice again.

'Daddy? Wake up,' her voice called.

Still half asleep, he turned his head and saw Jody standing beside him. But this wasn't part of the dream!

'Why are you sleeping in the chair, and Mummy on the bed asleep with her clothes on?' Jody asked.

Gary was unable to speak as he reached out and took her in his arms. As he cuddled her close to him, Jody responded by putting her arms around his neck. Although she was happy to be given such affection, she wondered why her father appeared so pleased to see her, and when she saw tears running down his cheek she became worried that something was wrong. Again she looked at her mother lying fully dressed and, assuming the worst, asked nervously, 'Has something happened to Mummy? Is that why she's lying on the bed?'

Gary wiped his eyes and smiled reassuringly. 'No, darling. Mummy had something to make her sleep. But she'll be awake in a little while. We must go and let Grandpa and Emma know that you're safe.' His voice had a nervous tremble in it.

Jody's face showed her bewilderment. 'What do you mean?'

Surprised by the child's question, he wondered if this *was* still a part of his dream. 'Jody, we've all been worried sick over you. Can't you understand that? None of us knew where you were or what had happened to you.'

Jody was confused by her father's concern. 'I was with David. Grandpa knew that. But when he telephoned to say that he couldn't come, he asked David to bring me home.'

Gary closed his eyes and tried to make sense of what Jody was telling him. 'But Jody ...'

'Jody? Where's Jody?' Alison was beginning to stir from her drugged sleep and her voice was husky.

Her disturbed daughter ran to the bed and took her hand. 'Mummy, what's wrong?'

Alison struggled to open her eyes but when she saw Jody became disorientated and distressed. 'Jody, is that really you?' she asked. 'Where have you been?' She started to cry. 'Did they hurt you?'

Jody was lost for words; she had no idea what her mother was talking about. She decided that her parents must have been drinking.

Gary kissed his wife on the forehead and smiled. 'Jody is fine, darling. Get yourself together and come to the house. I shall get Emma to make a hot drink for you.' Then taking Jody by the hand, he said, 'Come on. Let's go and see Grandpa while Mummy wakes herself up. He's been so worried about you.'

Jody wanted more than anything to see her grandfather. She was so confused by her parents' behaviour. He was the only person who could explain what was going on.

Emma and the judge were sitting in the living room waiting anxiously for news when they heard Gary rushing in through the back door of the kitchen.

As he ran into the room he was smiling. 'I've got a great surprise for you,' he said.

'Jody!' said the judge. 'They've found Jody?'

Gary couldn't stop smiling as he said, 'Actually she found us.' He turned to the hall and called, 'You can come in now.'

Jody entered the room, looking totally bewildered.

'Jody!' Emma gasped. 'Oh, darling! Come here.' She held out her arms and Jody ran to her.

Her grandfather's eyes filled with tears. 'Thank God you're safe.'

He reached out and, between them, he and Emma held Jody in their arms.

Gary looked on as if still trying to accept that he was no longer dreaming.

Jody eventually managed to free herself from the welcoming arms and ask, 'Will somebody tell me what's happened and why everyone is so pleased to see me? I've only been away for the day.'

'But *where* have you been?' asked her grandfather. 'And who have you been with, Jody?'

'You know where I've been, Grandpa. You arranged it,' Jody said, looking puzzled.

The others looked at the judge as if expecting him to give an explanation.

'What on earth do you mean?' he asked. 'What did I arrange, Jody?'

Before she could reply, Alison came into the room and, although still groggy from the injection, took her daughter in her arms and held her close. 'Oh, Jody. Where have you been, my darling?'

'That's what we all want to know,' said Gary.

'We'd better let the police know she's back,' said Emma.

Jody pulled herself free from her mother's arms and with a scream of frustration shouted, 'Please! Please! Please! Will someone tell me why you keep asking me where I've been? And what have the police got to do with it? I've come home to a madhouse!' She stood looking at everyone. Shaking nervously, Jody was a little girl desperate for an explanation of the grown-ups' behaviour.

For a moment there was confusion among the adults over her apparent ignorance of the anxiety her absence had caused. Gary took Alison's arm and guided her to a chair, where she sat, still unsteady and bewildered.

It was Emma who took Jody by the hand and spoke quietly to her in a calm voice. 'Jody, darling, something happened today that had us all worried and confused. The only person who can tell us what actually happened is you. Do you understand?'

'But Grandpa knows where I was. Why didn't you ask him? It was his idea.'

'Why don't you tell everyone exactly what happened after you left here to go to school this morning?' her grandfather said quietly with a gentle smile. He was trying hard to look calm as he waited for her answer.

'But you *know* what happened, Grandpa,' Jody insisted. 'You can't have forgotten!'

Gary was quick to seize the opportunity. 'That's exactly it, Jody. Grandpa can't remember exactly what he had arranged for you to do today.' He smiled. 'So he couldn't tell us about it, you see.'

'But Grandpa phoned Mrs Harper to tell her I wouldn't be going to school today.' Turning to her grandfather she said, 'You remember that, surely?'

'Yes dear,' said Emma, playing along, 'but he got a little bit muddled and couldn't remember the arrangement he'd made.'

Judge Thornton wasn't happy with them lying to the child and became distinctly uncomfortable.

Alison's head was clearing as the drug wore off. She took Gary's hand in hers and said to her daughter, 'Do please tell us what you did today, darling. We're all longing to hear about it.'

Jody sat on a footstool beside the fireplace and began to relate the day's events. 'Well, I was halfway to school when David's car pulled up.'

'Was it a nice car?' Emma asked.

'Well, yes. I suppose so.'

'Can you remember what sort of car it was?' asked Gary.

Jody thought for a moment. 'I don't know the make. It was a blue one though. Sort of dark blue.'

'So what did David say when he stopped the car?' the judge asked her.

'He told me I wasn't going to school today because Grandpa had arranged a surprise treat for me,' Jody said with a wide smile.

'And what treat was that?' asked Emma.

'About our trip,' Jody replied. Then with a puzzled look, she said, 'But what I don't understand is why Daddy said that you were all worried about me. He even said that we must let Emma and Grandpa know I was safe because nobody knew where I was.' Then looking at her grandfather she said, 'Why didn't you tell them?'

'Because he forgot,' said Gary, still trying to keep up the charade.

'It's no use,' said the judge. 'We can't go on pretending like this. Jody is grown up enough to be told the truth.' Looking straight at the child he said quietly, 'Jody, I did not plan any surprise treat, and I do not know this man that stopped his car and told you that story.' Then to Emma he said, 'Would you telephone James MacCormack and if he isn't there, make sure they contact him and tell him that Jody is home and that I would like to speak to him.'

'I'll use the phone in the hall,' Emma said as she got up and left the room.

Unable to hide her anxiety, Alison asked, 'This man. Did he do anything to hurt you?'

'Why would he want to hurt me?' asked Jody, still unable to comprehend the seriousness of what had happened.

'Because he wants to hurt *me*, that's why,' her grandfather said quietly. 'This David, or whatever his real name is, has been doing everything he can to annoy, upset or hurt me. His purpose in taking you away this morning was simply to make me believe that something nasty had happened to you and that we might never see you again.'

Her grandfather's explanation seemed ridiculous to Jody. With disbelief she asked, 'But *why*, Grandpa? Why would David want to hurt *you*?'

The judge gave a shrug as he answered, 'I wish I knew. I'd give anything to know why. But he obviously hates me.'

Emma came back into the room. 'They will get in touch with him as soon as possible. I also asked them to let Inspector Buckley know.'

'Oh yes. Thank you, Emma. I'd forgotten about *him*. They will need a complete description of this man.' Then to Jody he said, 'Do you think you can do that, dear?'

'Of course she can. Can't you, darling?' asked Alison.

'I suppose so,' Jody answered with reluctance.

Aware of his daughter's confusion, Gary said cheerfully, 'I bet Jody can remember if he had a wart on his nose and which side it was on. Eh, Jody?'

Jody giggled at her father's remark and Emma smiled as she asked the question they all wanted to know the answer to.

'Whereabouts did you go today, Jody? Somewhere nice?'

Jody's face brightened as she replied 'The funfair on Hampstead Heath.'

'I bet that was fun,' said Gary. 'Did you stay there all day?'

'We went to McDonald's first and had a cheeseburger. That was where David said Grandpa was going to meet us for lunch. But when the mobile phone rang, David said Grandpa couldn't come after all but to stay there and enjoy ourselves until it was time to come home.'

'That wasn't true,' said the judge. 'I'm afraid David told you that just to keep you with him all day.'

'You make him sound bad but he wasn't, Grandpa. Really he wasn't,' Jody insisted. 'In fact, he even said what a clever man you were at putting people in prison.'

'Where did he say he had met your grandfather, Jody?' Gary asked.

Jody was thoughtful before answering. 'Well, he didn't say exactly where. But I think it was in a court because he said how Grandpa could frighten an innocent man by just looking at him.'

Her grandfather looked at Emma with satisfaction. 'I was right, you see. This man is out for nothing less than revenge on the judge he considers guilty of an injustice to a friend or relative.'

'Like that John Porter, you mean,' said Emma.

'Exactly,' replied the judge, adding, 'I wish they would find him. And soon.' He turned to Jody and said, 'What did this David look like, Jody? Can you describe him for me?'

'He was taller than Daddy and had dark hair.'

'Did he wear glasses?'

'No.'

'A moustache?'

'No.'

'Did he remind you in any way of the man you saw outside the house the other day? The man who said he was checking on burglar alarms and had a funny moustache?' the judge asked.

Gradually it dawned on Jody who David was. 'Yes! That's him!' she exclaimed. 'I had the feeling I had seen him before when he stopped the car and told me about your surprise trip. But I just thought he was a friend of yours and that I'd seen him with you.'

Alison, who had been trying to take it all in, asked again, 'But he didn't hurt you at all? Not in any way?'

'No, Mummy. I've told you. David was very nice to me,' Jody said with frustration. 'He took me on all the rides and paid for me to have a go on all the stalls. And he bought lunch and ice creams. Why do you keep asking if he hurt me?'

Jody's eyes began to fill with tears and Gary held out his arms to her. 'Come here, sweetheart.'

She ran into her father's arms and buried her head in his chest, gently sobbing.

Her grandfather was about to say something when the phone rang. He quickly got up and went into the hall. He picked up the receiver, assuming it to be James MacCormack.

'Hello, James?'

A disguised male voice said, 'I've returned your little treasure unharmed, this time ... But I've not finished yet. You must turn to Isaiah ten.' Then he hung up.

'Hello! Hello!' The judge tapped rapidly but knew the caller had gone. He replaced the receiver and went straight to the study. Taking the Bible from the shelf, he turned to Isaiah 10 and read:

> *Woe to those who make unjust*
> *laws, to those who issue*
> *oppressive decrees.*

That uneasy feeling he had had when the first biblical quote arrived was beginning to return. He sat at his desk with the open Bible in front of him. He looked at the word 'woe' and knew that it was just another word for grief. He felt a cold chill run down his spine as he wondered what further grief he was to suffer.

He was now certain that all his troubles would end if the police could track down John Porter. He suddenly remembered his friend Reginald's advice to use a private detective. He took his diary from his pocket and found the name and telephone number he had written there. He was wondering whether to make the call when the phone suddenly rang. Taking up the receiver he said, 'Yes?'

'William, I just got your message,' said James MacCormack. 'What's this about young Jody arriving home safely?'

Relieved to hear his friend's voice, Judge Thornton said, 'Yes. It's true. She came home having apparently had a lovely day at the funfair on Hampstead Heath.'

'What about the man?'

'We were gradually getting the whole story from her when he telephoned.'

'You're joking!'

'I'd put the phone down a few moments before you called.'

'So what did he say?'

'Just that Jody coming home safely wasn't the end of the matter. Then he gave me another Bible quote. This one says, "Woe to those who make unjust laws, and to those who issue oppressive decrees".'

'So he hasn't given up.'

'On the contrary. He is threatening further grief for me. I really don't know if I can take much more of this.'

James sighed. 'I should have put a tap on your phone when this first started.'

'I don't think it would have been any use, James. He isn't on the telephone for more than a few seconds. Not long enough to trace, I'm afraid.'

'Perhaps you're right,' James admitted. 'Even so, we must do something to catch this lunatic. I don't suppose you could recognize his voice?'

'It was disguised. But I wish John Porter could be found. I feel certain that it's him.'

'There's something else you should know,' said James with reluctance. 'With Thelma Davis's death and no evidence that John Porter was actually involved with her in any crime, the conditional bail order you put on him has been rescinded. So now that he is no longer required to report daily to a police station, he could be difficult to trace.'

Judge Thornton shook his head despondently. 'Then he could be anywhere.'

'I've put out his description to other forces, so let's hope we hear something soon.'

'Yes. All we *can* do now is hope, I suppose.'

'So this man didn't do anything to the girl?'

'According to Jody, he was a nice kind generous man who took her on all the rides and bought her lunch and ice cream. He apparently did nothing that could be considered unlawful. It seems that this David, as he calls himself, is a careful fellow. Careful and very devious.'

'He used false pretences in order to get the girl into his car. And that wasn't clever. That was abduction. And *that* is against the law, as you well know,' James said in an official voice. 'I'm sure that if you were the judge in such a case, you'd throw the book at him.'

'Oh that I were in that position,' the judge said with envy.

'Try not to worry too much. I intend to catch this man. I know it seems as though he's winning at the moment but he'll make a mistake. They always do,' James said with conviction. 'You've got Jody back and that's the main thing. I think I'll call round and have a chat with her tomorrow morning. You don't mind keeping her off school for half a day, I take it?'

'Not at all,' the judge agreed. 'A good night's sleep is what the child needs now. This whole experience has been one that she doesn't fully understand the seriousness of.'

'See you in the morning then.'

'I look forward to seeing you then. Goodnight, James. Thank you for calling.'

As Judge Thornton replaced the receiver, he wondered again about Raymond Farraday the private detective and whether he was really as good as his old friend Reginald had said. But now that Jody was safely home, he would try and get some sleep – he would wait until tomorrow before deciding whether to call on his services.

As he closed the Bible and replaced it on its shelf, the word 'woe' came into his mind once more. Walking to the door of his study, he wondered what he had ever done to deserve this torment.

CHAPTER ELEVEN

Anne Lawrence was beginning to wonder if the practical joke he had told her he was planning was really a joke at all. But if it wasn't, then what else could it be? It was the way he had referred to the 'final act' and something that was a 'precious family treasure' that made her suspicious of his actual intentions.

At first, the idea of playing a practical joke on an old friend of his seemed fun; Anne was willing to be involved in an innocent prank. But the fact that she had not seen him for a while, plus his apparent fear of being caught doing something naughty by his minder, was more than she was able to understand. She knew that his marriage had not been satisfactory for some time. At least, that is what he had told her – and she had believed him, until now. But she was beginning to wonder why he had not left the woman in question if he was really that unhappy.

Anne looked back on their relationship and questioned why she had got involved in the first place. The loneliness after her husband died had been worse than she had imagined. Then one day she had gone into a local bar alone, something she had never done before, and there was this man who smiled and spoke to her and they were soon sitting together and enjoying each other's company. She learned that he was in the area once a week on business and heard about his unhappy marriage. When he asked if he could see her again she had said yes. Before she had time to realize what was happening, a relationship had begun. Although she only saw him at weekends, it suited her. She enjoyed their clandestine meetings, especially the regular sex. But recently he had not been down to see her as often and although he made various excuses as to why, she was no longer happy with the situation. And now all this talk about a plan that he had for her to dress up in a maid's costume was beginning to worry her. Anne wanted more than anything to see him and discuss things face to face, not just the brief phone calls and whispered conversations that had recently become the only contact they had. Yet despite her feelings, she knew that all her doubts would disappear once she could feel his arms around her and see his smile again.

Her thoughts were broken by the chime of the grandfather clock in the hall striking eleven. She checked it with her wristwatch and decided to go into Sherborne and get some food from the supermarket. She went to the kitchen to pick up the shopping list that she had written earlier. After slipping a bolt on the back door, she walked into the hall and took her coat from the hall stand. As she was putting it on, the doorbell rang and made her jump. When she opened the front door she couldn't believe her eyes.

'Johnny!'

The man standing there was smiling broadly and holding out his arms to her.

'Surprised?' he said, and stepped into the house, closing the front door behind him. 'Oh, I've missed you. Come here.'

He took her in his arms and kissed her passionately. Anne responded and held him tight. After a few moments he released his hold on her, his eyes sparkling. 'I've waited ages to do that.'

Anne still couldn't believe he was really there. All she could say was, 'I've been thinking about you all morning. How are you?'

'I'm fine.' He smiled. 'And I think about you all the time, my lovely.' With a soft, sexy voice he added, 'Especially at night.'

She blushed slightly as she said, 'Go on with you.' Taking his hand in hers she added, 'I've really missed you. In fact, I was beginning to think I wouldn't see you again, it's been so long.'

'I know. I couldn't get away before today. You know how it is.' He slipped his arm around her waist and pulled her near to him. As she was about to speak, he kissed her. His tongue began to explore her mouth and she willingly responded. Then moving her lips close to his ear, she whispered, 'Let's go upstairs. The shopping can wait.'

'We've traced John Porter,' Detective Inspector Buckley announced to his superior.

'Good work,' said the chief constable. 'Where is he?'

'At this moment we're not really sure. But we've found his home address and spoken to his wife on the phone.'

'So he's married?'

'Yes, sir. To an Irish lady with a fiery temper. No wonder he was seeing this Thelma Davis woman on the side.'

'Bad as that, is she?'

'Afraid so. She suspects he's had another woman somewhere but never had any proof. She said he's always going off to look for work on the mainland but can't seem to hold a job for long. Then he comes home and expects her to keep him till he goes off again.'

The chief constable raised an eyebrow. 'On the mainland?'

'Yes, sir. They live in Ryde, on the Isle of Wight.'

'So when is she expecting him home?'

'She's not sure. But the local lads are watching for him. If he shows up there they've promised to give me a call and I shall nip over and interview him.'

'Unless he's already skipped the country.'

'He won't have done that sir,' said DI Buckley, sounding confident. 'He doesn't have a passport. I checked.'

'Well, you've not wasted time, I'll say that. Good work.'

'Thank you, sir.'

'I'll give Judge Thornton a ring and keep him up to date with what you've done. If we can just pin all these letters and the abduction of the girl on Porter, the judge will be able to relax and enjoy life again.'

DI Buckley went to leave his governor's office but when he got to the door turned and said, 'I'm very glad the girl is home safe and unharmed. I've got a daughter about her age so I know what the family must have been going through.'

Bernard Thornton had collapsed in the street forty-eight hours earlier and been taken to St George's Hospital, Tooting. After several tests he was now sitting up in bed awaiting the results with trepidation.

As he looked at the four other men in the small ward, he wondered what turn of events had brought them here. One appeared to have tubes attached to every orifice. The other two men were sleeping and looked as though they might not see another day. It was all very depressing and Bernard would have given anything for a large whisky. As he sat wondering what was wrong with him, a porter arrived with a wheelchair.

'Mr Thornton,' he said in a quiet voice, 'Doctor Harrison wants to see you in his office, sir.'

'About time,' Bernard said as the porter helped him out of the bed. 'I don't need that cripple carriage, thank you.'

The porter shrugged and watched Bernard attempt to walk unaided. As he lost his balance, Bernard grabbed the porter's arm for support, his legs unable to carry him.

'Your carriage awaits,' the porter said with a smile.

Reluctantly, Bernard sat in the wheelchair and was taken into the hallway. As they reached a lift, Bernard felt nervous and his mouth dried up. The lift started going down and with his heartbeat quickening, he tried to appear casual.

'Haven't got a bottle of Scotch on you, I suppose?' he said with a forced smile. 'A chap could die of thirst in here.'

'Might be able to manage a glass of rubbing alcohol,' said the porter with a grin as the lift came to a stop.

Without saying anything in reply, Bernard was wheeled to an office. The porter knocked and entered, pushing Bernard up to a large desk where Doctor Harrison was sitting. A man in his fifties with receding fair hair, he looked up from his notes and smiled. 'Thank you, Martin,' he said to the porter. 'I shall ring when I'm ready for you.'

The porter nodded and left the office.

'Well, Mr Thornton, how are you feeling?' the doctor asked.

'Thirsty actually,' Bernard answered nervously.

Getting up from his desk, the doctor went to a wash basin and ran the cold water tap for a moment. Filling a glass with water, he returned to his desk and gave it to Bernard.

'Thank you,' said Bernard gratefully and drank the water in one go, putting the empty glass down on the desk. 'Pity it wasn't something stronger,' he said, trying to make a joke.

'I'm afraid drinking something stronger is the reason you are here, Mr Thornton,' Doctor Harrison said seriously. 'You told the nurse this morning that you live alone.'

'That's correct. Never found a woman that wanted to live with an old reprobate like me.' Bernard laughed nervously.

'And I see from her notes that your next of kin is a judge in Guildford,' the doctor said with surprise.

'Yes. He's just retired so he's not sending people to the gallows any more.' Unable to hide his fear he asked, 'What is it, Doctor? What the hell's wrong with me? I've never fainted in the street like that before, let alone been carted off in an ambulance. Please. No bullshit. What's the matter with me, Doc?'

'To put it bluntly, I'm afraid your desire for something stronger, as you put it, has been slowly killing you over the years. And now it's caught up with you.'

Bernard was frightened of the answer as he asked, 'So what is it?'

'I'm afraid your liver is no longer functioning properly. You are suffering from advanced cirrhosis. Which as I am sure you're aware, is caused by overindulging in alcohol.' Doctor Harrison gave a sigh. 'I'm sorry to be the bearer of bad news, Mr Thornton, but that is the situation.'

Bernard sat unable to speak for a moment while he tried to take in what he had been told. Then in a weak voice he asked, 'How long have I got?'

The doctor hesitated a moment, then answered, 'Perhaps six months.'

Bernard started to shake uncontrollably and as tears began to fill his eyes, he tried to smile. 'A large whisky wouldn't do me any harm then, would it? I mean, not now.'

The doctor smiled sympathetically, 'If you want to shorten your life even further.'

'No thanks.' He wiped his eyes with the back of his hand and asked, 'When can I go home?'

'I would like to keep you under observation for a day or so. But I suppose, providing you feel up to it, you could go home tomorrow. Although I'd be happier if there was someone there to look after you. Or perhaps you could stay with your brother for a few days. I could have a word with him if you'd like me to?'

'No need,' said Bernard. 'He'll look after me, no problem. He's a decent chap really. Look forward to having me stay a while he will,' he said convincingly.

'All right, in that case there's no reason why you can't go out tomorrow, as long as you're with someone for a while. I don't think it's a good idea to be alone at the moment.'

'Thank you, Doctor. And thanks for being so frank.' Bernard held out his shaking hand and Doctor Harrison took it firmly in his.

'I'm going to give you some tablets to take each day. They will make it easier for you to keep off the alcohol. Then I shall arrange transport to take you home.' The doctor let go of Bernard's hand. Going to the door, he called Martin to bring the wheelchair.

Once back in the ward, Bernard sat by his bed wondering what excuse he could give his brother for arriving uninvited at Four Oaks. One thing he was determined to do before dying was to ask William's forgiveness for causing him unnecessary hurt a few nights earlier. Then he remembered the excellent whisky his brother kept and the idea of a trip to Guildford became even more alluring.

Anne Lawrence had cooked lunch for two and having eaten every morsel of the pork chops and vegetables, they sat back on the two-seater settee and cuddled up together.

'You haven't told me why you've not been down for such a long time,' she said. 'And don't tell me the wicked witch of the wood stopped you going out.'

'Don't be daft,' he answered with a laugh. 'Although if she knew I was with you right now she'd stop my breath.'

'If she's really that horrible to you why don't you leave her?' Anne asked, realizing she had asked the same question on previous occasions. 'I know you've said she'd do something terrible to you if you did, but surely you can't go on living with a woman like her?'

He tried not to show his discomfort. 'I've told you before, my lovely. I've got to pick the right time. Trust me, eh?'

'I want to. You know that.' She kissed his hand and said, 'How long can you stay?'

'I'll have to get back this evening. I've got to make the final preparations for our practical joke. Which, by the way, will be very soon. I hope the costume fits you,' he said with a cheeky grin.

'Yes,' she said without enthusiasm, 'but I'm not sure about it. You aren't up to something you shouldn't be, are you? I mean something that would get us into trouble with the law?'

He pulled back from her embrace and gave her an innocent look as he said, 'Don't be silly. It's just a bit of fun, that's all. I'm doing it for a pal I owe a favour to.'

'So what was all that about a family treasure? You haven't stolen anything, have you?' Anne asked anxiously.

Again he laughed. 'Don't be daft. It was just something I

borrowed. It's gone back now. I only took it for the day to get him worried. That's all.'

Anne was only half convinced and asked, 'What did you mean by the final act? It sounded quite sinister.'

'Will you stop worrying, my love? Trust me.' He kissed her face and smiled. 'Let's go upstairs again.'

He took her hand. Although she wanted him again, Anne had the distinct feeling that she was getting involved in something she might regret.

Judge Thornton was in his study sorting out old papers to throw away. He hadn't properly cleared his desk for ages and wondered how he had managed to accumulate so much rubbish. It was as he opened the centre drawer too far that it almost fell into his lap. As most of its contents had dropped out, he decided to empty everything onto the desk top. He turned the drawer upside-down and saw the piece of paper that had been taped on the underside all those years ago. Carefully, he removed the tape and opened the folded paper. On it was a telephone number he had written almost thirty years earlier. The number of Caroline Wentworth, the woman he had secretly had an affair with after his wife had died.

As he remembered those clandestine meetings, he found it strange that he felt no guilt. Caroline had been divorced and was working as a temporary clerk at Kingston County Court in Surrey when they met. She was an attractive young woman and he was a young, ambitious but lonely barrister. Somehow they became soulmates and the inevitable happened.

Caroline had wanted to marry him but William Thornton did not want another woman in his home. Angela had given him the daughter he adored and he had found a housekeeper who took wonderful care of both her and the house. His thoughts went back to those secret trips to meet Caroline in London. The only person who knew of his liaison was convinced that the lady was Emma. Reginald was right when he said how attractive Emma Roberts was, the judge thought, and he had to admit that he had enjoyed being alone with her during these recent days. As he looked once more at the phone number on the piece of paper in his hand, he knew that he had no reason to keep it now. He threw it in the wastepaper basket along with other things from the past. It amused him to think he had hidden that phone number from the world by using a method normally associated with secret agents and Sherlock Holmes.

He sat thinking of Reginald and how selfish and untrusting he had been by not inviting him to Four Oaks.

Emma knocked and came in with a cup of tea and a biscuit.

'I thought you might like some tea.' Seeing the mess on his desk she said, 'Good heavens! Where on earth did all that come from?'

'It's rubbish I've been hoarding. But now it's time to get rid of it all.' He cleared a space for Emma to put the teacup and biscuit. 'Here we are. You can put them there.'

As she put them down she noticed the papers in the waste basket. 'And all that rubbish was in your desk?'

'I'm afraid so,' he said with a sheepish grin.

'Why is it that men won't throw things away? You're like little boys with their pockets full of apple cores, bits of toffee and conkers. Frightened to get rid of them in case you might need them,' she laughed.

'Yes, I suppose we are. But if we were as perfect as women, you wouldn't have anyone to nag, would you?' he retorted with a confident smile.

'I should know better than to start fencing with a legal brain. I bet you hardly got beaten when you were a barrister.'

'Ah, now, speaking of barristers, Emma, I was thinking that I would invite my friend and his wife to dinner one evening.'

'Not the one from Dorset?' She asked with surprise.

'Yes.'

'So there really is a friend in Dorset? I was beginning to think there was another woman somewhere,' she said.

'You're not serious?'

'Of course not. I was teasing you. I shall be delighted to meet this friend of yours at last.'

'I really should have invited him here before but he's in a wheelchair these days and I thought he might find the steps awkward.' He hoped he sounded convincing.

Emma wasn't completely taken in by his excuse but smiled as she said, 'You let me know when you want to have him here and I'll try and do something special.'

'Every meal you produce is special, Emma.'

'Flattery will get you anywhere,' she said, walking to the door. 'And don't let your tea get cold.'

As she left the room he picked up the cup and remembered how Reginald had been convinced that he and Emma were having an affair. The idea that anyone would think that no longer seemed to offend him. In fact, the opposite was now true, but he was not sure what to do about it.

The doorbell rang and he wondered who would be calling at three o'clock in the afternoon. When he heard the familiar voice of his brother in the hall, his heart sank.

Emma knocked and entered with a pained expression. Before she could announce their visitor, Bernard staggered in, looking unsteady on his feet.

'Before you jump to the wrong conclusion, old man, I've not had a drop. Mind if I sit down?'

'So how did you get in that condition?' the judge asked abruptly.

Emma went to leave as Bernard sat in a chair.

'Don't go,' said Bernard. 'I need a favour from you both. That's my reason for coming. I would have phoned but the old mobile has been disconnected. Bloody fools wanted paying for my use of it,' he laughed, in an effort to make light of the situation.

As he tried to get his breath, Emma watched him with some concern.

'If it isn't the drink, then what's wrong with you?' she asked.

'Yes, Bernard, what is wrong with you and why have you come here?' his brother asked impatiently.

'Firstly, I wish to apologize for my past behaviour to you both. To you, Emma, for my lewd conversation on the phone the other day. It was the drink talking, of course. Most uncalled for, nevertheless. Sorry,' he said, giving a humble nod. 'And to you, William. What I did was bloody childish revenge and I really am sorry. I just hope it didn't cause too much of an inconvenience. I felt quite awful about it afterwards.'

Judge Thornton was completely confused. 'My dear Bernard, I have not the slightest idea what you are talking about.'

Bernard suddenly looked relieved. 'You mean he didn't do it after all?' He laughed and said, 'The crafty little bugger. I paid him ten quid as well.'

'Will you please tell me what you are talking about?' snapped the judge, getting angry.

Bernard smiled as he replied, 'My neighbour's lad came down to Guildford for a pop concert that night. I asked him if he wanted to earn a tenner and he said yes. So I gave him your address and the money. I was angry, you understand. Anyway, I'm glad he didn't. Those tyres must be bloody expensive.'

Emma and the judge turned to each other in disbelief.

'Are you telling me that it was you that had my tyres cut up!?'

'Oh. He *did* do it then,' said Bernard regretfully. 'Sorry, old man. As I say, bloody childish of me. Getting my own back for that night in jail, you see. Sorry.'

'What about the break-in and the letters? Were they one of your childish ideas too?' Emma asked angrily.

'Break-in? Letters? I don't know what you mean, Emma. Cross my heart and hope to die,' replied Bernard. Then remembering the purpose of his visit he said with discomfort, 'That was a Freudian slip if ever there was one.'

'So you aren't responsible for anything other than my tyre destruction. Is that what you're saying? And I want the truth, Bernard. The whole truth and nothing but. Do you understand?'

'Look, old man, you have my word that I know nothing about any break-in or letters,' Bernard said with conviction. 'And as for the tyres, I'll make it up to you.'

'And how, may I ask, do you intend to do that?' the judge asked with sarcasm.

'I've been offered eight hundred for the old Jag and that should cover the tyres, eh?'

Looking at Bernard with a puzzled expression, William asked, 'And having sold your car to repay me, which I must admit is a noble gesture, what will you then use to travel with? A bicycle, perhaps?'

Emma was tired of listening to Bernard and made no effort to hide the fact. 'If you'll excuse me, I've things to do.'

She left the room and Bernard became agitated as he tried to explain the reason for his visit to his brother.

'The thing is, old man, I came out of hospital this morning after having some tests done. And, er, well, the fact is I'll not be needing the car or anything else.'

Realizing Bernard was genuinely worried, his brother was suddenly concerned. 'Why were you in hospital?'

'Had a touch of the old passing out on the pavement thing. Bloody awful feeling came over me and then suddenly I went. Lucky for me there was a kind soul that called an ambulance. Next thing I knew, I was in a hospital ward with three other old crocks.'

'You say you had some tests. What were the results?'

'That I've got advanced cirrhosis.'

'Oh dear. And what is the prognosis?'

Trying to put on a brave face, Bernard said, 'That I won't be getting a visit from Father Christmas this year. Shame. I was going to ask for a fire engine instead of another cowboy outfit.' Unable to keep up the pretence, Bernard put his head in his hands and sobbed. 'I don't want to die, William. I want to live.'

For the first time since they were children, his brother felt compassion for the man he had grown to dislike so intensely. He went to him and held him tight.

After a while, Bernard composed himself and explained the true reason for his visit. He repeated Dr Harrison's words verbatim, about not being on his own for the next few days.

'So you see, old man, I didn't really expect you to put me up after the way I've behaved. But there wasn't anyone else I could turn to. I wouldn't be any trouble. I promise.'

Judge Thornton had seen that pleading look in the eyes of many men standing in the dock while they waited to hear their fate. In most cases, he had had no hesitation in giving a severe sentence. Now here was his brother with that same anguished face, begging for leniency.

'You may stay here for a few days, Bernard. I shall ask Emma to prepare the single spare room for you.'

Bernard's gratitude was obvious. 'I told Doctor Harrison that you were a decent chap. And you *are*, big brother.' Taking his brother's hand he shook it vigorously and said, 'Sorry for all the trouble I caused you, old man. Been a bloody fool. Hope you can forgive me.'

The judge walked back to his desk and said quite calmly, 'I find myself pitying you, Bernard. To think that we both had the opportunity to make something of our lives. And now, here you are, turning to the man you only ever turned to when you were in trouble. The man you mocked for being a success, while you continued to travel on the road to failure. I can never forget the suggestive things you said about myself and Emma. The same Emma that you now expect to feed and care for you. Perhaps I *will* be able to forgive you, one day.

I don't know. But while you are under my roof I shall expect you to refrain from getting drunk and unpleasant. Especially in the presence of my granddaughter. Is that understood?'

'So she's safe.' Bernard sighed with relief. 'Thank heaven for that. When Gary told me that she was missing and might've been abducted, I was quite worried.'

'Yes. We all were. But about your drinking.'

'No problem,' said Bernard, trying to sound convincing. 'I can take it or leave it, old man. Doctor gave me some tablets for it, so no worries on that score.'

William decided to drop the subject for the time being and arrange with Emma to get the room ready for Bernard. But first he would have to tell her he was allowing him to stay and he knew that wouldn't be easy. 'I'll go and see about the room. In the meantime I think you will be more comfortable in the lounge.'

'Really do appreciate it, big brother. Really do.'

The judge opened the study door and held it for Bernard to leave. They were walking towards the lounge when Alison came from the kitchen.

'Uncle Bernard! I thought that was your car in the drive. What brings you here?'

'Hello, young Alison.' Bernard smiled. 'Your father's very kindly invited me to stay for a few days.'

Alison gave her father an inquisitive look.

'Your Uncle Bernard has not been well. He's staying here a few days until he feels stronger,' her father explained.

'Oh. Right. Good,' she said with surprise. 'Emma wants to see you when you have a moment, Father.'

'I was just about to see her. Perhaps I could ask you to keep your uncle company in the lounge while I'm gone.'

'Oh. Yes. Yes, of course,' said Alison. Taking Bernard by the arm, she was surprised at how unsteady he was. 'Come on, Uncle. Tell me what you've been up to since I last saw you.'

As she led Bernard to the lounge, her father took a deep breath and went to break the news of Bernard's stay to Emma. When he reached the kitchen, she was busy making one of his favourite apple and raisin pies. As he approached her, he gave a gentle cough.

'No need to cough,' she said without looking up. 'I heard you talking out there in the hall to Alison.'

'Good heavens. Did you really? You must have bionic ears to be able to hear that far away.'

He was about to inform her of Bernard's request when she casually asked 'So how long will he be staying?'

William was quite taken aback. 'You really are a woman of unexpected surprises, you know.' Then with admiration he said, 'You never cease to amaze me, Emma. But to be quite serious for a moment, my brother collapsed in the street and was taken to a hospital where they ran some tests. They have revealed that he has only a short period of time left. He is staying here just a few days until he gets his strength back. He has nowhere else to go, you see.'

For a moment, Emma was thoughtful. 'Yes, of course I see. After all, he is your brother. What is actually wrong? Did he say?'

'He has advanced cirrhosis of the liver, I'm afraid.' Then he added, 'I thought perhaps the single guest room?'

She wiped the flour from her hands onto her apron and with an affectionate smile said, 'You really are a lovely man, you know. That's why I hate what has been happening to you. I'll go and get the room ready.' She kissed him on the cheek and left the kitchen.

He stood touching his face where her lips had kissed it, wondering why he wasn't shocked or even embarrassed.

CHAPTER TWELVE

Detective Inspector Buckley was trying to catch up on all the paperwork that had accumulated. As he laboriously waded through it, he had a feeling it was going to be one of those days that went very slowly. He was filing some reports when the sound of his phone ringing gave him a welcome break. He quickly picked up the receiver. 'DI Buckley.'

'This is Sergeant Lawson, Hampshire police, sir. We were asked to let you know when John Porter showed his face here on the Isle of Wight.'

'That's right.'

'He came over on the late ferry last night. Do you want us to apprehend him?'

'Have your people spoken to him?'

'No, sir. Just kept him under surveillance.'

DI Buckley thought for a moment. 'If he tries to leave the island, hold him. I'll get clearance to come over myself and talk to him. If I let you know when I shall be arriving, do you think your people could meet me and take me to him?'

'No problem, sir.'

'Thanks. I'll get back to you.' This was what he had been hoping for. And now, with a bit of luck, he could tie up the loose ends and get his chief constable's thanks for all his efforts. Hoping this might be the next step up the promotion ladder, he made arrangements to go over to the Isle of Wight.

Within an hour he had reported the situation to the chief constable and was on his way to Portsmouth to catch the ferry to Ryde.

James MacCormack was cautious and didn't want to build up Judge Thornton's hopes of an end to the affair. As much as he wanted to inform his friend that John Porter had at last been found, he decided to say nothing until his inspector reported back to him. If Porter was their man, all well and good. But if it turned out that he was innocent of any involvement, the chief constable saw no point in saying anything at this time. The thought that kept nagging him more than anything was that if John Porter wasn't guilty, then who was? All he could do now was keep his fingers crossed and wait.

Hambledown Terrace was a narrow road tucked away behind the high street in Ryde. Number 7 was a small semi-detached property in need of some cosmetic repair. The cracked paint around the window frames and loose pointing in the brickwork gave the place a sad, uninviting appearance.

An unmarked car pulled up outside the house at 11.10 in the morning. Detective Inspector Buckley stepped out onto the pavement and spoke to the driver who had met him at the ferry terminal.

'I shouldn't be too long.'

'It's all right, sir. No need to rush.'

DI Buckley walked to the front door and, finding no bell, gave a sharp knock.

A woman of around forty opened the door. She had dark hair that was in need of brushing and brown eyes that appeared to have only recently opened from their sleep. Inspector Buckley couldn't believe this was the same woman he had spoken to on the telephone.

'Mrs Porter?' he asked.

'I am,' she answered sharply. 'And if it's the council you happen to be from, I'd like something done about it. And I'm not meaning next year!'

'I'm not from the council, Mrs Porter.'

'Well, if they don't send someone to fix it soon, the whole lean-to roof will collapse, so it will.'

'I'm sorry, but I'm Detective Inspector Buckley. I phoned you a couple of days ago, remember?'

She thought for a moment and then said, 'Sure now. You're the one who was asking if my husband was here. Said that you were anxious to speak with him.'

'That's correct,' he said smiling. 'And I believe he is here now? I would like to see him. May I come in, please?'

She grinned and said, '*Please*, is it? And here am I seeing policemen on the television only gaining entry to a house by smashing the door down.'

Despite her appearance, he enjoyed the lilt of her accent.

'That's television. But I'm real,' he said firmly. 'And I would like to speak with your husband, please.'

'There you go with that *please* again. And how can I refuse a polite and handsome gentleman like yourself? Come in.'

The narrow hallway was shabby, decorated with floral wallpaper that had obviously been there for several years. The stairs, dark, well-worn carpet gave any visitor a feeling of depression. The wooden door leading to the living room was open and revealed a place of complete contrast. Brightly coloured curtains and a three piece suite in cream and gold fabric greeted the eye.

'Sit down,' said Mrs Porter. 'I can't close the door cos the hinge is broke. And that's another thing the council have to put right. Quick enough to ask for the rent but slow as a tortoise to put things right, so they are.'

'If I could just have a word with your husband,' Inspector Buckley said. 'I know that he's here, and I've come rather a long way.'

'What's the sod been up to?' she asked in a quiet voice.

'I'm hoping he can help me with my inquiries,' he said.

She laughed and mimicked him. 'I'm hoping he can help me with my inquiries.' Then confidentially she said, 'That means he's as guilty as hell. Well, you can take the lazy good-for-nothing bastard and lock him away for ever. You'll be doing me a favour. And he won't be getting any spare crumpet behind bars now, will he?'

Before Trevor Buckley could reply, she walked to the door and shouted, 'Get your arse out of bed! You have a visitor.' Then, smiling, she asked the inspector, 'Would you like a cup of tea or coffee?'

'No, thank you.'

'Well, you won't mind if I do.' She left the room and went to the kitchen at the end of the hall.

DI Buckley stood waiting, then he heard an upstairs door open and John Porter coming down. He had obviously just woken up and dressed in a hurry. His shirt was hanging over creased trousers and he was wearing slippers. He tucked his shirt in as he walked into the living room.

'Are you the bloke from the council?' he asked.

'I'm Detective Inspector Buckley from Surrey Police.' He produced his warrant card and said, 'Can I have a word with you in private, sir?'

John Porter was clearly intrigued. 'Er, yes. Can't close this door, I'm afraid.'

'Perhaps we could talk outside?'

'Yes. Sure.' Calling to his wife, he said, 'Just going outside for a minute. I'll have something to eat when I come in. Shan't be long.'

Mrs Porter shouted from the kitchen, 'If you think I shall be cooking breakfast at this time of day, you've got another think coming, you lazy sod!'

John Porter gave a sheepish grin and led the inspector to the front door and opened it. 'You mustn't mind her,' he said as they left the house. 'She's got that Irish temper but her bark's worse than her bite. Now, what can I do for you?'

Inspector Buckley was surprised at his apparent innocence and wondered if his trip had been a wasted one. 'You were the boyfriend of Thelma Davis, I understand?'

Suddenly John Porter became agitated. 'Keep your voice down, eh? Let's move away from the house. Moira's hearing can even penetrate brick walls.'

'I've got a car. We can sit in there.'

He opened the rear door of the car and the two men sat in the back. The inspector closed the door and instructed the driver to move away.

'Anywhere in particular, sir?' asked the driver.

'No. Just drive around. Away from here.'

Moira Porter watched from the living-room window and looked worried as the car moved out of sight.

Once they were out of the terrace, Inspector Buckley began his questioning. Not wanting to waste time, he decided to try a direct question, hoping the bluff would pay off.

'Firstly, Mr Porter, what made you choose Glasgow to send the letters? Why not London?'

John Porter looked bewildered. 'Glasgow? Letters? What are you on about?'

'You deny sending letters from Glasgow?'

John Porter started to laugh. 'I've got to hand it to you. You had me going there for a minute. Even that warrant card had me fooled. Who set this up? Was it Dave?'

Inspector Buckley wasn't sure whether he was the one being taken for a ride or not. He waited for John Porter to settle down before asking, 'How long were you Thelma Davis's lover?'

The smile quickly left John Porter's face. 'Thelma's dead, for Christ's sake. Can't you leave her to rest in peace?'

'Not while you try to avenge her death with threatening letters and phone calls, Mr Porter.'

'Who the hell *are* you? And who's he?' he asked, indicating the driver.

'I'm a police officer and he is a police driver. This is a police car and you are a suspect in a case I am investigating, Mr Porter. I will show you my warrant card once more and then I would like you to answer my questions. Is that clear?'

Inspector Buckley was becoming impatient as he showed his warrant card again. John Porter suddenly seemed nervous.

'All right. So you're a copper. But what's all this cobblers about letters and threats? And who is it I'm supposed to be sending these letters to?'

'Does the name Judge Thornton mean anything to you?' The inspector watched for any telltale sign of recognition.

John Porter didn't hesitate in answering. With hatred in his voice he said, 'That bastard. If it wasn't for him my Thelma would still be alive.'

'That's not the way I expected a religious man like you to react, Mr Porter.'

Porter was clearly confused. 'Who says I'm religious?'

'The way you can quote the Bible, I naturally assumed that you were. I haven't read mine for years I'm afraid.'

'Me! Quote the Bible? You must be joking. I was dreading going into the witness box for Thelma in case I got struck down for just *holding* one when I was sworn in,' he laughed.

'And if I told you that the young man who broke into Judge Thornton's house has given your description as the man who paid him to commit the offence?'

John Porter gave a sigh of boredom. 'How much more of this crap do I have to listen to? Letters, threats, and now we've got a break-in for good measure. I've never heard such a load of bollocks in all my life!'

'Then you wouldn't object to being in a line-up so that he can identify the man who paid him?'

John Porter hesitated, and for a moment Inspector Buckley thought he might be on the right track after all. But he was soon to believe that he was on a wasted errand.

'As long as you don't mention Thelma in front of Moira. If she hears her name she'll go spare and start smashing things. Most of them over my bloody head.' John grimaced. 'Deal?'

'Then you are prepared to come and let this young man have a chance to identify you?' the inspector asked with surprise.

'Certainly. I can't wait to meet the lying bastard. And I shall want a lawyer present, just in case you lot are trying to fit me up. Understood?'

The inspector tried to hide his disappointment. 'Well, we shall be in touch if we decide to hold an identity parade, Mr Porter.'

John Porter smiled and said, 'Any time. And I'll tell you one thing you can do.'

'And what's that?'

'When you find whoever has been putting the frighteners on the judge, give him a medal. If I'd had my way at the time, I would have strangled the old bastard. If it wasn't for him me and my Thelma would be together now.'

'And what about your wife?'

'Stuff her,' said John with a supercilious grin.

For the return journey to Hambledown Terrace, neither man said a word. As the car pulled up outside the house, John got out. Moira came to the front door and sneered at him.

'Not locked you up then? Pity,' she said in a loud voice. 'Get inside, you dozy bugger.'

Moira Porter pushed her husband into the house and waved to the inspector as his car pulled away.

The moment the door was closed, her husband took her in his arms and kissed her.

'Everything go all right, me darlin'?' she asked anxiously.

'Couldn't have been better,' he said smiling. 'He talked a lot about letters and religion at first. Then when he mentioned Thelma I gave him a bollocking and played the poor distraught lover. You'd have been proud of me.'

'I *am* proud of you, Johnny boy. And when our little plan is complete, I'll buy some lovely new clothes and make you fancy me like you've never fancied me before.'

'What with all the excitement and you talking like that, I fancy you right now.' Taking her hand, he whispered, 'Let's go upstairs.'

As he led the way to the bedroom, she gave his neck a lovebite.

John winced and then smiled as he took her in his arms and carried her into the room. He threw her down on the bedspread and slapped her. 'That's for what you just did to my neck, you randy little bitch,' he said grinning.

Moira reached out and pulled him down on top of her. 'Be rough with me, Johnny. I love it when you're rough with me.'

They embraced in a passionate kiss and started to undress each other.

When the car reached the ferry terminal, Inspector Buckley thanked the driver and made his way to the waiting ferry. He wasn't looking forward to informing his superior that John Porter was not their man. Neither was he happy about starting the investigation from square one again.

It was almost a week since Reginald Byers-Wheatley had had the visit from his old friend and he wondered if his problem had been sorted out. He picked up his desk directory and dialled William Thornton's number.

Alison happened to be on her way from the sitting room to the hall when the telephone rang. She picked up the receiver and answered it. 'Hello.'

'Is that the Thornton residence?' asked Reginald.

'Yes. Who do you wish to speak to?'

'Your voice sounds too young to be the housekeeper, so am I correct in assuming that you're Alison?'

She laughed as she replied, 'I assure you our housekeeper isn't old and doddery but, yes, you are correct, I'm Alison.'

'This is an old friend of your father's. Is he there by any chance?'

'He's in the garden. Who shall I say is calling?'

'Tell him it's Reggie, will you? But if he's busy I shall call back later.'

The name suddenly registered with Alison. 'You must be his friend that lives in Dorset.'

'Good heavens!' he laughed. 'So he's been talking about me, eh? Well, don't believe a word he says.'

'I'll try not to,' she said jokingly. 'I heard Father say something about inviting you up when he was talking to Emma. That's why I assumed you were *that* Reggie.'

'Oh, I see. Well, it would be nice to come up and meet you. And to see Emma again.'

'You've met Emma?' she asked with surprise.

'Years ago. An attractive woman. Damned attractive.'

Alison smiled to herself at his apparent admiration of a woman he hadn't seen for years. 'Yes, she is. I'll go and get Father for you.'

'Only if he's not busy. I ...' He heard the receiver being put down and waited. A few moments later he heard voices and recognized one of them as his old friend.

'Reggie,' said the breathless voice, 'how nice of you to call. Is everything all right?'

'Everything's fine with me. How about you?'

'I was just out looking at the roof. I think there's one or two tiles that need replacing.'

'Well, get them fixed before I come up. Don't want the rain dripping on me while I'm in bed. I assume you're intending to put me up for the night?'

Surprised by the remark, the judge asked, 'How did you know that I intended asking you up here?'

Reginald laughed. 'Sixth sense, old man,' he teased. 'Runs in the family. Mother was a witch. I say, that daughter of yours sounds a lovely girl. Lucky she takes after her mother and not you, eh?' He laughed again.

Judge Thornton smiled. 'Is the purpose of this call to try and annoy me, Reggie? Because if it is you are failing to do so. How are you? And how's Katherine?'

'We're both fine. The real reason I've called is to ask if there has been any further development regarding your mystery correspondent?'

'No, I haven't received any more of those letters, thank goodness,' he said quietly. 'I think I'll hang up and take this in the study. Hold on a moment.' He replaced the receiver and went into the study. Closing the door, he went to his desk and picked up the receiver of his extension. 'Still there, Reggie?'

'Still here. I gather you haven't been in touch with young Farraday?'

'Oh, the private investigator?'

'Yes.'

'No, Reggie, I haven't. Though I have thought about it.'

'Well, if I were you I'd give him a buzz. He really is the most discreet chap and very reliable. I assure you that there would be no leaks to the press, if that's what's worrying you, old friend. Heard any more about when the sword might tap the shoulder, by the way?' he asked with interest.

'No. Not yet. It will be sometime next month I understand. And please remember that only Alison knows about that. One is not supposed to tell a soul, of course, so whatever you do be careful not to let the cat out of the bag.'

'My lips are sealed, William. Even Katherine knows nothing of your good fortune. You have my word. Now when do you want us to visit the stately home?'

'Actually, it's a bit difficult at the moment, Reggie,' he said with embarrassment.

'Here you go putting it off again,' Reggie laughed.

'The fact is, my brother's turned up unexpectedly, Reggie, and it might prove difficult having you both here together. He's rather ill, you see, and it wouldn't be fair on Emma to have extra people to cater for at this moment. I do hope you understand.'

'Of course I do. And quite right you should be concerned for your Emma. Bad enough having an old invalid like me to worry about but with your brother as well ... What's wrong with him, by the way? Nothing serious, I hope?'

'His illness is terminal, Reggie,' William said gravely. 'He's been told that it's a matter of a few months I'm afraid.'

'Oh, William, I am sorry. Well, of course you can't have us there. Another time, old chap.'

'Yes, of course. I promise.'

'But do think carefully about hiring Farraday, won't you? I guarantee that if anyone can get results, he can.'

'I shall give it some thought. Thank you for being so understanding about coming here at the moment. My love to Katherine.'

'I will. Bye for now, William.'

'Goodbye, Reggie.'

After he had hung up, William went back into the garden to inspect his roof once more. As he stood looking at the gaps where the tiles were dislodged, he wondered whether to take his friend's advice and call Raymond Farraday.

CHAPTER THIRTEEN

The single guestroom was ready. Emma had placed clean towels on the rail beside the wash basin and the judge's old dressing gown on the bed. To add more colour she had placed flowers in a vase on the chest of drawers and with the pale blue curtains and matching bedspread the room had an atmosphere of comfort and relaxation. Although it was not a large room, here was ample space for a small armchair.

Bernard was shown to the room by Alison while Gary went and brought the suitcase in from the car. 'I hope you'll be comfortable, Uncle,' Alison said. 'If you need anything just ask.'

Bernard was impressed with his new surroundings and showed it. 'What a lovely room. I can see that I shall be as happy as Larry here.'

'I hope you will,' she said. 'I'll leave you to it.'

As Alison left the room, Gary arrived with Bernard's case.

'Where would you like this?'

'Oh, just lay it on the bed.'

Gary put the case on the bedspread and was about to leave when Bernard stopped him. 'I'm glad that no harm came to your little girl. Are they any nearer to catching the man?'

'Not at the moment, I'm afraid. But the chief constable is your brother's friend so I'm sure he's doing everything that he can. Do you need anything else?'

'No thanks, Gary. Unless you can get me a ticket for your show. I'd like to see what you do for a living,' he said with a friendly smile. 'Must be exciting being an entertainer, old son.'

'It is sometimes,' Gary laughed, 'but not when they get up and walk to the bar.'

'It's when they walk out with your money you need to worry, Gary-boy,' Bernard chuckled.

Gary nodded in agreement. 'That's not happened so far, I'm glad to say. Give us a shout if you need anything. See you at lunch.'

When Gary had left the room Bernard closed the door. He opened his suitcase and took out his pyjamas, which were rolled up. Carefully, he removed the litre bottle of whisky they had been protecting and unscrewed the cap.

Licking his lips in anticipation, he held it to his mouth and took a good swig. With a sigh of contentment, he replaced the cap and looked for somewhere to conceal the bottle.

After rejecting the chest of drawers and the wardrobe, he lifted the fitted cushion from the armchair and pushed the bottle under the webbing at the rear of the seat. He smiled with satisfaction as it perfectly fitted the space. Replacing the cushion, he sat very carefully to see if the bottle would be noticeable. To his delight the seat felt comfortable and he was happy with the chosen hiding place.

Bernard put the rest of his things in the chest of drawers and then took his washing bag to the wash basin and brushed his teeth. Cupping his hand to his mouth, he breathed into it and sniffed. Satisfied that his breath had no hint of whisky, he went to the window and opened it. The view of the garden was beautiful and Bernard was just taking deep breaths of air when he saw his brother in the garden below. He was about to wave and call to him when Emma appeared. She was obviously following his brother to a secluded area of the garden where they both stopped. Although he was unable to hear what they said, he felt they did not wish to be observed. Then, to his surprise, Emma took his brother's hand and appeared to place it around her waist. Although his vision was partly blocked by the trees, he was certain they were locked in an embrace and kissing. After a while they became free from each other's arms and stood talking quietly, still holding hands. Bernard had often wondered if his brother and Emma were involved in a secretive relationship but what he saw had surprised even him. He thought of the things he had said to them both about their sexual desire for each other when he was the worse for drink. The thought of them making love amused him. The idea of his pious brother and Emma romping about in bed together was something he couldn't quite visualize. As he watched, they moved further into the wooded section of the garden and out of sight. After a minute or two, Bernard gave up watching for them and went downstairs to see if anyone else was about.

Gary was oiling the hinges of the dining-room door. The heavy footsteps of Bernard descending the stairs made him look up. 'Everything all right up there?' Gary enquired.

'Everything's fine. What are you doing, Gary-boy?'

'Getting rid of the squeak. Pops has been going to do it for ages but he never got round to it. He might have been an efficient judge but he's useless at DIY,' Gary said. Then lowering his voice he added with a grin, 'Doesn't know a nail from a screw doesn't Pops.'

Bernard said with a chuckle, 'Oh, I think he knows what a screw is.'

Gary didn't understand Bernard's remark and just smiled politely as though he did. Opening and closing the door, he was satisfied with his efforts. 'That's better. I'll get rid of this oil can and we'll have a coffee, eh?'

'Sounds good to me,' Bernard said. 'Any idea where William is?' he enquired innocently.

'He's in the garden looking at the roof. He'll be in soon. Make yourself comfortable in the living room while I ask Emma to make some coffee.'

Bernard chose not to make any reference to her being in the garden; he simply nodded and went into the living room. He sat in the biggest armchair, picked up the newspaper and had just begun to read it when Jody appeared.

'Hello,' she said cheerfully, 'I'm Jody. You're Grandpa's brother Bernard, aren't you?'

He put down the newspaper and smiled. 'That's right. I must say you've grown since I last saw you. Quite the young lady now, aren't you?'

Jody liked being called a young lady and went and sat in a chair near Bernard. 'I was trying to work out what I should call you,' she said thoughtfully. 'What does someone call the brother of a grandfather? It can't be uncle because an uncle is the brother of someone's parents.'

Bernard understood her dilemma. 'You're quite right,' he said, stroking his chin with a look of uncertainty. 'Mind you, there is a simple answer to the problem.'

'What's that?' she asked.

'Why don't you just call me Bernard? Then we'll both know who you mean.'

'OK,' Jody said. 'That will save a lot of trouble.' She gave a contented smile and decided she was going to like her grandpa's brother Bernard. 'How long are you staying?' Jody asked him.

'I'm not really sure. Why?'

'I just wondered,' she said. 'Only nobody actually said if you were staying days or weeks.'

'Probably a few days,' he said. 'Then I shall be able to go back to my flat. Not that I wouldn't want to stay here a lot longer if I could.'

'Then why can't you?' she asked.

'I'd be in the way if I overstay my welcome.'

Gary entered the room and asked, 'Have you seen Emma, Jody?'

'No.'

'Never mind. I've put the kettle on. Coffee won't be long, Bernard.'

As Gary turned to leave, Bernard said, 'No hurry. I've got this lovely young lady to keep me company.'

Gary looked around the room and teasingly said, 'I can't see a lovely young lady. Is she hiding somewhere?'

'He means me,' said Jody, with a chuckle.

Gary turned to Jody and made a funny face as he left the room. Jody giggled to herself and asked Bernard, 'Do you pull faces at your children?'

'I don't have any children,' Bernard replied.

'Don't you?'

'No. As a matter of fact I don't have a wife either.' He sighed. 'Never found a woman that I wanted to spend the rest of my life with. Or who wanted to spend the rest of her life with me.'

'But don't you get lonely?'

'Not very often. I know some married people who get lonely even though they're not on their own. On the other hand, I've known people who live alone and are happy. Look at Emma. She isn't married but I don't think she's lonely, is she?' Bernard asked.

'No. But she's not lonely because she lives here with us,' Jody stated with conviction.

'Yes, of course. You're absolutely right,' he said. Unable to resist using her as a sounding board he said, 'I imagine that she and your grandfather are very fond of each other. Am I right?'

'Oh yes. They've been friends for a long time. Emma is one of the family really,' Jody said.

'Almost like a married couple when you think of it, aren't they? All these years of living under the same roof together. Perhaps they'll *get* married one day?'

Jody gave an incredulous look and said, 'Grandpa and Emma? Don't be silly.'

Bernard heard someone coming and quickly smiled and said, 'I was only joking.'

Gary entered the room with two mugs of coffee and a sugar bowl on a tray. 'Here you are,' he said, handing Bernard his mug. 'Help yourself to sugar. Oh, I forgot the milk.'

'I take it black,' Bernard said.

Gary put the tray down on the coffee table and sat on a nearby armchair. Taking his mug he held it up and said, 'Down the hatch.'

'Isn't "down the hatch" usually associated with something stronger than coffee?' asked Bernard with an enquiring grin.

'A bit early for alcohol, isn't it? Or can't you last till lunchtime?' Gary asked.

'Only kidding,' Bernard said. Then raising his mug to Gary he said sarcastically, 'Here's to the coffee growers.' After a sip he said, 'I thought my brother always played golf on a Saturday.'

'He does usually. But his partner couldn't make it today.'

'Oh? Well, William can't be very popular if he only has one person that'll play with him,' Bernard laughed. 'Who is this partner? Another judge?'

'The chief constable actually,' Gary said. 'They've been friends for some time and he's the one person that Pops can beat. And you know how he likes to win.'

'Don't I just,' Bernard said. Then changing the subject he asked, 'What did you think of the last budget?'

'Not a lot. It was the usual performance by a chancellor. Full of figures that nobody can understand and promises of a wonderful life if you vote for his party at the next general election. They're all the same, if you ask me.'

'Absolutely. When a politician tells you that he's got a clear conscience, he's got a bad memory,' Bernard laughed.

As the two men discussed politics, Jody sat thinking about Bernard's reference to her grandfather and Emma. She tried to imagine them being married and realized that if Emma was married to Grandpa she would become her grandmother! Bernard's suggestion seemed totally ridiculous, so she erased it from her mind and went to the kitchen to get some fizzy orange. When she had finished it, she washed the glass under the tap. As she placed it on the drainer she glanced through the window and saw Emma and her grandpa appear from the trees. As they walked towards the house Jody opened the back door and went into the garden, waving to them. Although they waved back, she had the feeling that they were being secretive about something.

'We've been looking at the wild section beyond the spinney and wondering what to do with it,' explained Emma.

'Thought of cutting it back and perhaps putting something useful there,' said William, taking Jody's hand. 'Any ideas what would go there?'

'What about a swimming pool?' she asked as they walked to the kitchen. 'Then Daddy could get some exercise and I could have friends round in the summer.'

Emma laughed and said, 'That's typical, that is! Your daddy gets his exercise and you and your friends can splash about all day. What about your grandpa and me? Don't we even get a paddle?'

Jody gave a sheepish grin and said, 'You know what I mean, Emma.'

Putting her arm around the girl's shoulder, Emma said, 'Of course I know. But there's one snag with a swimming pool.'

'Only one?' said the judge. 'I can think of at least *two*. We would need to run electric power for the heating and build changing rooms with lighting and so on. And it's the furthest distance from the house so the drainage alone would cost me a fortune.' He stroked her cheek and said, 'Sorry, Jody. Now I'm retired I can't spend a fortune on a swimming pool. You do understand?'

Seeing the logic of his objection, she reluctantly nodded. 'Yes. I just thought it was a good idea.'

'I'm sure we'll think of something. There's no rush,' Emma said. 'Where is everyone?'

'Daddy and Bernard are in the living room talking about boring stuff, so I left them alone. I think Mummy's in the flat.'

'And what are you doing?' asked her grandfather.

'Nothing.'

'Then how will you know when you're finished?' he joked.

Emma whispered a reply in Jody's ear and the girl giggled as she said, 'Because I won't be doing *nothing* any more.'

Being Saturday, the post arrived late. As Emma was on her way to the dining room to lay the table for lunch, she heard the letters drop onto the mat. She went to the front door and picked up four letters and three lots of junk mail. It was as she sorted out the envelopes that she saw the name *Glasgow* on a postmark. Although she had been prepared for another letter to arrive, the sight of the envelope made her stomach queasy. For a moment she was uncertain as to what she should do. Then she hurried to the dining room before anyone else appeared. Closing the door, she put the rest of the mail on the table and stood staring at the envelope. After a few moments, she knew that there was no point in putting off the inevitable, and headed to the living room.

Judge Thornton was talking with his brother and Gary when Emma got to the door. She looked at the judge. 'Can you spare a moment, please?'

'Yes, of course,' he replied. 'Perhaps you will join us for an aperitif before lunch, Emma?'

'Yes. I could do with one.' Then to the others she said, 'I won't keep him long.'

The judge stood up. 'Excuse me. Help yourself to a drink, Gary. And give Bernard what he wants.'

'Thank you, old man.' Bernard's face brightened.

'I thought you were off the booze,' said Gary.

'Only when he's not drinking,' the judge said caustically.

As William went to join Emma, Bernard tried to hide his discomfort over his brother's remark. 'Doctor said I can drink within reason, Gary-boy. A large whisky would be good for me. Medicinal, you know.'

Gary looked at him and shook his head in despair. 'You'll never change, will you....'

He proceeded to pour the drinks, while Bernard sat licking his lips like a child waiting to be fed.

The note in the envelope was as brief as the others. This time the quote was from Leviticus 26.28:

I will continue, hostile to
you in fury; I in turn will
punish you myself sevenfold
for your sins.

Emma had her arm around her employer's shoulder as they sat looking at the Bible.

'Oh Emma,' he said wearily. 'I can't take much more.'

'I know. Why hasn't John Porter been found? He can't have disappeared so he must be *somewhere*.'

'One would have thought so.'

'Are you going to phone the chief constable?' Emma asked.

'Oh yes. I must. But then I shall call someone else, Emma. Someone that perhaps I should have called much earlier.'

Raymond Farraday was in his mid thirties with auburn hair and hazel eyes. His average height gave him the advantage of being able to lose himself in a crowd, unlike a taller person who would stand out conspicuously. Over the years he had appeared as a window cleaner, a chauffeur and a business man, to name but a few.

He had just parked his car and was putting the key in the front door lock when he heard the phone ringing. He ran to answer it.

'Raymond Farraday?' asked a man's voice.

'Speaking,' he said breathlessly.

'I was given your number by Reginald Byers-Wheatley.'

'I see. And who am I speaking to?'

'I was told that I could rely on your discretion and I am relying on discretion, Mr Farraday.'

'You can rely on that, sir. Now perhaps you would like to tell me who you are and how I might be able to help. Or, if you would prefer, we could meet somewhere.'

'Yes. I think that would be preferable to talking on the telephone.'

'OK. I could come to you or you could come to me. Other than that we could meet at a pub somewhere between the two. I really don't mind which.' Farraday waited to hear his caller's decision. After a slight pause he spoke.

'I think it better that you came here. My house is tucked away in a quiet road and it would be safer than my being seen calling on you. If that were to happen it would only add to my problem.'

Farraday was intrigued by his caller's obvious reluctance to give his name. 'I understand. And when I arrive at your house, who do I ask for?'

'Once we have agreed a time, I shall be waiting for you. I would like our meeting to take place as soon as possible. My home is just outside Guildford.'

Farraday looked at his watch. 'I could be with you at any time after 2.30 today. Would three o'clock suit you?'

'Excellent. Have you a pen handy?'

Taking the biro by the message pad, Farraday said, 'Ready when you are.'

'The name of the house is Four Oaks. It's the sixth house on the right as you turn into Clover Avenue in the village of Bell Green. Once you get to the church you take the second on the left into Mayfield Road. Clover Avenue is first right.'

'I'll find it,' said Farraday as he finished writing. 'See you at three o'clock.'

'Yes. I do hope you're able to help, Mr Farraday. I really need to put an end to this dreadful business.'

'If I can, I will. Can you give me an idea as to what your problem is?'

'I shall explain everything when I see you. Just one other thing.'

'Yes?'

'Only my housekeeper and son-in-law know about this. So if you don't mind, I shall introduce you as a friend of a friend who is bringing me up to date on his wellbeing. You're just passing through. That sort of thing. Is that all right?'

'Er, yes. Yes, anything you say.'

'Thank you. Three o'clock then.'

When the caller had hung up, Raymond Farraday thoughtfully put the receiver down, wondering what Mr Byers-Wheatley was getting him into.

It was five minutes to three as Judge Thornton checked his watch. He was sitting at his desk in the study, making notes of all the things he wanted to discuss with Farraday when he arrived. He had left the dining-room table just a few minutes earlier, having made the excuse that he had some paperwork to sort out.

The doorbell rang and the judge was pleased that Farraday was a few minutes early, rather than late. He walked to the front door and opened it to find not Farraday but James on the doorstep.

'Sorry to call on you like this but I'm on my way to HQ and wanted to tell you personally rather than phone,' he said with an air of apology. 'May I come in for a moment?'

Trying not to show his frustration at James's timing, William said, 'Yes of course. Let's go to the study.'

As James entered the house, the judge glanced at his watch. It was almost three minutes to the hour.

When they got to the study and closed the door, James said with regret, 'I'm afraid Porter isn't our man.'

'You found him!'

'Yes. Trevor Buckley went over to the Isle of Wight to his home. He's married with an Irish wife who apparently would've loved Buckley to arrest him and lock him up. But that's all to do with Porter's womanizing. As far as the letters to you and the break-in, he's in the clear. Sorry.'

Judge Thornton was deeply disappointed. 'Well, it looks as though we'll have to start all over again. And I was convinced it was Porter.'

'I can't stop, I'm afraid, or I'll be late. But if you get any idea of who else it might be, or if you receive another one of those Bible quotes, let me know straightaway.'

Without saying a word, the judge picked up a piece of notepaper from his desk and handed it to the chief constable. It was the quote he had copied from that morning's letter.

'When did you get this?' James asked.

'This morning.'

'I'll take it and see what the lab boys can come up with.'

'No ...' the judge said, taking it back from him. 'I've got a criminal psychologist coming to study them all. That way we might get a better idea of the sort of man we're looking for, you understand.' He wondered how he had made such a spur-of-the-moment fabrication of the truth.

'Good idea. Though he won't have much to go on, will he?'

The doorbell rang and the judge anxiously ushered James to the door. He was about to open it when James asked, 'Where did you get this chap from?'

'An old sparring partner of mine from Dorset.' He opened the door and saw Farraday standing there. Quickly introducing the two men, he said, 'Farraday, isn't it? This is a friend of mine, James MacCormack.'

The two men acknowledged each other and James walked to his car. The driver got out and opened the door for him.

'I'll be in touch. Let me know what he makes of the Bible quotes,' he called. The driver closed the door, got behind the wheel and drove away.

The judge waved goodbye and then turned to Farraday. 'I'm sorry about that. He's a friend who happens to be the chief constable here. He called to give me some bad news. Do come in.'

Judge Thornton ushered Farraday into his study and offered him the only comfortable chair other than his own. Once seated he got straight to the point and gave Farraday a detailed account of the events that had begun with the retirement card.

Raymond Farraday listened carefully but the judge wondered why the man was not making any notes and apparently relying on his memory alone to store the details being given to him.

'And there you have the whole story,' he finished. 'The various biblical quotes are on the desk in front of you.'

Farraday studied the quotations for a few moments. 'There's one thing that puzzles me.'

'What is that?' Judge Thornton asked.

'You didn't mention your name when you telephoned me. You introduced me to your chief constable and yet, despite being in your home and listening to your problem, you still haven't told me your name, Judge Thornton.'

The judge was taken aback. 'I apologize, Mr Farraday, but I was anxious not to give away my identity until I knew whether you would act on my behalf or not.'

'I see.'

'I suppose that seeing my name on the envelope was rather a surprise.'

'Oh, I like to know who it is that I'm doing business with. I knew who you were *before* I came here.'

The judge was intrigued. 'Really? May I ask how?'

'It's very simple. I telephoned Mr Byers-Wheatley and told him I had received a call from someone he had recommended to me. You were the only person to whom he gave my number that lives in the Guildford area.'

The judge gave a quiet laugh. 'As you say, very simple. I must say there is something about *you* that puzzles me.'

'And what's that?'

'Throughout this meeting you have not made one single note and yet I assume you will remember all the facts I have given you?'

Raymond Farraday pointed to an innocent-looking pen in his top pocket and smiled. 'With this I don't forget anything. In fact it's the best investment I ever made. James Bond himself couldn't have asked for anything better.'

'You mean *that* has recorded everything we have said? I have heard of these things, of course, but never actually seen one. Amazing.'

'Getting back to this adversary of yours, Judge. This man, John Porter. You said that the police had questioned him but eliminated him from their enquiries.'

'That is correct.'

'And yet you were convinced that he was your man.'

'I was, yes.'

'Well, with nothing else to go on, perhaps I should see if there is anything the police overlooked. Would you like me to do that?'

The judge hesitated for a moment then asked, 'Do you really think that the police overlooked something? I mean, with all the resources that they have, surely if he was guilty they would have brought him in for further questioning.'

'Perhaps. On the other hand, he might be smarter than your friends in the police force. In my experience they are rather inclined to go by the book and often overlook the obvious.'

'But I'm sure that in this instance James MacCormack and the inspector have done everything possible,' the judge said in the chief constable's defence.

'Then why did you call *me*?'

Judge Thornton knew the answer to that question only too well. He knew now why his friend had given this man his recommendation. Trying to hide his discomfort, he said, 'Perhaps we could discuss your fee, Mr Farraday.'

Emma and the others had all left the dining table and were having coffee in the living room while the judge continued in conference with his visitor.

'So who is this man that's with Grandpa?' Jody asked Emma.

'Yes,' said Alison, 'who *is* the mystery visitor? Father's being very secretive about him.'

'He's a friend of your father's friend in Dorset,' Emma explained. 'That's all. So there's no secret about it. Would anyone like some more coffee?' she asked, casually changing the subject.

'I'd love some, Emma,' said Bernard. 'Especially if there's a nice brandy to go with it to aid the digestion.'

'Aren't you supposed to be off alcohol?' Emma asked.

'Only when there's an "X" in the month,' he laughed. 'Besides, it would keep my tongue from wagging about any bit of gossip I might have come upon while looking from the old bedroom window.'

Emma showed no sign of embarrassment but looked Bernard in the eye with an inquisitive grin and said, 'Do tell if you've got some gossip to impart, Bernard. Providing it's not gossip that's unfit for Jody's ears.'

Her stare made Bernard back down. 'Only kidding, old girl. Just an excuse to try and get a drop of the happy juice, you understand.'

Emma smiled and said condescendingly, 'I know it was.'

'I know some gossip that would really surprise you all,' Jody said dramatically. Then, about to leave the room, she continued, 'But I was sworn to secrecy. So I can't tell you what it is.'

The adults looked at each other and tried not to laugh as she went from the room.

'What was that all about?' Bernard asked.

Alison put a finger to her lips and whispered. 'A small girl who wants to get attention.'

'Ah yes. Understood,' Bernard said, as he waited to see if Emma was going to respond to his request for a brandy.

Having replenished the cups with coffee, Emma was about to sit down again when the front door closed and the judge came into the room. She filled a clean cup and gave it to him.

'Thank you, Emma,' he said, sitting in an armchair. Then to the others he explained, 'That was a friend of Reggie's. I didn't bring him in here as he had to get back to London.'

'Who's Reggie?' Bernard asked.

'An old friend from my early days in law, Bernard. Friend privately, that is. But once we got to court it was a battle of skills.

He would have been a judge but for an unfortunate accident. Nevertheless he still has a fine legal brain.'

'I'd like to meet him,' said Alison.

'So you shall. I shall be inviting him and his wife for a weekend.'

'I'm glad there really is a friend in Dorset,' said Gary. 'I was beginning to think you'd got a secret lover tucked away down there,' he laughed.

Emma glanced quickly across at the judge but said nothing. Judge Thornton gave her an embarrassed smile that Bernard was quick to notice.

'The only women he loves are right here, aren't they, old man?' he said pointedly.

'Not all of them,' the judge retorted. 'Jody is missing. I think I'll have a brandy. Care to join me, Gary?'

'Why not?' Gary replied.

'Remember you're working tonight and you've got to drive,' Alison reminded him.

'One brandy won't do him any harm,' said Bernard. 'In fact, most doctors prescribe it.'

The judge raised an eyebrow and said, 'But not *your* doctor, I understand, Bernard. Quite the opposite, in fact.' The look of dejection on Bernard's face made him relent. 'But perhaps one glass wouldn't do any harm.'

Bernard's face brightened up as he watched Emma go to the decanter and pour brandy into three balloon glasses. 'No harm at all, big brother. Do me the world of good, in fact.'

As Emma gave Bernard his drink he winked, and she wondered what he had actually seen from his bedroom window. For just a brief moment she felt like putting something stronger into his glass, something that would stop his unpleasant jibes.

'Where is Jody, by the way?' asked her grandfather.

'I think she was bored with grown-ups talking,' said Gary. 'I expect she's watching TV back at the flat.' Then seeing the anxious expression on his father-in-law's face, he said, 'Probably watching that cartoon DVD you bought her, Pops.'

'As long as she isn't watching one of those naughty ones from Sweden.' Bernard grinned. 'If she is, can I borrow it when she's finished with it?'

'That isn't funny,' Alison snapped.

'I'm afraid my brother has a sick mind that alcohol seems to stimulate,' said the judge with contempt.

'That remark was certainly uncalled for,' said Emma with a cold glare.

'Sorry ... Didn't meant to offend. Stupid thing to say. Hope you can forgive a silly old fool,' Bernard said with obvious embarrassment.

Gary looked at his father-in-law and said, 'I think I'll go and check on Jody.'

'I'd be grateful if you would. I may sound over-cautious but under the circumstances, when she's out of our sight and we aren't sure where she is, it would put our minds at rest.'

Alison was quickly on her feet. 'I'll go,' she said. 'I've got to pop back to the flat anyway.'

As she left the room, Bernard looked at the judge and in an effort to make up for his earlier faux pas and win back some respect he asked, 'You don't think that chap would try and abduct the girl again, do you? I mean, not in daylight.'

'I think your brother is simply being careful. And rightly so,' Emma said reproachfully.

'Pops is absolutely right,' said Gary. 'We can't be too careful while that maniac is still on the loose.' He stood up. 'I think I'll just stretch my legs after that lunch. Shan't be long.'

Bernard sipped his brandy, wondering how long it would be before the judge and Emma made an excuse to leave.

'I didn't mean to break things up,' explained the judge. 'But I do worry when Jody is out of our sight for long. She has no idea of the danger she was in when this David fellow took her away. Although I feel sure he would not dare to try and abduct her again, I don't want to take any unnecessary risks with her safety.'

'Absolutely,' Bernard agreed. 'Bloody man wants stringing up if you ask me.'

Judge Thornton sat thoughtfully, remembering the times that he had given maximum sentences to criminals he wished he could have had strung up. So many evil men and women who had committed horrific crimes and yet could only be given a life sentence under the law. But many of them were now free and at least one of them might be seeking revenge on the judge that had sent him to prison. He wanted more than anything for the man responsible for these threats to be caught. And then sent away for a very long time.

Emma put the empty coffee cups on a tray and walked to the door. 'I'll go and get the dishwasher on,' she said, leaving the room.

Once they were alone, Bernard took the opportunity to talk to his brother about Emma. 'She's a lovely woman is Emma. And obviously very fond of you, as I'm sure you are of her.'

'We are *all* fond of Emma,' Judge Thornton replied.

'I must say that together you two look as though you're a real couple. If you get my drift,' said Bernard with a wink.

'Oh yes, Bernard. I get your drift,' William said with a disapproving scowl. 'But I would be obliged if you refrain from speaking that way about Emma as long as you are a guest in my house.' Then added firmly, 'Do you get *my* drift?'

Bernard looked uncomfortable as he replied, 'Absolutely. Say no more.'

'And I hope you won't,' said the judge curtly as he began reading his newspaper.

Bernard picked up his brandy glass and finished his drink. He went to speak but seeing his brother apparently engrossed in an article, thought better of it and went to his bedroom and the concealed bottle of whisky.

William looked up from his paper as Bernard left the room, wondering if he had done the right thing in allowing him to stay.

After a while his thoughts went back to that moment in the garden when he had decided to tell Emma about the knighthood. How thrilled she had been – and the way she had held him and given him that unexpected congratulatory kiss! He was thinking of Emma and his feelings for her when he heard Jody's laughter from the kitchen. Knowing that she was safe, he was able to relax once more and read his newspaper.

CHAPTER FOURTEEN

Moira Porter answered the knock on her door and saw the young good-looking man holding up an identity card.

'Electricity company, ma'am. There'll be a cable change over at the local power unit today and we're checking to make sure that your fusebox will stand any sudden power surge. Can you show me where the fusebox is.'

'Under the stairs,' said Moira, standing aside to let the man in.

'Thank you,' he said, and opened the stair cupboard door. Kneeling down, he shone a torch at the fusebox. Then opening the cover he made his inspection with Moira watching him.

'A sudden surge of power, you say? It's a long time since I experienced such a thing, so it is.'

The man smiled to himself at her brazen remark and carried on with his work. He took a screwdriver from his pocket and made some adjustments. Then replacing the cover, he got up and closed the cupboard door.

'I'd like to check the light fittings if I may,' he said.

Giving him a provocative smile, Moira said quietly, 'You can check anything of mine that takes your fancy. And while you're doing what you have to, I'll make us a coffee.'

'Thank you. I shan't be very long.'

'Be as long as you want, petal. My husband's away so there isn't any reason for you to hurry. If you know what I mean.'

Moira went to the kitchen while the man went to the front room. He stood on a chair and placed a minute object between the flex at the top of the lamp holder. Then quickly making his way to the bedroom, he repeated the same procedure there. He went down to the bottom stair, where he stood to reach the hall light. Placing the small object in the exact position, he moved through to the kitchen.

'I'll just check this one and then I'll be off,' he said.

'You'll have your coffee now that I've made it with loving care especially for you.' Moira grinned.

'Of course.' He smiled. Able to reach the fitting on the low ceiling, he did what he wanted while Moira's eyes had turned away. 'Well, everything seems OK,' he said.

As she passed a mug of coffee to him, she smirked. 'Oh dear. Does that mean I shan't be getting the sudden surge of power after all?'

'Afraid so,' he said in mock sympathy. 'Husband's away, is he?'

'Only till tonight, darlin'. So it's as well you didn't go arranging to stay the week,' Moira laughed.

That was the information Farraday wanted. He walked up the path of the next house to convince Moira that he was calling there too. As soon as she had closed the door he walked back to the street, giving a nod to the driver of a small van that was parked a few yards away. Farraday then travelled back to the ferry in the unmarked police car.

Later that evening, Raymond Farraday made the phone call he had planned. When he heard the man answer he spoke in a soft, quiet voice.'

'Is that John Porter?'

'Yes.'

'I know about you and Thelma Davis. And I know everything you've done.'

'Who is that?' Porter asked nervously.

Farraday rang off. Now he had to wait for his associate on the Isle of Wight to contact him with the recording of John and Moira Porter's conversation – a conversation that Farraday was convinced would make interesting listening.

As usual, the Monday morning post consisted of nothing but junk mail and the odd letter. On this occasion there were two offers of cheaper gas, an advert from a landscape gardening company and an invitation to a dinner party at the House of Lords on the 24th, which was in eight days' time. The dinner was to be preceded by a cocktail party at 22 Somerville Crescent, Chelsea, at 6.30 p.m. A letter printed on official-looking cream notepaper said: 'This dinner is to be a surprise gathering of friends and colleagues of one of our most respected high court judges. There will be no publicity, and therefore the identity of our honoured guest must remain confidential until the occasion. For security reasons you are requested to bring this invitation card and letter with you.' It was signed 'The Viscount Sisemen, Committee Chairman'. In the corner of the card was printed 'Dress code: Black Tie'.

There was no RSVP and Judge Thornton realized that it was more a command than an invitation. As he sat wondering why he had been selected to attend such a prestigious affair, Emma entered with his morning coffee.

'Look at this,' he said, showing her the invitation card.

Emma's face broke into a proud smile as she read it. 'This sounds like quite a posh function, doesn't it? Any idea who it is that they're honouring?'

'Not only have I no idea who it is, I have no idea why I'm being invited.'

'I should have thought that was obvious.'

'Really? Then would you mind enlightening me?'

'What did you tell me this morning when we were alone in the garden?'

'About the knighthood, you mean?'

'Yes. If you have no idea who this judge is then they must be inviting people like yourself who are about to receive the tap on the shoulder.'

He was amused at her description of such a solemn ceremony and began laughing. 'My dear Emma, I wish I had your command of the English language.'

'What do you mean?'

'I wonder if Her Majesty refers to the ceremony as "a tap on the shoulder"?' He grinned, remembering that his friend Reginald had used the same phrase.

Emma laughed. 'I bet Phillip does.'

'Probably.'

'How many people know about the knighthood?'

'Only Alison and yourself in the family.'

'Not Gary?'

'Not unless Alison has told him on the quiet.'

'You said "only Alison and myself in the family". Anyone outside the family know?'

'Reggie. But he won't let the cat out of the bag. I had to tell him in order to explain my concern over his advice. You see, he suggested that I feign illness in order to bring this Bible quoter out into the open.'

'I don't understand.'

'Well, his idea was for me to have the press announce that I was ill, so that this person would feel that his threats no longer had any point. It was then that I explained the harm a story like that might do to my receiving a knighthood. And it could so easily.'

'In what way?'

'Well, supposing, just supposing, that the press did print a story of my being ill. I would have friends coming to visit and sending cards. Think of Jody and how she could let slip a remark at school that would show me to be simply pretending I was ill. Then the press really *would* have a story. And once it became public knowledge I would be saying goodbye knighthood. And who knows what this person would do next? In any case, I'm totally against the idea of lying about my health in order to bring this person into the open.'

'I agree. That would be tempting fate. Let us hope that we hear something positive from Raymond Farraday.'

It was nine o'clock on Tuesday morning when the package was delivered by special messenger. It contained the recording he had been waiting for and when Farraday played it, even he was surprised at what it disclosed. Without hesitating, he went to the telephone and arranged an immediate meeting with his new client.

Soon after 11.30 he arrived at Four Oaks where he was met by an excited Judge Thornton.

'Thank you for coming so quickly, Mr Farraday. I can't wait to hear what you have. This way, please.'

He led the way to his study and once inside, Farraday put a small tape machine on the desk. 'I think you will find this most interesting, Judge. After what you told me about the way the Thelma Davis trial had gone, I was more than surprised at what this tells us. I shan't bother with the earlier stuff as it's just normal boring chat. It was after he received a call from a stranger, i.e, me, saying that I knew everything he'd done regarding Thelma that we hear his reaction.' He pressed the start button and they heard John Porter's voice:

'Hello ... Hello! Who is that?! ... Bastard's hung up.'

Moira was then heard asking, 'What is it, John? What's all the shouting, for God's sake?'

'He knows!'

'Who knows what?'

'About Thelma. He said he knows what I've done. Moira, he knows!'

'Don't talk crap. How could he know?'

'I tell you, he knows!'

'You keep saying he knows but you won't tell me who he is! Tell me, for Christ's sake!'

'I don't know, do I? It was a man that knows about what I did. Somehow this bastard knows. Christ, I could be right in the shit if anyone finds out. I could end up in prison!'

'Calm down, Johnny. She was cremated, wasn't she?'

'Yeah.'

'Then how the fuck can they prove anything? They can't dig up ashes. Have a drink and let's be calm about this.'

There was the sound of glasses clinking and liquid being poured.

'It's all right for you to say be calm, Moira. It wasn't you that killed her, was it? It isn't you that benefits from her death, is it?'

Judge Thornton sat listening in disbelief at what he heard and stared at the tape machine as it continued.

'I'm in this just as much as you, Johnny. Wasn't it my idea for you to give her the stuff in the first place? And why did we choose Emophadene? Because there was no way that they could ever trace it.'

'Yes, yes. I know all that. But it was me that kept giving it to her. So in any court in the land I'd be the one getting life. Not you!'

'Listen to me, will yer? This man who phoned knows nothin'. He's one of these people that try frightening you in the hope that he'll strike lucky one day and be able to get some hush money. Now isn't that the truth of it?'

'Maybe. But when the will is out of probate, or whatever they call it, suppose someone gets nosey and wonders how I've come to get the house and everything. And suppose this bloke that phoned starts digging deeper? Then I'll be in the shit. And so will you.'

'Not threatening me, are you, Johnny? Cos if you are you'd be a sorry man when I've cut yer balls off, so you would.'

'And you'd be a sorry woman if I wasn't able to screw you, so you would.'

There was nervous laughter from both of them. Then it was Moira that spoke.

'Oh, I think I could be happy with the young man who I had to myself this morning.'

'And who was that, you randy little bugger?'

'The handsome devil from the electric company who was here alone with me. 'She was clearly enjoying teasing him.

'And what did he want?'

'Apart from me, you mean? He was checking the lights around the place in case of a sudden surge. At least that's what he said. In truth I think he was after my body.' She laughed.

There was a moment's silence before John Porter asked in an anxious tone: 'What did he do exactly?'

'To me or the lights?' She laughed again.

'I'm serious, Moira!'

'He got up to examine the lights, that's all. Here, in the hall and kitchen. Oh, and he went upstairs.'

There was the sound of a chair being moved and after a few seconds an amplified scraping noise.

'What are you standing on the chair for?'

'Just checking … Shit!'

'What is it?'

'He wasn't a fuckin' electric man. We've been bugged!'

'Oh Jesus!'

'What with that copper who came asking about some judge's bleedin' Bible or break-in or some such crap, and now this. I think we'd better disappear for a while.'

Farraday switched the tape machine off.

'The rest is just Porter removing the mike from each of the flexes I placed them in. I checked up on Emophadene and it's a tablet that, taken gradually, weakens the heart to the point where it finally stops. With it being almost untraceable the natural assumption would be that the patient had a weak heart and that any stress would bring on a fatal attack.'

'We must obviously hand that tape over to the police. With a confession of unlawful killing, Porter and his wife must be prevented from leaving the country and brought to trial,' the judge said with a look of determination. 'At least some good has come about from your involvement. But unfortunately the tape also shows that Porter had no knowledge of either Bible quotes or breaking into my home.' With a despondent sigh, he said, 'I was convinced that Porter was the man. What on earth do I do now?'

'This man is quite obviously someone with a grudge. And we can be fairly certain that it has to do with your time on the bench. Agreed?'

'It would seem to be the only logical conclusion, yes.'

'Then as you are unable to think of anyone else who might be responsible, why not let me go over the transcripts of the more recent cases that you dealt with. Perhaps they might give me an idea. It's a long shot I know but it's all I can think of.'

'Well, it might be possible to arrange that. How far back would you need to go?'

'Assuming this person was convicted and is now released, I would think that would be a very time-consuming task. But if, as you suspected in the case of John Porter, it's a friend or relative of a convicted felon, we would need to look at more recent cases. Say those you presided over in the past year.'

'Very well. I shall make arrangements for those documents to be put at your disposal. But do you really think it will prove successful?'

'As I said, it's a long shot but it's worth trying. After all, there's nothing else to go on.'

'No, I suppose not.'

'Unless ...'

'Unless what?'

'I was just wondering if we're looking at the probable and ignoring the possible.'

'How do you mean?'

'That perhaps this menace is actually being instigated by somebody closer to home. Someone you consider to be a friend, for example.'

The judge considered that possibility for a moment, then rejected the idea. 'I cannot believe that any of my friends would do such things. And what on earth would be the point of it? No, no. The whole idea is quite ludicrous.'

'It was just a thought. I'll wait to hear from you and as soon as you arrange for me to see the transcripts of the last few cases I shall get started on them.'

Judge Thornton opened the study door and saw Farraday out. Now all he had to do was inform James MacCormack about Porter and his involvement in Thelma Davis's death. The one thing he wasn't looking forward to was telling his friend how he came to be in possession of the tape. He returned to the study and dialled James's direct line.

'Chief Constable.'

'Thank goodness you're there, James.'

'Hello, William. Anything wrong?'

'Er, yes, but I think it would be better if we could meet. I have something for you that you will want to hear and act upon rather urgently.'

'You make it sound very mysterious. What is it?'

'A verbal confession by John Porter that he and his wife were responsible for Thelma Davis's death.'

'You're joking!'

'Far from it, I'm afraid. I strongly advise that you arrest them both as soon as possible. They may well be abroad by now but they must not be allowed to remain free for long.'

'But Trevor Buckley was convinced that he had nothing to do with this business.'

'With the letters to me and the break-in, that's true. But I'm talking about the premeditated murder of a young woman. I must ask you to act quickly. And then perhaps come and hear the evidence for yourself.'

'Give me half an hour and I'll be with you.'

'Thank you.'

The judge replaced the receiver, wondering how much he had jeopardized their friendship by employing Raymond Farraday, a *private* investigator.

James arrived within twenty-five minutes and was met by his friend at the door.

'I've put out a call to have Mr and Mrs Porter picked up and held. I hope you're right about them, William, because if you're not I'm going to look bloody silly.'

'Come into the study and listen to a recording that I have received. It's Porter's admission of guilt.'

James sat while the judge put the tape on an old machine. As he listened to it, James was clearly astonished at what he heard. When the tape finished, he gave the judge a quizzical look.

'When was this recorded and how did you manage to get hold of it?'

'It was recorded yesterday evening at their home in Ryde.'

'May I ask by whom?'

The judge became uncomfortable. 'By a private investigator that was recommended to me.'

"Well, he's used a method that could cost him his licence. If we wanted to wire a house we would have to go through the proper channels.' William looked worried and James gave a wry smile. 'But I have to hand it to your man. We've got our friend Porter by the short and curlies. I won't have to use this tape with a bit of luck.'

'Why is that?'

'Because once Porter knows we've got this confession, he'll make a statement. Although his lawyer is sure to question the method by which it was obtained.'

'I certainly wouldn't want to get this investigator into any trouble. I just hope you understand why I employed him.'

Jokingly, James replied, 'Because you didn't trust *my* chap, I imagine.'

'Oh no, it wasn't that, James.'

'I was just kidding. The only time I object to the private eye is when they get under our feet during an investigation. But now we're back to square one as far as your letters from Glasgow are concerned.'

'Yes ... I know.'

'Can't you think of anyone else who might be behind them? Anyone at all?'

The judge shook his head. 'I've thought of everyone that I could. I was sure it was Porter but like Phillip Burns, he is in the clear.' Suddenly a thought crossed his mind. He was about to speak but then decided otherwise.

'What is it?' James asked.

The judge hesitated and then with reluctance said, 'I was just thinking about your Inspector Buckley.'

'What about him?'

'Well, I know he checked up on Burns and discovered that he was not anywhere near Glasgow when the letters were sent. And that he checked on the printer and paper et cetera. But I wonder if there was something that he might have overlooked?'

'Ah. I see what you're driving at. You think your private Sherlock Holmes might have done better.'

'Please don't misunderstand me, James. I'm sure that your Inspector Buckley is most efficient.'

'But you'd like your chap to double check Mr Burns, yes?'

'Well, I ...'

'Why not? You never know. It could be worth a try.'

'You really wouldn't mind?'

'I want to see an end to this matter as much as you do. If your chap can find something that we missed I'm all for it. But I shall deny I ever said that.' He smiled. 'All I ask is that you keep me informed all the way.'

'Thank you, James,' the judge said with relief. 'Thank you for not reprimanding me for going behind your back. It's just that I must do everything I can to put an end to this matter. I really don't think I can take much more.'

James gave him a friendly pat on the arm. 'I look forward to getting back to our Saturday golf again.'

'So do I. Really I do. But while this business is hanging over me, I simply don't feel like it.'

'I understand. But I warn you,' James joked, 'I shall be on top form and thrash you unmercifully.'

The judge smiled and with a hint of sarcasm asked, 'Been getting some secret practice in, have you?'

'Oh, that does it.' James grinned. 'When I get you out on the first tee you'll wish you hadn't said that. The mood I'm in, even Tiger Woods would tremble with fear.'

The judge laughed as he walked James to the front door. 'I shall keep in touch. And thank you for coming.'

'Chin up,' James said as he got into the waiting car and drove away.

The judge closed the front door and wondered if he should telephone Raymond Farraday regarding Phillip Burns. But then Farraday's words came to his mind: *'Perhaps this menace is actually being instigated by somebody closer to home. Someone you consider to be a friend, for example.'*

The thought of anyone close being responsible seemed a

completely ridiculous suggestion, yet he could not help remembering how his brother Bernard had behaved when he first called at the house after his years abroad. When William had refused to show any sympathy for his brother's involvement with the girl in that Lagos hotel. Bernard had become very angry. He had admitted responsibility for having the tyres cut and had been very unpleasant to Emma. Yet despite everything that Bernard had said and done, he could not believe that all these threats were the work of his own brother.

CHAPTER FIFTEEN

The next few days were uneventful. There were no letters of a threatening nature and Bernard had not been any trouble. Even his drinking appeared to be under control, much to the judge and his family's relief, although they were not aware of Bernard's private supply. His afternoon rest had become a regular daily ritual, his sleep always induced by the hidden whisky bottle. But the contents had been rapidly depleted and Bernard had to wait for the right moment to replenish it. The last thing he wanted was for anyone to discover his secret because Four Oaks had become a proper home to him, something that had been sadly missing from his life during the past years, and he had no intention of jeopardizing it.

Jody was enjoying Bernard's company and he kept her amused with stories of his adventures, most of which were fabricated but sounded exciting to a small child. Her mother and father appreciated the time Bernard spent with their daughter and he seemed happy to entertain her. Even Judge Thornton had begun to trust his brother more and wanted to make Bernard's last days as pleasant as possible.

But Emma remained suspicious of Bernard, convinced that a leopard never changes its spots, and despite his efforts to appear friendly towards her, she was unable to forgive him for the way he had spoken to her in the past. Having come from a working-class background, she had always assumed that a man of middle-class upbringing would behave better.

On one occasion Emma had been cleaning the single spare room and was about to change the sheets when she realized that she had forgotten the clean pillowcases. She left the door open while she went up to the next landing where she kept the fresh linen in the airing cupboard. Taking the pillowcases from the shelf, she was about to close the door when she saw Bernard hurrying up from the hall. He was carrying something in a plastic bag but trying to conceal it from view by holding his jacket over it. He reached the open bedroom door and, obviously assuming someone was in the room, took the plastic bag from under his jacket and held it behind his back as he went in. Emma made her way from the landing and was about to enter the bedroom when the door was shut in her face. Determined to have her curiosity satisfied, she opened the door to see the plastic bag on the bed and the armchair cushion being removed. Bernard turned around with a look of surprise. 'Emma! I didn't hear you knock.'

'I was getting clean pillowcases. I didn't know that you were back,' she said innocently. Then throwing the sheets onto the bed, she went to the armchair. 'I'll do that, Bernard. Wants plumping up, I expect.'

As Emma went to take the cushion from him he quickly put it back on the chair. 'It's fine now. No problem. Can I help you make the bed?'

'No need. I can manage.'

'Right ... I'll, er, leave you to it then.'

He picked up the plastic bag from the bed and took it to the chest of drawers. 'I'll just put this away,' he said with a casual air. Hurriedly putting it in a drawer, Bernard made his way to the door. 'I'll leave you to it then.'

'I won't be long,' Emma said.

Bernard nodded and managed to force a smile as though he had nothing to hide.

Emma waited for him to leave before going to the chest of drawers and opening the one containing the plastic bag. When she saw the whisky bottle she knew that she was right about a leopard never changing its spots. She closed the drawer again and then remembered what Bernard was doing when she came into the room. Going to the armchair and removing the cushion, she found the hidden bottle. It contained very little whisky and she realized he was intending to replace it with the one he had smuggled into the house. After putting the cushion back, Emma finished making the bed and left the room. She wondered whether she should tell anyone what she had discovered or simply let Bernard continue to accelerate his own death.

She finished doing the other bedrooms and went to dust and tidy the study. She carefully lifted the papers from the desk and replaced them once she had finished dusting it. When she began cleaning the mantelpiece she saw the invitation card to the dinner at the House of Lords. Beside it was the official-looking envelope it had arrived in. Emma took the card down and read it. She couldn't resist removing the letter from the cream envelope and reading it. She imagined all the important people that would be gathered there and felt a sense of pride that the man she loved and respected had been invited. It was only when she was thinking about the invitation later that morning that something began to disturb her. For some reason she couldn't explain, Emma had the feeling that something was wrong. The more she tried pushing the feeling aside, the more she felt that something unpleasant was about to happen.

Raymond Farraday had begun the laborious task of reading through the transcripts of all the cases that Judge Thornton had presided over in the past twelve months. As he read the first transcript, he could understand why certain people would wish the judge harm. The trial of Martin Saunders was the one that Farraday was reading at that moment.

Saunders was accused of running his business partner down with a van, killing him instantly, despite evidence by eight witnesses, including a priest, that it had been an accident and that Saunders was a caring man who raised money for local disabled children, and was a good employer. The prosecuting counsel had managed to twist the evidence to show Saunders as a cunning man who had lied under oath:

'Mr Saunders, have you ever in the past used a vehicle to dispose of another human being?'

'Good God, how can you ask such a question?'

'Because I require you to answer either yes or no. Shall I repeat the question?'

'The answer to your question is no!'

'Really?'

'Yes, really.'

'Then you deny being in a red Ford Cortina when on 7 August 1989 it ran down and killed one George Denton?'

'But I wasn't driving. Dave Morten was.'

'So you claimed at the time.'

'It was true!'

'But Dave Morten was unable to corroborate your story as he died from a heart attack, suffered at the time.'

'Because he was driving. That's why. The police knew that he was driving.'

'Because he was in the driver's seat when they arrived?'

'Yes.'

'But was he in the driver's seat *before* they arrived?'

'What are you trying to say? That I changed places with him?!'

'Your words, Mr Saunders. Not mine.'

Farraday went on to read the transcript and was surprised at the weak argument put up by the defence counsel. But when he read the Judges summing up he felt that an injustice had been done:

'Ladies and gentlemen of the jury. You have heard how the accused was driving the van that killed his business partner. Defence counsel is claiming that it was an accident. Yet it has been shown that on the death of his partner, the accused benefits considerably. By becoming free to sell the business premises and the surrounding land for development, he would be an extremely wealthy man. You have also heard how he was once involved in another incident where a car he was in struck and killed another person. I must instruct you that this incident and whether he was driving or not on that occasion cannot be allowed as evidence in this case. Your duty is to look at the facts regarding this particular case, not whether the accused is guilty of any earlier incident which is irrelevant to your consideration of a verdict. A verdict that I trust will be a true one, based on the facts you have heard.'

It was Judge Thornton's reference to the *earlier incident* and the way he was reminding the jury of it, while seemingly instructing them to ignore it, that bothered Farraday. And when he went on to read of the guilty verdict and Judge Thornton's maximum sentence for manslaughter, he began to understand the enemies he had made.

When he read the transcript of the next trial he found the judge equally harsh. Could this really be the same man whose fear of retribution was causing him sleepless nights? The man who would have sent men to the gallows had the death penalty still existed? These questions were starting to bug Farraday, but Judge Thornton was his client and he intended earning his fee. As he sat making a list of those people who *could* be responsible for the threatening letters, he realized what a mammoth task lay in front of him.

It was while he was reading the transcript of yet another case of violence that he was interrupted by the telephone. He reached out and picked up the receiver. 'Farraday.'

'This is Judge Thornton.'

'Hello, Judge. I'm going through the transcripts and making a list of suspects at the moment.'

'Good. But I had a thought and wondered if you might think it worth following up.'

'What is it?'

The judge went into detail about Phillip Burns and the way Inspector Buckley had made enquiries about him, without being able to tie him in as the Bible quoter. Farraday listened and when the judge had finished asked, 'And you really believe he might be your man? Just because you angered him when he was a defence counsel in some of your cases?'

'Yes I do. There's the Glasgow connection for one thing. I still think that despite Inspector Buckley believing Burns to be innocent, there might be something he had overlooked. Just as you discovered the connection John Porter had in that poor woman's death. Something Buckley didn't even know about.'

'Yes, but the idea that a barrister would hate a judge so much he would send biblical quotes doesn't sound likely. If that were the case, then having read transcripts of the first three you presided over twelve months ago, any one of those defence lawyers might have a grudge.'

There was a pause before the judge said, 'I don't think I quite follow.'

'Well, according to what I've been reading, you were not exactly keen on hearing anything in the accused's defence. On the contrary, you appeared to be doing everything to help the counsel for the prosecution.'

'Then you must be misinterpreting the transcript of that particular case, Mr Farraday.'

'I get that impression from all three cases that I've read so far, quite frankly, Judge. You have even planted the thought of guilt in the minds of the jury while instructing them that they must ignore that very point.'

It occurred to Farraday from the silent response that he might be dropped from the case. But instead of an argument, the judge was remorseful as he replied, 'Perhaps I have been overzealous at times, but that doesn't excuse the way I am now being persecuted, surely? I mean, this person cannot be of sound mind to do these things. And that means that he is a dangerous man, does it not? A man that might suddenly become violent, either to me, or worse, to one of my family. I beg you to follow any lead that you think might bring this affair to a conclusion, Mr Farraday. I just want this business to be finished so that my family and I can get on with our lives in peace.'

Despite the evidence he had read, Farraday was beginning to feel sorry for his client. 'Send me all the details you have on Phillip Burns and I'll check him out.'

'Thank you. I'll see that they are with you very shortly. Oh, and Mr Farraday?'

'Yes?'

'Despite what you may have read in those transcripts, I am not a vindictive man. Really I'm not. I shall be in touch.'

The judge hung up and Farraday replaced his receiver. As he continued to read the transcript in front of him, he looked for something that would prove the judge really wasn't as bad as he appeared. But all he found was evidence to the contrary, with Judge Thornton apparently a very biased man.

As he left his study after phoning Farraday, the judge saw Bernard coming down from his room.

'Ah, Bernard. Can I have a word?'

'Won't take long, will it?'

'Not long. Why? Are you off somewhere?'

'Only to the flat. Gary's invited me over.'

'Then I won't detain you.'

'It's all right. What did you want me for?'

'Let's go in here for a moment,' he said, ushering Bernard into the sitting room.

As he walked towards an armchair, Bernard wondered if Emma

had discovered his whisky bottle and informed his brother out of spite. He sat down, expecting to be reprimanded. The judge closed the door and sat in his favourite chair.

'How are you feeling, Bernard?'

'Bloody awful to be honest. It's no fun knowing you don't have much time left.'

'No. I'm sure it isn't. Bernard, we haven't always seen eye to eye but I would like to ask you a question that I need an honest answer to. Not one that you *think* I might want to hear, but a truthful one.'

'Fire away.'

'The reason I ask is because I have just had a rather rude awakening as regards to my character.' He hesitated before he asked, 'Would you say that I was an uncaring and vindictive man?'

Surprised by the question, Bernard was confused. 'I always admired the way you cared for your family, old man. And I'm grateful for your kindness to me now, despite the differences of the past. So to answer your question, no. I couldn't say you were uncaring or vindictive. Quite the reverse, old man.'

'Thank you, Bernard. And now I must ask a question that you have already been asked. But I need an honest answer. Apart from damaging my tyres, was there anything else that you did? Anything at all?'

'Good Lord, no. I admit to arranging the tyres business but I was not responsible for anything else.' Giving a quizzical look, he asked, 'What did you think I'd done?' Then suddenly an expression of disbelief came over him. 'My God, William. You don't think I had anything to do with Jody's abduction!'

'Oh, good gracious, no. I was thinking more of sending me a biblical quote. Something like that,' he said.

'Sorry, big brother, you've completely lost me now. Can you imagine me having anything to do with biblical quotes? Bloody hells bells.' Bernard broke into laughter. 'The only thing I ever remember that had anything to do with the Bible was when our old nanny got annoyed with me for making fun of that bit "Gladly the cross I'd bear". Remember?'

'I don't think so?'

'Of course you do. When Mother asked what we'd learnt that day I said, somewhat facetiously, "About a bear called Gladly who was cross-eyed." Surely you remember that?' he chuckled.

The judge smiled as he said, 'Yes, I do remember now. You always were incorrigible, even at Bible class.' Then becoming serious he said, 'I hope you didn't mind me asking about the biblical quotes. It may sound silly but to be perfectly frank they have become rather a worry.'

'In what way, old man? Someone playing silly beggars with you, are they?'

'I think it's more serious than that, Bernard. I have good reason to believe that whoever it is wishes to hurt me to get revenge for something I may have done. In a funny sort of way I was hoping it *was* you that had sent them. At least then it would have made this business less sinister.'

Seeing that his brother was genuinely perturbed, Bernard asked, 'But what sort of revenge? And for what?'

'Possibly someone or the relative or friend of someone who considers the judge of their case to be a monster that needs punishing.' He gave a sigh and said, 'I won't burden you with my problem. You go and keep your appointment with Gary.'

With a dismissive wave of his hand, Bernard said, 'There's no hurry, old man. I want to hear more about this business of someone wanting to harm you. I may be an old alcoholic who's done bugger all to be proud of in his life but I want to be of help if I can. Tell me more about this Bible thing.'

Judge Thornton was reluctant to involve his brother but as Bernard was the only member of the household who was unaware of what had been going on, he decided to tell him everything.

He gave Bernard the full story to date. Somehow Bernard's apparent understanding was a strange comfort to him. Judge Thornton suddenly regretted that only when death threatened to part them were they becoming closer to each other.

CHAPTER SIXTEEN

It was past midnight when Gary turned into the drive. Bernard was sitting in the passenger seat and although looking tired, had obviously enjoyed his night out. As the car stopped, Gary said in a quiet voice, 'Try not to make a noise, Bernard. The girls will be fast asleep and I don't like to wake them when I get home this late.'

'I'll be as quiet as a lamb,' Bernard whispered. 'Thanks again for getting me a seat, Gary-boy. Thought the show was a bloody sight better than some of the crap we get on TV. Why aren't you on the box? You'd give that Bremner chap a run for his money.'

'Thanks. But I'm happy doing what I do. Wouldn't want all that pressure. Besides, I get a lot of work and some of it is cash in hand.' Gary winked.

'Say no more. Well, thanks again, Gary-boy. Good night.'

Bernard quietly opened the door and got out, closing it carefully behind him. Giving Gary a wave, he made his way to the house. Although he had enjoyed four large whiskies during the evening, he was remarkably sober and able to turn the key and let himself in without making a sound. As he cautiously crept through the hall towards the stairs he could see a light shining under the sitting-room door. Curious as to who was up, he looked in and was surprised to see Emma sitting quietly on the sofa. Wearing only a dressing gown over her nightdress, she was staring into space. She was holding a brandy glass that was almost empty. As Bernard entered the room and closed the door, Emma jumped with a start. 'Bernard! I didn't hear you come in.'

'Tried not to wake anyone. Surprised to see you up, Emma. Is anything wrong?'

'Should there be?' Emma asked, sounding unconcerned.

'Finding you here in your night attire with a brandy seems unusual, that's all.'

She straightened her dressing gown and put her glass down on the coffee table. 'I couldn't sleep so I thought a brandy might help.'

'Good thinking. Mind if I join you in a nightcap?'

'Please yourself. I shall go back to my room. Try not to wake your brother. He's got a lot on his mind and needs his rest.' Emma got up from the sofa and was about to leave when Bernard commented on the forthcoming tribute dinner.

'Emma, this House of Lords shindig he's going to. Do you think there's something odd about it? Because I do.'

His comment was unexpected because it reflected her own thoughts. 'What made you say that?'

'Well, for a start I can't believe an official dinner at the Palace of Westminster is to be preceded by a booze-up in a house at Chelsea. Not only that but the invite doesn't have an RSVP.' Bernard took a good swig of whisky then added, 'I find that very strange. Don't you?'

'Yes,' she said thoughtfully. 'To be honest I've had some doubt as to its authenticity for some time. And the fact that you have doubts about it as well makes it even more worrying. And there's something else.'

'Really?'

'Yes.'

'What's that?'

'I tried to get the telephone number of Viscount Sisemen but without any luck. At first I assumed he was ex-directory.'

'Naturally. A chap like him would be.'

'Yes. So then I rang the House of Lords and spoke to their catering department.'

'And?'

'I asked about any functions they had on that evening but at first they wouldn't give any information. So I said I was ringing on behalf of Judge Thornton who was unable to find his invitation and wanted to check the time of arrival.'

'What did they say?'

'The woman said that she could not give out information of private dinners for security reasons. And that was that. But I'd subconsciously been doodling on the telephone pad and had written the name Sisemen. It was then that I saw it.'

'Saw what?'

'The name Sisemen is an anagram of Nemesis.'

Bernard looked shocked as the name dawned on him. 'Christ! That's the name of the Greek goddess of whatsit.'

'Of retribution and vengeance,' Emma said.

'Yes, that's her. Bloody hell!' Bernard exclaimed.

'Then I did something that would infuriate your brother if he knew.'

'What was that?'

'Promise me you won't say a word, Bernard. Promise.'

Bernard couldn't wait to hear what she had done. 'Hand on heart, old love.'

'I telephoned the chief constable and told him what I had done. He assured me that my call would be in confidence and said that he would check the address in Chelsea.'

'And?'

'The house belongs to a Francis Styles who is in Canada on business until the end of next month. So he won't be there at this gathering on the twenty-fourth of *this* month. And there's another thing that bothers me. When James MacCormack checked the list of viscounts, there was no one named Sisemen. Perhaps it's silly of me to be so suspicious. But with this other business going on I've really been worried.'

'Ah, you mean this Bible chappie? I'd forgotten about him. But I doubt *he'd* be arranging dinners for the noble Lords. A sandwich at the Little Chef is more in his league, I shouldn't wonder.'

Emma managed a smile. 'You're probably right.' Seeing that there was still some brandy left in her glass, she picked it up and drank it. 'I'll be off now. Good night, Bernard.'

'Good night. And don't worry. Everything will be fine, you wait and see.'

As Emma left and closed the door, Bernard poured himself a drink. Even in her dressing gown and slippers she had looked attractive and he wished he knew the truth of his brother's relationship with her. He finished his whisky and looked at the empty glass, wondering whether to have one more for the road. Deciding to drink his own supply instead, he switched the lights off and went upstairs to his room.

Sitting in bed with a glass of whisky beside him, he was

thinking of his night out with Gary and how impressed he was with his nephew's performance. His voice characterizations had been remarkably accurate. Gary's vocal skill, plus the use of wigs and false moustaches, made his subjects come to life. But despite his admiration, Bernard began to understand his brother's reluctance to see his son-in-law perform. The club that Gary appeared in was not the sort of place that a judge could very well frequent, he decided. Finishing his drink, he put the empty glass on his bedside table and switched off the light. As his head touched the pillow he found it difficult to get off to sleep. His thoughts were of the person sending his brother the threatening quotes and the dinner invitation. Were the two really connected as Emma had suggested? And if so, was his brother in some sort of danger? After tossing the situation round in his mind, he made a decision. Tomorrow he would find out if the dinner invitation was genuine. And if it wasn't, Bernard knew exactly what action he would take. At least he would do one decent thing for his brother before he died. As he thought about his plan, he closed his eyes and fell asleep.

It was before breakfast the following morning that the chief constable telephoned with the news that Moira and John Porter had been arrested while boarding a ferry to Lymington. Their plan to sail to France and travel on to Spain had been foiled by the police, who had spotted the pair at Yarmouth on the Isle of Wight. Pleased with the news, the judge could now enjoy his breakfast, knowing that the Porters would spend a lot of their remaining years in one of Her Majesty's prisons. And all because Raymond Farraday had used unorthodox methods of investigation. The judge was now hoping Farraday would have the same success in discovering the identity of the man sending the Bible quotations.

As he sat waiting for breakfast, the judge wondered why Bernard was late coming down. It was only when Emma brought in his coffee that he was informed that his brother had eaten earlier and left the house, saying that he was going to London. Intrigued by this news, Judge Thornton wondered why Bernard had said nothing of the intended visit to *him*. It was when Jody came to say good morning before going to school that her grandfather was to become even more intrigued.

Jody told him that Bernard had gone to the flat earlier and after talking with her father, the two men had driven off in Gary's car. Apparently they had *both* gone to London.

CHAPTER SEVENTEEN

Twenty-two Somerville Crescent was a large terraced house with expensive curtains at the windows. After driving round the crescent, Bernard and Gary headed for the town hall. They had no difficulty in checking the voters' register and seeing that the house was occupied by Francis and Megan Styles.

Returning to Somerville Crescent, Gary parked the car on the opposite side to number twenty-two so that Bernard had a clear view of the house across the crescent. Taking a pair of spectacles and a beret from his jacket pocket, Gary put them on. Then carefully placing a false moustache on his upper lip, the transformation was complete. He was now a French visitor, looking for his cousin. As he left the car and walked towards number twenty-two, Bernard sat nervously watching his nephew as he rang the doorbell. A man of medium build opened the door. After some conversation and head shaking, the man closed the door again. To Bernard's surprise, instead of Gary coming back to the car, he called at the house next door. A woman in her fifties answered and spent some time in responding to her caller's enquiry. Gary thanked the woman and returned to his car. As he got in, Bernard was impatient to know why Gary had called on the neighbour. His nephew drove out of the crescent before removing his disguise and replying. 'I had a feeling there was something not right about the man at number twenty-two.'

'In what way?' Bernard asked.

'Something about him didn't ring true. So I went next door and pretended I had a message for Mr Francis Styles. The lady explained that I'd got the wrong house and then told me that the Styles were away in Canada. I said I had seen someone at the window next door and she said that he would be the house sitter.'

'House sitter?!"

'Yes. Apparently Styles got someone from an agency to look after the place while he was away.'

'And why would a house sitter be giving pre-dinner drinks to people dining at the House of Lords tomorrow evening?'

'Exactly,' said Gary. 'It looks as though your suspicions could be right, Bernard.'

Bernard was thoughtful for a moment. 'Yes … Yes, it does. And if I *am* right, this whole business is worrying. Very worrying indeed.'

'So what do we do now?'

'Make one more call. Then get back to Four Oaks.'

Anne Lawrence was watching television when the phone rang. She turned the sound control down and picked up the receiver. The voice of the caller was unmistakable. She had been expecting him to phone and make sure she would be on the morning train to London, as arranged. Although she was used to him fussing over detail, Anne thought he had sounded more tense and excited than usual. She confirmed her arrival time and after telling her that he would go over the details of her performance when he saw her, he blew a kiss into the receiver and hung up.

She sat staring at her suitcase that was packed and ready by the front door. Anne was looking forward to seeing Johnny and spending the whole night with him. Whatever else he was, Johnny was the only man who had made her feel a real woman when they were in bed together. With him she had lost all her inhibitions and felt young again. But she still had a nagging feeling that this practical joke he was planning was not the innocent prank he had made it out to be.

It was just before lunch that Bernard joined his brother in the sitting room for an aperitif. Looking tired and trying to hide the fact that he was in pain, Bernard explained his trip to London as going to see an old friend who was in town and who he hoped to meet again tomorrow.

The judge did not question his brother's meeting with his friend; what was concerning him was not where he had been but his health. He had noticed it slowly worsening in the past days and was about to discuss the subject when the telephone rang. Excusing himself, he went to the hall phone and answered it. After a few moments he returned and appeared upset. Bernard saw the look on his brother's face and knew exactly who his caller had been. He kept his fingers crossed that William would believe what the caller had told him.

Lunch was almost over when the doorbell rang and Emma left the table to answer it.

The delivery van from the local florist was in the drive and standing on the doorstep holding a wreath was the girl from the shop. 'I'm so sorry to hear about Judge Thornton,' she said with professional solemnity. 'At least it was sudden and he didn't have to suffer.'

Emma looked at her in total disbelief. 'I'm sorry. I think there's been a mistake. He isn't dead!'

The girl checked the attached delivery note. 'But it's to be delivered today, it says here. And the Interflora shop in Fulham where they were ordered made me repeat the message on the card to make sure I'd got it right.'

Emma removed the card from the wreath and felt sick as she read the words printed in the centre of its black border:

IN DEEPEST SYMPATHY
to
Judge Thornton
Whose passing will be unexpected.
Isaiah 3.11.

Emma was shaking but tried to hide her feelings. She told the girl to take the wreath away as it was a sick joke.

She stood for a moment, not sure what to do. She felt that the judge had been through enough for one day. First there was the upsetting phone call before lunch and now this. She made up her mind to keep this latest incident from him, for the time being anyway, then went to the kitchen and hid the card in a drawer.

Returning to the dining room, she said the delivery girl had come to the wrong house by mistake. Emma then finished her lunch without the incident being mentioned again.

Once Bernard and the judge had been served coffee in the sitting room, Emma cleared the dining table and returned to the kitchen.

She put everything into the dishwasher then took the card from the drawer and went quietly to her room. She searched for her old Bible and found it among some books on her wardrobe shelf. It had been years since she had opened it and loose pages fell out. Sorting through them, she finally found Isaiah 3.11 and read the quotation:

> *Woe to the guilty!*
> *How unfortunate they*
> *are, for what their*
> *hands have done shall*
> *be done unto them.*

She stood looking at the page for a moment, knowing that despite her intention to keep this latest one from the judge, somebody would have to be told. She thought of Farraday, the man who had been more successful in his investigations than the police. But his telephone number was in the judge's desk directory in the study and if he caught her there pretending to clean at this time of day he might become suspicious. Emma was wondering what to do for the best when she heard Bernard on his way upstairs. With Gary out at a luncheon in Kingston, Bernard was the only one she felt able to turn to.

When Emma had finished telling him about the wreath and this latest Bible quote, she waited for Bernard's reaction.

He was sitting on the edge of her bed and although still catching his breath from the climb up to his room, his answer was instant. 'This bloody maniac wants shooting. The man must be as unstable as hell and that means he's bloody dangerous.'

'I know. And that's what worries me. But what are we going to do?'

'You said your first instinct was to phone this Farraday chap.'

'Yes.'

'Then that's what you do. It's a woman's first instinct that's usually the right one. So phone this chap and explain this latest development and see what he says. Otherwise you must give that chief constable wallah a buzz and ask him to get off his arse and do something. He's supposed to be my brother's pal but appears to have done sod all up to now.'

Emma spoke half-heartedly in James MacCormack's defence. 'Oh, I'm sure he's doing all he can.'

'Yes, chasing motorists! Anyway, let's not argue over him and his army of Mr Plods – we've got to do what's best for my brother. I may not have long to go but before I do I want to see the evil sod that's sending these things behind bars.'

His anger wasn't helping his breathing and as Emma watched him struggling for air, she felt sorry for him. For the first time since being on the receiving end of his unpleasantries, she was seeing the other side of Bernard Thornton. Something about him made her feel that he was sincere when he said he wanted to help his brother. Even Bernard's bad language no longer offended her.

'If we phone Raymond Farraday I'll have to get his number and I shall need your help to do that,' Emma said.

'I don't follow.'

'His number is in the desk directory in the study and I'll need you to keep your brother out of the way while I go and get it.'

Bernard got to his feet. 'Consider it done.'

'Don't you want to rest a bit longer first?'

'No, no. Going downstairs is no problem. Its climbing up the bloody things that gets me a bit puffed.'

Emma opened the door and ushered him out of her room. She watched him go and waited a moment before she left.

A few minutes later they were downstairs, Bernard in the sitting room with his brother and Emma in the study. She was not long finding Farraday's telephone number and writing it on a piece of paper. She took it back to her room and dialled the number.

The voice on the answerphone apologized for being absent and asked the caller to leave a message. She hung up and wondered whether she should call James MacCormack. She knew his phone number off by heart but wasn't sure whether it would do any good to call him. Bernard may have been somewhat cruel in his reference to the chief constable doing 'sod all' but Emma felt that he had got a point. She finally decided to do nothing until she had spoken to Bernard and explained why she had been unable to contact Raymond Farraday.

Emma left her room and made her way back downstairs. She found it strange to be treating Bernard as a confidante after all the years of disliking him.

Suddenly she thought of the wreath and a cold shudder came over her. Then, remembering the message on the card, she became frightened. The thought of William dying before Bernard had never occurred to her, until now.

It was late afternoon when Gary got home from his luncheon. As he was parking his car he saw Bernard at the sitting-room window, signalling him to wait. With his brother safely in the study, Bernard walked quietly to the kitchen and out through the back door.

He brought Gary up to date with what had happened during his absence.

'So there you have it, old son. This bastard has now got us really worried with this wreath business. He's obviously mad and wants locking away. And the sooner the better.'

Gary thought for a moment. 'This Farraday's bound to have a mobile phone as well as his home number.'

'Hadn't thought of that. But surely Emma would have seen it if it had been in the directory.'

'Perhaps. In any event I think the chief constable should be told. I mean, if anything happened to Pops we'd never be able to forgive ourselves.'

'No. Well, perhaps you *should* give him a call,' Bernard reluctantly agreed.

'Look, I'll ring James MacCormack on my mobile. That will save Emma using the house phone,' Gary said.

'OK. Do you have his number?'

'No. But as soon as I've said hello to Alison, I'll come over and get it from Emma. Ask her to write it down for me, will you, Bernard?'

'Will do.'

'And check that she didn't see another number when she was looking up the one for Farraday.'

'Right away.'

Gary went into his flat, leaving Bernard to make his way back into the house via the kitchen.

Both before and after dinner that evening, Gary had tried to contact Raymond Farraday several times but without any luck.

Emma had managed to go into the library and check to see if there was a mobile phone number but there wasn't. And why

Farraday had not picked up his phone messages was a mystery to Emma and the others. They assumed he must be away on an overnight trip.

When James MacCormack was told of the wreath being sent, he agreed that the judge should be spared further worry until the culprit had been identified – something the police were no nearer to achieving. Even his attempt to discover the name of the person that ordered the wreath from the florist in Fulham had drawn a blank. That person had sent the order by post and enclosed cash for payment. The only comfort he could offer was that the man responsible would slip up sooner or later and be caught. 'They always do,' he assured Gary. But Bernard was far from convinced and reiterated his lack of confidence in James MacCormack.

Judge Thornton had gone to bed early and was trying to read a P.G. Wodehouse novel, a birthday gift from Gerald and Patricia Turvey. Normally he would read a complete book in a matter of three to four nights but tonight he was unable to concentrate properly. His mind kept wandering from the Wodehouse humour to the abduction of Jody and the threatening biblical quotes.

He was paying Raymond Farraday a substantial fee and was becoming impatient to hear that he had been successful in his search for the culprit.

Then he thought of the House of Lords dinner invitation and wondered who and what it was actually in aid of.

By the time the police arrived, the ambulance men had already managed to free the driver from the wreckage. An eyewitness said that the driver swerved to avoid a fox and ran into the parked van that showed signs of a violent impact.

First aid was administered but within minutes the driver of the car was dead.

The policeman searched his pockets for identification and found his driving licence. The name of the driver as Raymond Farraday.

CHAPTER EIGHTEEN

The train from Guildford had arrived at Waterloo station a few minutes late. By the time the taxi had pulled up outside 22 Somerville Crescent it was just after 6.30. The Victorian-style streetlights gave the property a luxurious appearance.

The house was a large semi-detached four-storey building with three stone steps leading to an impressive front door. Even the bell-push had a highly polished brass surround. As he rang the bell, he was aware that this was the home of a wealthy person.

The door was opened by a maid who greeted the caller with an enquiring smile.

'Good evening, sir.'

'Good evening. I believe you are expecting me. I'm Judge Thornton.'

'Yes, sir. Please come in. Do you have your invitation card and letter?'

'Of course,' he said, giving them to her as he admired the spacious oak-panelled hall with its staircase leading to a gallery landing. Dominating the antique furniture was a gilt Victorian mirror hanging above a seventeenth-century oak coffer. He removed his hat and overcoat and gave them to the maid before being shown into the impeccably furnished sitting room which was void of people. Looking at his watch he asked, 'Am I the first to arrive?'

'If you'll excuse me I'll tell Eric that you're here,' the maid said, deliberately avoiding his question.

As she left the room he looked around, admiring the very expensive and tasteful decor. There were five original oil paintings hanging with their own picture light above. He was studying the work of a Dutch artist when the door opened and a man entered, wearing dark grey trousers and a black jacket. From his voice and manner this was obviously Eric the butler.

'Judge Thornton, sir. May I offer you a drink?'

'Thank you. A whisky would be most welcome. Tell me, have the others been delayed?'

'What others would that be, sir?'

'The other guests, of course.'

Eric looked confused as he replied, 'As far as I am aware, you are the only one expected, sir. I'll get you that drink.'

Eric left the room, leaving his visitor nonplussed.

He was trying to make some sense of the situation when the maid entered the room holding an envelope.

'This arrived for you this morning, sir.'

He took the envelope from her and saw that it had a first-class stamp and a Glasgow postmark.

'The letter arrived this morning, you say?'

'Yes, sir.'

'Thank you,' he said, forcing a polite smile.

When she left the room he opened the envelope and removed the contents. It was the familiar plain paper with the words *Leviticus 24, verse 20*.

As he sat staring at the paper, a cold shudder ran down his spine. Unless the sender was party to the dinner invitation, how would he know where to send the letter? However, he had walked into the house determined not to show any sign of apprehension and so he tried to appear as natural as possible.

Eric entered with a crystal glass on a silver tray. In it was a large measure of whisky.

'Did you want anything with it, sir?'

'No. No, thank you. I'll take it neat. No sense in spoiling good whisky,' he said. Then in a calm manner he asked, 'Have you such a thing as a Bible anywhere?'

Eric looked surprised. 'A Bible, sir?'

'Yes. I, er, I want to look something up. If it's no bother, that is.'

'Not at all, sir. I think I know where there is one.'

He watched Eric leave, wondering what this biblical quote would be. As he drank his whisky he had the feeling that the evening would not be as pleasant as the invitation suggested. Tapping his pocket to check its contents, he wondered what these latest quotes might be, and whether the maid and butler were simply innocent servants or part of something far more contrived.

Eric arrived with a Bible and offered to replenish the now empty tumbler. Gratefully accepting the offer, he handed Eric his glass. With the butler gone from the room, his fingers flicked through the Old Testament until he found Leviticus 24 verse 20. He began to sense a feeling of impending danger as he read:

> *Fracture for fracture, eye*
> *for eye, tooth for tooth.*
> *The injury inflicted is the*
> *injury to be suffered.*

The colour drained from his cheeks as he nervously re-read the quote. Why had this quotation been sent to this house of all places? he wondered. And why had the sender gone to the trouble of getting an invitation card printed? Was all this simply to get Judge Thornton to Somerville Crescent on this particular evening? And if so, why number 22 and for what reason?

When Eric returned with another large whisky, he asked, 'Are you all right, sir? You look pale.'

Slipping the paper into his pocket, the visitor replied, 'Probably something I had at lunchtime.'

As Eric handed the whisky to him, he said with relief, 'Oh, I thought perhaps you'd received bad news, sir.'

'No, no. Tell me, what is the name of my host?'

'Viscount Sisemen made this evening's arrangement, sir.'

'And what time are you expecting him?'

'Difficult to say, sir. He's a law unto himself as far as time goes.'

'But if, as you say, he made the arrangements for this evening, he should be here surely?'

Before Eric could answer, the maid came in and handed the judge a brown envelope. 'A gentleman left this for you, sir. I was asked to make sure that Judge Thornton listened to it in private.'

Inside the envelope was an audio cassette. The label was blank, giving no indication as to what the tape might contain. Eric informed him that the mahogany cabinet standing against the wall was a music centre that included a tape machine. He showed the judge how it worked and then both he and the maid left the room.

As the tape started there appeared to be nothing on it until a male voice spoke with a sinister, breathless huskiness.

'*Good evening, Judge Thornton. I'm so glad you came. Are you sitting comfortably? I hope you are, and that my servants are taking good care of you.*'

He sat listening intently as the voice continued.

'*Now that you have read my note, you are wondering why I send you quotations from the good book. You see, I wanted you to go through some mental turmoil. The way you did when I had your granddaughter for the day. How could a nice little girl like her have the genes of a bastard like you, hmm? I would have kept her longer but couldn't risk being caught, could I? And I'm sure you lost sleep when your study was broken into. I do hope that you lay awake at night wondering why you were going through all this. Well, let me try and answer that for you. Cast your mind back to the days when you sat wearing the wig and robe, pontificating on the rights and wrongs of those standing before you. Some completely innocent, yet trembling as you distorted the truth so that they would be convicted in order that your sick mind would be satisfied.*'

As the voice became more threatening, the listener became nervous. He finished his whisky as the voice continued in anger:

'*Just think of all the innocent people who have languished in prison because you wanted the pleasure of destroying their lives. But why? For what reason did you, the judge, ignore the truth? Was it perhaps that you hated people of the lower class? Did you feel nothing but contempt for their families as you willingly destroyed their lives? I wonder how you would feel if your daughter suffered as they have. You must be feeling tired now. I added something to the whisky so that you would become helpless.*'

Realizing that he had been drugged, he desperately tried to get out of the chair but without success. His eyes became heavy and his body weak as the voice continued. '*And now I am the judge. And you have been found guilty of ruining the lives of innocent people. Therefore, it is my duty to pass sentence. You will go from here and spend the rest of your miserable life in fear. Every day you will wonder where and when I will strike. You will spend sleepless nights wondering who I am. But you will never know. Never ... And that is to be your punishment. And my retribution.*'

Fighting to stay awake, the voice became distant and his vision hazy.

'*I shall haunt you. Until your dying day … Sleep well.*'

Unable to stay awake, his eyes closed and he fell asleep.

Anne Lawrence didn't like what had happened. When she saw the man slumped in the armchair she was very uneasy. Johnny turned his back to Anne while he removed something from the man's pocket and placed it in his own.

'I don't like this, Johnny. I don't like it at all.'

'He's all right,' he whispered. 'I only gave him a harmless sleeping draught.'

'This wasn't a practical joke, was it? What the hell have I got myself into? And him a judge! Christ! I could end up in prison.'

'It's just a joke, like I said. Now give me a hand to get him to the back door and into the car.'

'Then what are you going to do with him?'

'Drive him to a lonely spot and leave him. When he comes round he won't know where he is. And that's it. Joke over.'

'What happens when he remembers that he was here and comes back to the house?'

'We won't be here, will we? I shall be long gone and you'll be on your way home, so don't worry.'

'But it was my glowing reference that got you the job of house sitter, remember? It was Mrs Anne Lawrence of Sherborne that told them *Eric Sheldon* was trustworthy and reliable. So what happens if they get on to me? What will I say?'

'Don't get your knickers in a twist.' He grinned. 'How can you be held responsible for the reliable Eric that you knew becoming a shit? Tomorrow Eric will have vanished and you'll have nothing to worry about. For God's sake, don't panic. Now, give me a hand with the judge. I've got to get him away from here before he comes to.'

Reluctantly, Anne helped Johnny ease the unconscious body from the armchair to the floor. Getting a grip on the judge's ankles, Johnny dragged him across the carpet and towards the sitting-room door. He had just stopped to get his breath when the doorbell rang. Johnny froze and signalled for Anne to keep silent. For the first time he looked nervous. He had not bargained for an unexpected caller.

Anne was frightened as she stood there, hoping the caller would leave. Suddenly the doorbell rang again and it became obvious that one of them would have to answer it. Anne was in no fit state to face anyone and Johnny signalled to her to stay in the sitting room out of sight.

Johnny looked round desperately. Being near the cupboard under the stairs, he opened the door and managed to force the body inside.

Again the doorbell rang and Johnny took a deep breath to regain his butler persona before answering it. When he opened the door he was rendered speechless. The similarity between the man standing there and the one under the stairs came as an unpleasant shock. The caller then introduced himself.

'I'm Judge Thornton. I believe you are expecting me.'

The judge knew from Johnny's expression that he was *not* expected. As he stepped into the hall, Anne appeared from the sitting room and was unable to hide her shock at seeing him.

'Is something wrong, my dear?' the judge asked calmly. 'You look as though you've seen a ghost. Surely you were expecting me?'

'We ... we weren't expecting *anyone*.' Johnny said, trying to compose himself and sound credible. 'Are you sure you've got the right house, sir?'

'This is twenty-two Somerville Crescent, is it not?'

'Er, yes, but.... '

'Then I have the right house.' Fixing his eyes on Johnny, he asked, 'Where is your other visitor?'

Before anyone could stop him he walked to the sitting-room door where Anne was standing. Finding his piercing blue eyes unsettling, she threw an anxious glance to Johnny, who put a finger to his lips, warning her not to speak.

The judge entered the sitting room and seeing no one there looked to the hall and called, 'I would like an answer to my question. Where is your other visitor?'

Johnny came into the room and managed an innocent smile. 'Oh, there was a gentleman who called earlier. And he said that *he* was Judge Thornton. I must say you look very alike, sir.' Anxious to know the truth, he said, 'And the gentleman had an official invitation to a cocktail party. A hoax, I'm afraid. But he must have believed it as he was dressed for dinner.'

'And as I am not, you no doubt assume that he was the real Judge Thornton and that I am an imposter. Is that it?'

'I'm naturally curious, sir.'

'The other gentleman was my brother and the dinner suit he wore was mine. Does that satisfy your curiosity?'

Johnny became flustered, wondering if he had drugged the wrong man. 'Yes ... Thank you, sir.'

'And now perhaps you can satisfy *my* curiosity. Where is my brother?'

'Well, sir. As soon as he realized he'd been the victim of a practical joke, he left.'

Picking up the empty glass on the side table next to the armchair, the judge sniffed it and asked sharply, 'Then who was sitting here drinking whisky?'

Johnny thought quickly. 'Oh, that was your brother, sir. He asked if he could have one before he left.' Smiling and now regaining his composure, Johnny said, 'No doubt your brother is on his way home again. I'm sorry you have both had such a wasted journey, sir. Stupid things, practical jokes.' He went back into the hall and waited to open the front door, anxious for his visitor to leave.

Judge Thornton began to wonder if the invitation to the cocktail party really *had* been an annoying hoax. Then as he went to follow Johnny into the hall, he noticed the Bible on the side table. Something made him look at the armchair where Bernard had been sitting and he noticed an envelope that had become wedged between the seat cushion and the side of the chair. He removed the envelope and when he saw the postmark hurried to the hall where Johnny was waiting.

'This envelope is addressed to *me* at this address! Can you tell me what happened to the contents?'

'Your brother must have taken it with him, sir.'

Judge Thornton stared at the envelope, realizing that the invitation was more than a harmless hoax. Convinced that his brother's suspicions were right, he went to Johnny. 'Please open the door.'

Johnny knew that once the judge had gone he could make his getaway. His plan was turning into a disaster and all he wanted now was to get out of the house and disappear. Opening the front door, he gave a sigh of relief as the judge stepped out. But instead of leaving, Judge Thornton signalled to the driver of a waiting car and stepped back into the hall again. Johnny watched as the driver of the car walked briskly towards the house.

'What's going on?' Johnny asked, becoming agitated.

'That is what I intend to find out,' replied the judge in a determined voice. 'This is my son-in-law. And now I suggest we all go into the sitting room.'

Gary Hanley entered the hall and as the judge closed the door he indicated for Johnny to precede him. As he passed the stair cupboard, Johnny thought of its occupant. If these men didn't leave before he regained consciousness, he'd be in trouble. Suddenly he remembered the whisky and wondered if it might get him out of the predicament he found himself in. At least the two men would fall asleep until he and Anne had got away. Then he would have to think of a way to keep Anne from talking. Things had become too dangerous for him to rely on her keeping her mouth shut, he decided. But he knew that he'd have to appear calm in the presence of the two men.

'Can I offer you gentlemen a drink?' he asked smiling.

'No, thank you,' the judge answered brusquely. 'There are a few questions I would like answered.'

'Questions?' Johnny asked. 'Certainly, sir. If I can.'

'I know that the owner of this building is in Canada. May I ask how long you have been in his employ?'

Johnny was surprised that the judge knew of Francis Styles' whereabouts.

'I've been with Mr Styles for some time,' he said proudly, then trying to sound convincing, 'I hope you don't think he had anything to do with this silly practical joke.'

'I played a practical joke yesterday morning. One I'm sure you'll find very amusing,' Gary said with a smile.

'Really, sir?' Johnny said politely.

'Yes. I pretended to be a Frenchman looking for his cousin at this very house. Only the man I spoke to wasn't a butler. He was from an agency that provide house sitters. Now isn't that interesting?'

Johnny didn't answer. He was desperately thinking of a way to get himself out of trouble when Anne lost her nerve.

'Tell them, Johnny. Tell them the truth!' she begged.

Her outburst was the one thing Johnny had feared. 'Shut up, Anne!' he commanded.

'I think I would prefer to hear what the lady has to say,' Judge Thornton said. 'Please go on, my dear. Tell us what this charade is in aid of.'

Anne purposely avoided Johnny's eyes as she spoke. 'Johnny told me he wanted me to help him play a joke on someone and I thought it was just going to be a harmless bit of fun. I had no idea the victim was going to be a judge until today. Even then I didn't realize what was intended.'

'Neither did I,' Johnny insisted. 'The man who put me up to it said it was only a joke on a friend. Otherwise I would not have agreed to it,' he said innocently.

'Go on, my dear,' Judge Thornton continued.

'All I knew was that I was to pretend to be a maid. Then when the gentleman arrived, give him a letter and then a tape. I was to tell him that someone had left it for him. I swear I had no idea what was in the letter or on the tape.'

'And where is this tape?' Judge Thornton asked.

As Anne went to speak, Johnny was quick to answer. 'Your brother said it was a personal message and took it with him.'

Gary noticed Anne look anxiously in the direction of the mahogany cabinet and wondered why. He walked over to it and saw the tape in the machine. 'Is this the machine that was used to play the tape on?'

'Yes,' Anne said.

'Then what's this tape on here?'

'Just some music I was playing before you arrived. That's all.' Johnny smiled.

His rapid reply did not impress the judge, who saw Johnny slowly moving towards the door. Judge Thornton quickly closed the door and stood in front of it, giving Gary a nod to start the tape.

Gary pushed the rewind button and noticed Johnny becoming nervous. Anne stared at the cabinet, wondering what she would hear. There was a silence in the room until Gary pressed the start button and the message finally began.

Anne listened to the threatening, husky voice, with total disbelief that Johnny had got her involved in this mess. What she had understood to be a harmless joke was now turning into a nightmare.

Judge Thornton felt a chill when the voice began, but then his fear turned to hatred and anger. Whatever grievance this person had against him, the judge knew that he would never be content until this madman was locked away. As the tape ended, he managed to regain his air of authority. Looking at Johnny, he said in a commanding voice. 'I should like to know who it was that made that disgusting recording.'

'I have no idea, sir. I was simply asked to—'

'Please don't play innocent with me. You were given the recording to give to Judge Thornton. Well, *I* am he. And I want to know who this person was!'

'I know who it was,' said Gary, who had been listening with deep concentration to the recorded message.

'You do?' said the judge with surprise.

Gary was confident. 'Yes I do. And despite him making an effort to disguise the voice, occasionally the natural timbre came through. And that was the giveaway.'

'So who was it?' the judge asked impatiently.

Before Gary could answer, there was a tapping sound from the hall that took everyone's attention. As the judge opened the door, the tapping was clearly heard coming from the stair cupboard. He went quickly to the cupboard door and opened it. His brother was crouched on the floor, looking weak. 'My God! Bernard! Give me a hand, somebody.'

Anne ran to his aid and as Gary went to help, Johnny saw his opportunity to make his getaway. As he quickly ran from the sitting room into the hall, Gary dived at his feet in a rugby tackle and brought him down. 'No, you don't, Johnny, or whatever your real name is.' He pulled him to his feet and, gripping his arm firmly in a half lock, pushed him into the sitting room and forced him into an armchair. 'Don't move,' Gary said threateningly. 'There are some questions that we shall want answered. Make a run for it and I'll break your neck. And that's a promise.'

Gary went back into the hall, closing the door behind him. He saw the judge struggling to help Bernard stand up, while Anne looked helplessly on. Despite the lack of space offered by the cupboard entrance, Gary managed to get his arm around Bernard's waist and with his father-in-law's help the two of them got Bernard to his feet.

'I'll get him some water,' Anne said, and hurried to the kitchen. Gary and the judge watched anxiously while Bernard slowly regained consciousness. After a few moments, Anne came with a glass of water and held it to Bernard's lips. Although tired and breathless, he managed a smile as he whispered, 'I never thought I'd be glad to taste water. Thank you.'

With the feeling returning to his legs after his ordeal of being bundled into such a small space, he was helped back to the sitting room and put comfortably on the settee.

While the judge sat consoling his brother, Gary stood by the door, which he had closed firmly behind him. His voice was full of contempt as he spoke to Johnny. 'The next time you want to make an anonymous recording, get a professional!'

Johnny's lips became dry as everyone stared at him.

Bernard's eyes squinted in an effort to focus. 'It was you! I could have died in that cupboard. You bastard.' He fought for breath while his brother tried to calm him. Apologizing to Anne, Bernard said, 'Forgive my French.'

Anne shook her head in despair. 'Christ, Johnny. What have you done! Why did you get me involved in this awful mess?' She sat with her head buried in her hands.

There was a look of confused disbelief on the judge's face. 'Why? Tell me why? What in God's name have I ever done to you to make you say those terrible things on that recording?'

Johnny felt in his pocket and appeared to regain confidence. 'Yes. All right. I'll tell you. My marriage wasn't exactly great but that didn't bother me. These things happen. But at least she gave me the son I always wanted and that made me happy. Then one night my son tried to help a man who had been injured in a robbery. He even phoned for an ambulance. He never laid a finger on the poor sod, but the police had to pull someone in so they arrested my boy. When this man died, my son went to court charged with manslaughter! And I watched the judge, an inhuman, uncaring swine, ignoring the fact that my boy was innocent. I watched that judge convince the jury that my son was guilty by reminding them that he had a previous record. A previous record of burglary, yes. But he never hurt anyone in his life. But you got him put away for twelve years! Twelve years for something he hadn't done!'

Gary and Anne looked at the judge, expecting him to defend himself, but he sat silent and thoughtful. And as he recalled the trial of Nicky Bains, tried to remember the facts of the case.

'Every time I went to visit him I watched him suffering,' Johnny continued. 'So I made a promise that the judge who put him there would suffer too. For at least twelve years!'

Anne suddenly realized how unstable he was. 'You planned all this just to get revenge!'

Johnny tried to justify his actions. 'Don't you see? It was perfect. The quotations from the Bible. Giving his little granddaughter an adventurous day out while he sat at home in a state of mental torture. While he wondered whether he'd ever see her again, she was having rides and enjoying herself at the funfair. If his brother hadn't come and messed everything up, it would have worked out exactly as I planned. And no one would have ever known.'

Gary grabbed him and pinned him against the door with his forearm held firmly at his throat. 'What about her mother and me? What about what we went through because of your twisted mind?'

Something was sticking into Gary's stomach and the smirk on Johnny's face made him release his hold on him. As Gary stepped back he could see the pistol pressed against him.

'Johnny! Don't be a fool!' Anne cried. 'Don't make things worse for yourself. Put the gun down.'

Bernard's hand went to his pocket. 'That's my pistol!'

'What on earth made you bring a gun with you?' exclaimed his brother. 'You know it's illegal to carry firearms over here. And I take it you don't have a licence either.'

'Still the judge, eh, William?' Bernard mocked. 'Bought it in Spain, years ago. Thought I'd bring it with me in case I needed to frighten somebody. Had no idea what to expect when I arrived for the unpleasant charade this bugger had set up for us. Didn't dream anyone would mess up a decent whisky by putting some sleeping potion in it.' He began coughing and winced with the pain it was causing him.

His brother became concerned. 'Can I get you anything?'

As he fought to get his breath back he managed a grin. 'I wouldn't say no to some of your excellent whisky, old man.'

'When we get home, which won't be long now,' William promised. 'There are just one or two things I want to clear up before we leave.'

Bernard's breathing was becoming steady again. 'I should call the police if I were you, Gary-boy.'

'And get myself shot!'

'He won't shoot you,' Bernard said confidently.

'Don't bet on it,' Johnny threatened.

'But I *do*,' Bernard said smiling. 'You see, the firing pin's been filed off, so you couldn't shoot it if you tried. Apart from that, it isn't loaded.'

As Johnny tilted the pistol towards the floor to examine the chamber, Bernard gave Gary the signal to jump him. Gary lunged at Johnny, and gripping the gun with his right hand, threw a swift left hook to Johnny's chin. As he fell to the floor his hands automatically opened to break his fall and he released his hold on the gun. The pistol dropped to the floor and Gary quickly took possession of it.

'Be careful with that gun, Gary-boy,' Bernard said with a grimace. 'Bloody thing might go off.'

Gary quickly moved his fingers from the vicinity of the trigger. 'You said it wasn't loaded!'

'I know what I said. Give it here.'

Gary carefully put the gun in Bernard's lap, only too happy to be rid of it.

Seeing the door unguarded, Johnny got to his feet and made a run towards it. As he reached the door the sudden gunshot made him stop in his tracks. Nervously, he turned to see the pistol Bernard was aiming at him. 'The next one won't miss. Now sit down, there's a good chap.'

As Johnny sat, Bernard gave his brother a surreptitious wink.

'Shall I call the police?' Gary asked.

'Later, perhaps,' said the judge. 'First I want to ask this man a few questions. What is the name of your son?'

'Nicky. Nicky Bains.'

'Ah yes. I remember him. Tell me, Mr Bains. If your son is innocent and you feel there has been an injustice in his case, why have your legal advisers not made an appeal?'

'They have.'

'But if that is so, why do you not wait for the result of that hearing before inflicting your hatred on me? If, as you say, your son is innocent, he will be deemed so by the court and set free. Surely that is the way to do things?'

'You don't understand, do you? My son was put away because of you and that prosecuting counsel ponce. Between the two of you, you had him all confused and scared. Scared because none of you wanted to believe he was innocent. He pleaded with you but you wouldn't listen. And now you tell me to wait for the appeal hearing? Don't make me laugh. It could be months until that happens. And in the meantime, Nicky has to live with the knowledge that if he gets another judge like you, his appeal will be turned down and he'll be left to rot. And while he's inside, you'll be living in your fancy house with your family and wealthy friends to keep you company.'

Judge Thornton remembered Raymond Farraday's words after he had read the transcripts of some earlier cases:

> *According to what I've been reading, you were not*
> *always too keen to hear anything in the accused's*
> *defence. On the contrary, you seemed to do everything*
> *to help counsel for the prosecution.*

Those words of condemnation had been haunting him from the moment he first heard them. Now he was once again accused of using his position on the bench to put away a young man who, despite his police record, might be innocent of the crime for which he was sentenced. With the others waiting for him to speak, he cleared his throat.

'As you are aware, Mr Bains, you have committed a serious offence. And because of your determination to carry out this personal vendetta against me, you have caused great anguish to my family.'

'What do you think you've caused to mine!'

'Please let me finish. In any court of law you would be sent to prison for the offences that you have committed. But I am prepared to offer you a way out of your dilemma.'

The others were puzzled by his statement and waited with eager curiosity to hear the offer he was about to make.

'What sort of offer?' Johnny asked with suspicion.

'I shall study the transcript of the case. And I give you my word that if, as you say, I said or did anything to cause an unfair influence on the verdict, I shall do everything to right that wrong and get your son his freedom.'

The others couldn't believe what they were hearing.

Raising an inquisitive eyebrow, Johnny asked, 'What's the catch?'

'The catch, as you put it, is this. In return, you will never again contact, harm or threaten either myself or any member of my family.

And if you did, it would be in the certain knowledge that you will spend the rest of your life incarcerated in one of Her Majesty's prisons.'

His unexpected offer angered Bernard. 'After what he did to me you want to let the bugger off scot-free!'

'And what about what he did to Jody!' Gary shouted. 'You haven't forgotten that, surely?'

Judge Thornton spoke quietly. 'Please let us calm down. I know what he did to you was unpleasant, Bernard.'

'Too bloody right it was. I could have died in that bloody cupboard!'

'But remember, he thought it was *me* he was punishing. And as for what he did to Jody, Gary, he didn't actually do one thing to harm her. In fact, on her own admission, she had a wonderful day. Again, it was *me* he was trying to hurt. And there is something else. Now that we know the identity of Mr Bains, should anything occur in the future to cause us any grief or harm, I shall make arrangements for him to be taken immediately into custody.'

'But why in God's name don't you have him arrested? I know what I'd do with him. He wants stringing up!' Bernard cried, his hand twitching with the pistol.

'Be careful with that firearm,' his brother pleaded. 'Put it away before you do one of us or yourself an injury.'

Johnny became visibly more relaxed as Bernard reluctantly put the gun back into his jacket pocket.

The judge looked across at Johnny. 'You heard my offer. I should like to have your answer.'

'You'll really help Nicky get out?'

'You have my word.'

Johnny was looking at the judge's eyes and couldn't help noticing how sad they were. For a brief moment he felt sorry for the man he had hated so much. 'But suppose you can't get him released?'

'Oh, I think that once the transcripts are read and I make my recommendations, there is a good chance that your son will gain his freedom. I may be retired, Mr Bains, but I do still have influence. Do you accept my offer?'

Johnny's hesitation gave the judge concern. He knew that he couldn't afford the publicity Johnny's arrest would bring. And the thought of having his knighthood offer withdrawn was too unbear-able for him to contemplate.

Anne Lawrence sat willing Johnny to agree to the judge's terms. She longed to get back to her home in Sherborne where she would try and forget this man, the man with whom she had been so infatuated but now despised.

After a moment's serious consideration, Johnny made his decision known. 'All right. It's a deal. You get Nicky free and you'll never hear from me again.'

Judge Thornton managed to conceal his relief and simply nodded in acceptance of their agreement.

Gary and Bernard exchanged a look of total confusion at what had just taken place.

'And that's it!' Bernard exclaimed. 'I get drugged and shoved in a bloody cupboard and that's it! Forgotten. Case over and done with. Jury dismissed. All rise and sod off? Why not stick *him* in the cupboard and let the bastard rot!'

The judge raised his hand in a request for calm. 'Please, Bernard. Trust me. I assure you this is the best solution to all our problems.'

Gary stood shaking his head in disbelief. 'OK, Pops. I suppose you know what you're doing. Though personally I'd like to be alone with Johnny-boy for a few minutes after the grief he caused us.'

'Please, both of you, calm down,' Judge Thornton pleaded. 'I shall explain the reason for my decision later. But before we go I should like Mr Bains to satisfy my curiosity on one or two things. For instance, why were your communications all posted from Glasgow?'

'My cousin lives there,' Johnny explained. 'I told her it was a running joke I was playing on a friend and naturally she believed me.'

Anne looked at him with contempt. 'That's what you told me too. Only you said it was a joke that you were playing on *behalf* of a friend. Well, if your precious son is anything like his father, prison is where he belongs!'

Johnny wanted to physically strike her for the remark but knew that he would be safer using a verbal attack. 'But you didn't mind giving his father your frustrated, ageing body in bed, did you?'

Anne's eyes filled with tears at being humiliated in front of the other men.

Judge Thornton went over and took her gently by the arm. 'Why don't you go and get changed, my dear. I'm sure you will feel happier in more suitable attire.'

He led her to the door and opened it. As she left the room she gave him a grateful smile. Closing the door, he continued his questioning of Johnny Bains.

'Another thing that I am curious about, Mr Bains. The lad that broke into my study. Where did you find him?'

Johnny shrugged. 'Chance meeting in a pub when I came to Guildford to see where you lived. I heard him talking to his mates and boasting about his ability to get into any house, no matter what locks they'd got. And let's face it, fifty quid comes in handy if you're on drugs, as he probably was.'

'So the young man was telling the truth after all,' Judge Thornton said pensively.

'How do you mean?' asked Johnny.

'He *was* caught, Mr Bains. And he corroborated your story when the police arrested him. Now, as he sits alone in his cell, I am sure that he will remember you long after you have forgotten *him.*'

Johnny had lost his arrogance and was less confident as he asked a question that was obviously bothering him.

'Do you mind telling me how you and your brother *both* came to be here tonight? Because if you hadn't turned up when you did, your brother would have woken up on Clapham Common none the wiser as to who I was. Eric the butler would have simply vanished into thin air, as though he'd never existed.'

The judge was only too happy to explain. 'My brother came to the Crescent with my son-in-law yesterday morning and was suspicious of this whole cocktail party deception. They were worried for my safety and between them they came up with a plan of their own. Gary telephoned me, using a convincingly official voice, to inform me that due to illness the whole function had to be cancelled. Then my brother and housekeeper conspired for him to wear my dinner suit and come here in my place. My housekeeper filled me in not long ago and I decided to follow them.' He frowned at the suit. 'I think it would fit much better if you lost some weight, Bernard.'

Bernard started to laugh but had difficulty in breathing and his face became distorted with pain.

'I think we should leave,' the judge told Gary, unable to hide his anxiety over Bernard's health. 'I hope that you will forgive us, Mr Bains, and that you will keep to your word. Oh, and just one other thing that intrigues me. Why did you send biblical quotations?'

Johnny's answer was intentionally irreverent. 'I went to a religious school where they made us eat, drink and sleep the Bible.' An insolent smile appeared. 'Besides, I wanted you to have sleepless nights worrying about them. Be honest, they were more effective than cut-out letters from a magazine or newspaper. My idea was more original, don't you agree?'

The judge didn't bother to reply. He and Gary managed to get Bernard to his feet. They helped him to the door and as they passed Johnny, Bernard's eyes were full of hatred. Weak as he was, he couldn't resist taunting him.

'I hope you rot in hell, you bastard,' he whispered.

Seeing Bernard's hand still holding the gun that was in his pocket, Johnny stepped nervously aside, allowing the men to leave. When they reached the front door, Gary made sure that his father-in-law could manage alone for a moment and hurried back into the sitting room. Ignoring Johnny, he went straight to the cabinet and removed the tape. Putting it in his pocket, he went back to the hall and rejoined Bernard and the judge who were waiting for him.

Without saying a word, they left the house and made their way to Gary's car outside. Making sure that Bernard was settled comfortably in the passenger seat, Judge Thornton got into the back seat and they drove away.

On the journey home to Four Oaks, Bernard reflected on an evening that had been intended to expose the person sending the Bible quotations. But the plan to impersonate his brother had almost cost him his own life. He understood Gary's fear of letting him go to Somerville Crescent alone but wondered what might have happened had his brother not arrived when he did.

Then another thought crossed his mind. He wondered about Anne, the maid, and hoped she would be all right. Sick though he was, the thought of her legs in those black stockings made him feel better.

Gary noticed Bernard's hand was fidgeting with the pistol in his pocket and became nervous. He suggested Bernard gave it to his brother for safety, whereupon Bernard removed the weapon and, smiling to himself, passed it over his shoulder. Although he couldn't see his brother, he could tell that he was handling it with extreme caution.

'Be careful with that,' he said quietly. 'Blank cartridges can still give a nasty burn if you're careless.'

He could sense the surprised reaction and began to laugh, which made him cough again. But this time the coughing almost choked him and as he gasped for breath he passed out.

Without hesitation, Gary increased speed and made for the only hospital he knew of in that area, St Stephen's, which was only two minutes away off the Fulham Road.

Gary called Emma on his mobile phone to inform her where they were and that Bernard was in the intensive care unit where he had been placed on a life support machine.

After Emma had got over the shock, she broke the news that she had received from James MacCormack – that Raymond Farraday had been killed in a tragic road accident the previous night.

Digesting the news of Farraday's death, Judge Thornton reflecting on the irony of the situation. The man he had paid to find Johnny Bains was dead, while his brother had exposed Bains and risked his own life to do so. A life he was now in danger of losing.

It was just nine weeks since he had attended his brother Bernard's funeral. William Thornton wished they had been able to spend more time together. During the last weeks of his life, Bernard had mellowed from the brash drunkard to a much nicer human being. William would never forget the danger that his brother had faced by going to Somerville Crescent, a visit he had made, despite being unwell, simply to expose the person that had made his brother's life a living hell. Exactly what Bernard had intended to do on his own would remain a mystery.

Judge Thornton was sitting in his bedroom, acutely aware that it was through his own actions that he and his family had suffered over the past months. He could not forget that it was his personal prejudice that had sent an innocent boy to prison. And even though Nicky Bains would soon be free to commit burglary once more, it was Bernard's death that would remain on his conscience. The guilt he had felt over Raymond Farraday's accident had been removed when he learned that he had been travelling on a personal matter and not on behalf of his client.

Now William Thornton was wearing dark clothes once more. This time it was a black morning suit for his investiture at Buckingham

Palace. He would have given anything if Bernard could have lived to see this day.

Three guests were allowed at the ceremony, one of which could be a child of school age. And that was his problem. Much as he would have loved Jody to be there, he wanted his daughter and her husband present. Alison was his own flesh and blood and he felt he owed it to Gary to be there too. It would have been unthinkable not to invite him after all his help with the business at Somerville Crescent. And there was Emma. He could not possibly go through the ceremony without her there, a woman who had become so important to him since he had retired and got to know more intimately.

He had just finished dressing when there was a knock on his bedroom door. He opened it to find Jody standing there. She was wearing her prettiest dress and the happiest grin on her face.

'I'm coming to the palace with you, Grandpa!'

'I don't understand.'

Alison followed her daughter into the bedroom, wearing the new dress she had bought for the occasion. 'I'm afraid Gary has twisted his ankle, Father. I've bandaged it up but it's too painful to stand on. So it looks as though you'll arrive at the palace with three ladies. Unless there's someone else you'd rather bring instead of Jody?' she teased.

Her father looked concerned. 'Does this mean that Gary won't be able to come to the celebration dinner?'

'Have you ever known Gary miss the chance of getting a meal?' Alison laughed. 'Don't worry, Father. As long as he keeps his weight off the foot during the day, he'll manage to get into Guildford by this evening. By the way, is the chief constable definitely going to be there?'

Before he could answer, Emma appeared, looking lovely in a dress she'd had made. William felt immensely proud of the ladies who were about to share this special occasion with him.

Having called to make sure that Gary was all right, the four of them set off in the Bentley for London.

Alison sat in the back with Jody, which was unusual and left Emma sitting in front next to her father. As he glanced into the rear-view mirror, his daughter gave a knowing wink. Rather than be embarrassed, he felt happy. William Thornton was about to receive a knighthood from the Queen.

As they drove along the dual carriageway of the A3 he remembered Bernard and the day he was stopped and arrested. He found it difficult to understand how his brother could be so unpleasant to him on his return to England, and then spend his last hours going out of his way to help expose a man that had caused so much anguish to the family.

Then he recalled how Bernard had goaded him about his relationship with Emma and he realized that the reason he became angry was because Bernard was right. He really *did* feel something for her. Something deeper than admiration.

The future Sir William Thornton thought how nice it would be to have a wife to share his title. And he wondered if perhaps he and Emma might attend a more private ceremony in the not-too-distant future.